The Voyage Of The Evangelist

By
Harry Gandy

Published by Hemingway Publishers
Cover design by Hemingway Publishers
ISBN: Printed in the United States

PROLOGUE
ALEXANDRIA, EGYPT –
YEAR 49 C.E.

"There it is. The Pharos."

"Where?"

"Over there- the Pharos lighthouse."

"Yes. I see it now."

The barge creaked as it rolled slowly side to side under the still, hot African sun, making its way into the oily waters of the western harbor of Alexandria, Egypt. Hearing the excited voices of other passengers Mark forced himself to sit up against the hull to look at the famous Pharos. Any sign of land was welcome; he hated sailing and had been sick for most of his voyage from Palestine. Even so, despite his nausea, the lighthouse was indeed as impressive as he had heard, soaring four hundred feet into the sky, a light glimmering at its top.

Hugging the eastern Mediterranean shore, the barge carried fifty or so passengers on its journey to Africa, where it would soon be loaded with Egyptian grain for a return to Rome to do its share in feeding that city. Mark considered whether it would be better for him to take that return voyage himself. For he had failed in his earlier mission to Cyprus, proving himself unworthy of the trust Peter, the Apostle closest to Jesus, had in him and had returned to Palestine alone. He grimaced at the recurring painful memory....

He was with the Apostles Barnabas and Peter, preaching to a group of Cypriots in a small village at midday on a humid, windless day. The townspeople were pagan and Greek speakers. Peter had begun and spoke of their ancient beliefs, ridiculing them. He then spoke of the availability of everlasting life, but only for those who adopted the Way.

What is this 'Way' as it must have appeared to these Cypriots? That only through a profound belief that an obscure Jew in Palestine named Jesus was the son of the Hebrew God? That this Jesus had been crucified, died and then resurrected by this God and then taken to a perpetual paradise? And, finally, this death and resurrection allows for all people of faith access to everlasting life also. On its face, it sounds absurd. But...

A group of five men at the back of the crowd stood with arms folded across their chests, muttering angrily to each other. Three left before Peter was through and returned to find that he, Mark, was now speaking. They had brought with them a roughly hewn wooden cross, seven feet tall, as well as a hammer and long iron nails. One burly man taunted him. "Jew, if it's true that this Jesus rose from the dead and is coming back soon for his faithful, let us help you. We'll nail you to this cross and watch you die. Let's see if you really believe."

Two of them started moving through the crowd towards him. Fear suddenly took hold of him, and he couldn't speak or move. As they approached, he backed away slowly and finally cried out, "Leave me alone. Please." They kept coming, and as they neared, he began to cower and cry. Suddenly, Peter stepped between Mark and the pagans.

"Take me instead," Peter offered, and he began to pray aloud, raising his arms towards the sky, his face flushed and his eyes closed, repeating, "Take me... take me." The three men stopped before Peter, staring at him in surprise. The burly man glanced around at his companions and said, "He must be insane. Leave him be." They glanced indifferently at Mark, still bent over in fear, crying, before leaving silently. The crowd began to disperse as Peter went on praying, saying over and over, "Take me." Soon, only the three Jews remained, and Peter stopped. Neither Peter nor Barnabas spoke as he sank to the ground.

That evening, Peter tried to convince him that it was just a moment of weakness, nothing more, that all of them had felt similar moments of fear and that he still loved him like his son. Mark replied, "Yes, maybe." But the others were cool, or so it seemed, and he felt that he could no longer continue with the mission.

###

He shortly thereafter left Cyprus and returned alone to his mother's home in Jerusalem. He thought how Peter, Barnabas, and the others were possessed of a conviction that he did not have. They *know* that the world will end soon, perhaps even tomorrow and that they will then be raised and know unending life. No death. They are convinced that there is very little left of their current existence, and they are willing to give up what is left of it. He was aware that perhaps he had mouthed similar words, but he realized that then, in Cyprus, he did not want to die, that this life was all he really had. He recognized that his belief paled in comparison with the others.

Over the next months, he rarely left his mother's house and spoke very little about what happened in Cyprus. He stopped meeting with other followers of the Way, fellow Christians. What did he believe, really? Could he ever have a conviction for which he would be willing to die? Was it true what Peter said, that all of them had similar moments of weakness? Perhaps there was hope for him. Occasionally, his mother tried to console him. But he couldn't forget that moment of fear of a violent death in Cyprus.

A year passed when Peter one afternoon unexpectedly appeared at his door and asked to speak to him. They sat alone in silence on carpets in the dark, hot house.

Peter, staring at the ground before him, began, "I know what happened in Cyprus remains with you and that this past year has been hard. Your mother told us. No, I don't wish you to be angry with her. She's only acting as any mother would. She and I are worried about you."

"There's nothing to be said. You know that I am too much of a coward. It's undeniable that I don't have your courage or faith and probably never will."

"But I believe in you even if you don't. And so does your mother."

Mark wearily shook his head as Peter continued. "Just hear me out. I'm here because I want you to take on another mission, this time to Alexandria.

"I know you were born in Africa and lived there for many years. You know what the people are like and can speak to them in their own language. We would like you to go to Alexandria to spread the gospel there. You would be alone and would send us reports as to your progress. What do you say?"

Mark sat silently for a moment. "Why me? There are many others more capable than I am."

"I don't see it that way. We want someone who can speak directly to African pagans and tell our story. We're not seeking conflict with the pagans. We want to build a church there, and offer our story to any nonbelievers. I think you're the person to do it. Not necessarily as a hero, but as a builder."

Mark remained silent, staring at the wall in front of him. "I'll think about it."

After Peter left, his mother gently tapped as she pushed open the door and stood looking at him apprehensively.

Mark asked, "Do you know why Peter came?"

"Yes."

Mark slowly rose and began pacing aimlessly about the room.

"So you think I should go?"

His mother nodded. "I've never doubted my faith in the way. Nor yours. I know you. Anyone could have reacted as you did in Cyprus. But you and I both *know* that this world will come soon to an end and that we have been charged to act." Mark looked at her silently and said, "Perhaps."

###

Two months later, Mark left Palestine for Alexandria, first walking to the port of Tyre and then taking passage on the empty grain barge. The barge entered the western harbor at dusk, and Mark disembarked with the other passengers. He was then thirty years old, short and thin, and had already lost most of his hair. He shifted his bag to his shoulder and walked down the mole towards the town. When he stopped to reattach the strap to his right sandal, it snapped in two. He frowned and pushed his foot as far as possible into the broken sandal and strode off into the bustling city of Alexandria.

He had been given the name and location of a local follower of the Way, a Jew named Levi. He made his way to the Jewish quarter, asking for directions from time to time from those walking the city's streets in the relative cool of an African evening. Upon arrival, a sullen middle-aged woman warily opened the door a crack and upon hearing who he was seeking, went to fetch Levi. After a few moments during which Mark could hear the murmur of agitated words spoken between husband and wife, Levi appeared. He quickly looked over at Mark and admitted him to the small house.

Mark was offered a glass of table wine and water, from which he quickly took a sip and turned to notice Levi looking intently at him. "Didn't you expect me? I'm sorry to have arrived so late in the evening."

"I was expecting someone older. How was your voyage here?" Mark confessed to seasickness and not enjoying travel by boat generally.

"Tell me, who sent you here?"

"I was asked by Peter, Peter of the original twelve apostles of Christ." Levi nodded; he understood. Mark paused before asking, "Tell me, how are things for the followers of Christ here?"

Levi frowned. "The pagans here are a hard group. My family and I try to keep to ourselves and a few other families. We meet quietly in each other's houses and do not bring attention to ourselves." He paused and added, "Forgive me if I'm being rude, but I feel I must make sure of who you are. I'm sure you understand. There is much animosity here towards us."

Mark handed the cup back to Levi, saying, "Thank you. I'm here, sent by Peter, to spread the word, the gospel. I know that many pagans, as well as some Jews, don't wish to hear our message. But I have to do what I was sent to do. To establish a church here in Alexandria and to seek new followers. I understand how you feel, but I have to ask you to help me begin by introducing me to the other followers. Will you do that?"

Levi silently toyed with the empty cup before looking up at Mark, saying, "Of course."

The next day, Levi gave Mark directions to the shop where he could get his sandals fixed cheaply. "Ask for Anianus. He is a pagan but a good man."

Mark left the Jewish quarter and followed Levi's directions, which led him to a door opening into a small courtyard with a shop area off to the side beneath a rough wooden covering and adjacent to a stairwell to a second story. There, Mark found a man about his own age repairing a leather whip.

"I've been sent by a man named Levi who tells me you are the one to mend my sandal." Mark removed the damaged sandal and handed it to the seated man, who looked at him appraisingly. "Are you Anianus?" Mark asked.

"Yes. Let me see what can be done with this sandal." Anianus appraisingly peered at the sandal and said, "You've walked many miles in this, I can see. But I think it still has some life in it, the gods willing."

Mark hesitated before blurting out, "You mean if God so wills it."

Anianus looked up at Mark, who was peering at him uncertainly. "Yes, I suppose that may be what I meant. I see you're a follower of the same path as Levi. But more vocal perhaps."

"Yes, I suppose that's true." Mark paused momentarily and then went on, "I am here to bring the story of the Way of Jesus Christ to the people of Alexandria. I intend to start a congregation that will meet openly, and God's message will be made available to all. I understand that I may not be welcome here by many, but my message needs to be spread. There is one God, not many. God raised one man from the dead and took him to heaven. He shall return soon, and our present world shall pass away like a bad dream. Those who believe will live forever as God's children. That is my message."

Anianus silently absorbed Mark's words while examining his sandal, nodded and said, "I see. Simply put and well spoken. I've heard bits and pieces from your fellow followers here. I, too, wonder whether there are as many gods as people claim. Perhaps there is just one, as you say. Anyway, let me see what I can do for your feet, and then we can talk some more later."

####

Subsequently, Mark succeeded in starting a congregation in Alexandria of what would someday become known as Christians. Anianus became his first convert, his primary assistant, and his best friend. Over the next nineteen years, Mark became more and more vocal, indeed an evangelist, and had been ordained a bishop when his world did come to an end. While preparing a sacrament honoring the day of the resurrection of Jesus Christ, he was forcibly taken by a group of pagans who put a rope around his neck and led him through the town, all the while mocking him. The next day, they dragged him through the streets until he died. In due course of time, he was sanctified and became St. Mark, the Evangelist. Meanwhile, his body was interred in the church he founded, where it lay for hundreds of years.

###

As the body of St. Mark subsequently lay in repose under the care of priests of the Egyptian Coptic Church, life in the world of the Mediterranean Sea changed completely. During Mark's lifetime, Roman emperors had ruled as despots, and there may have been only a few thousand followers of Jesus Christ. By the fourth century, however, Christians made up approximately twelve percent of the population of Roman Italy, and their religion was legitimated by the emperor Constantine.

In 324 CE, Constantine founded what he envisioned as a "New Rome" on the site of the Greek city of Byzantium, renamed, unsurprisingly, Constantinople, which was to be the home of a second emperor. Eventually, Rome grew less and less important, so by 476 CE, there was no longer even a pretense of an emperor in Rome. And in Alexandria, the Christians had become a dominant force and began to persecute pagans much like Christians had been persecuted during Mark's life.

After the fall of the western Roman empire, Italy was invaded over and over again by peoples who migrated west, largely in response to the various tribes who swept into central Asia and Europe from Mongolia. As a consequence, native Italians from areas such as Padua, Aquileia, and Treviso became refugees and made their way to a remote section of the Italian peninsula located at the top of the Adriatic Sea. Here they inhabited lands largely isolated from the meddling of the various neighboring kings and emperors and included the islands of Malamocco and Torcello. Some form of a common government for these islands began as early as the sixth century. And a powerful ruler emerged from this process, resembling an Italian duke, or 'doge' in the Venetian dialect.

CHAPTER 1
THE GULF OF VENICE, JANUARY 828 CE.

On a dreary winter morning, cold, damp wind blew steadily from the Alps, sweeping south across the overcast Gulf of Venice. A freshly painted galley, black below and red above, had been drawn onto the beach on the island of Torcello, its prow facing the Venetian lagoon. Rustico, a short, wiry man with black eyes and thick, curly hair, slowly walked around it. Stony-faced, he studied the galley, running his fingers behind him along the sides. Occasionally, he would stop, peer at a spot, and then move on. Gianni, his son, stood beside the boat's builder, watching this procedure with equanimity; he knew when Rustico was satisfied.

After completing his inspection of the galley, Rustico joined his son and the builder, Ariosto, who waited for him to speak. Rustico gazed emotionlessly, then looked at the galley and said, "It seems acceptable."

Exasperated, Ariosto turned and looked directly at Rustico. "What do you mean? It's beautiful."

"Yes. Perhaps it is." Rustico nonchalantly replied. "We need to take it out on the lagoon and see how she does."

Ariosto asked, "Of course. When? There might be rain tomorrow."

"I expect that there will be many occasions when it will rain on it at sea," Rustico responded.

Ariosto nodded and said, "I'll need to get a crew ready unless you already have one arranged."

"Go ahead and arrange it. But no promises are to be made that anyone will necessarily be hired for its first sailing," Rustico replied.

After Ariosto and his men left, Rustico and Gianni secured the galley and covered the hold against rain. Then they walked the short distance to the house they shared with Rustico's father, Leo. The house was an old, single-story, unpainted wooden structure with a gap in its thatched roof for smoke. Sitting adjacent was a storage shed, and behind that, a windmill and four long trenches for drying and harvesting salt. A short, heavy door opened into a large rectangular living and dining area, with a fire pit for heat, light, and cooking at one end and three separate areas for sleeping at the other. Leo, balding with a fringe of grey hair, sat by the fire, warming arthritic hands, and nodded to his son and grandson as they entered. The walls were bare except for a crucifix hanging behind the fire. Leo slowly rose from his bench, rubbing his back.

"How is the boat?" Leo asked.

"It looks quite good," Rustico said. "We'll have to see how she performs, though. Perhaps in two days."

Leo nodded. "I'll look tomorrow. After the sun warms up." He motioned toward the fire. "Signora Luchesse has left, but she brought some fish soup."

Gianni, rubbing his still-cold hands, leaned over the pot and inhaled deeply. "I'm famished." He was pleasantly surprised that she had made dinner for them. She usually only had time to clean the house and do the laundry for the three men. Before he was born, there had been two girls - his sisters- who each died before reaching one year old. His mother died when he was five, so he had little knowledge of women except for the Signora. Her cooking was always a treat for the household.

Leo ladled soup into bowls while Gianni fetched bread, and the three men began eating in silence.

Rustico asked his father, "How was the Signora? Still in pursuit of you?"

"A woman's presence in this house might make a nice change," Leo replied thoughtfully. "We've been widowers a long time. Haven't we?"

Rustico shrugged and said, "Perhaps. Anyway, Gianni and I will be gone for some time. A wife could keep you company and provide some warmth at night."

"I suppose so," Leo added, studying his soup, "So, will this galley be able to carry salt up the Po River into the mainland?"

Rustico, chewing his bread, leaned back and sighed. "You are quite aware that this galley is for sailing south out of the gulf and not for river travel."

"I was just wondering if it could be used for our normal business dealings upriver afterward," Leo responded.

"Now, Father, I know you are not convinced about this, but I think we can do well selling to the Romans at Constantinople or perhaps even the Moslems in Africa. There are many others who will continue to take our salt inland," Rustico explained.

"But they will need to be paid. And how can I know that they will make the best deal for me. I could get cheated, you know," Leo replied heatedly.

"Yes, I know," Rustico replied, nodding, "Everything will be arranged with honest boatmen. Believe me, they will not cheat you or me."

"Gianni is 17 years old now. He could help with the salt works and continue our present trade up the Po. He's been with you and knows what needs to be done. And I can trust him," Leo stated.

Gianni interrupted, "But I want to go with my father."

"Is it safe for you?" Leo asked, turning to his grandson. "Your father fought against the Franks and knows the ways of the world. He knows sailors, fishermen, and merchants too."

Rustico interjected, "You think it's safe for him to sail inland? You forget. More than once, I had to fight thieves off to keep them from stealing our salt and our boat, too."

"There are difficulties there, I know," Leo admitted. "But the sea is much more dangerous, full of pirates. And even the so-called Christians of Dalmatia will cut your throat in an instant. What can you expect from heretics? Who knows what you'll run into in Constantinople? Greeks, of course. Jews. Maybe even some pagans."

Gianni looked at his father. "I want to go with you."

"I know. Your grandfather is concerned, and rightly so." Rustico said as he turned to Leo. "Father, you need to trust me in this matter. I know there are risks, but the rewards could be enormous. The Romans we know pay well for pelts, lumber, and perhaps salt, too. I've been thinking of taking some of the glassware made on the islands. Much of their work could sell for good prices in Constantinople."

Leo, unconvinced, merely nodded, responding, "Perhaps."

"I want to go," Gianni reiterated, and the three finished eating in silence.

###

The next day, Gianni and Leo, after storing newly harvested salt, made their way to the galley. Leo walked around it, shaking his head. "It's too big for going up the Po."

Gianni shrugged, "Probably."

Leo paused and sighed and began to explain, "I know I'm old and set in my ways and that the two of you have made plans to trade with the Romans. Your father is as ambitious as I was when I was his age. He is

15

a very good sailor and wants to see how this new galley does in the sea. But change is hard for an old man. I may not be here when you return."

"You should marry Signora Luchesse," Gianni suggested, smiling at the idea.

"You think so? Why?" Leo questioned.

"Why not? She's a nice lady. She puts up with you when you're cranky. Why wouldn't you want to marry her?" Gianni asked as he explained.

"All you say is true. But what you don't know is that women change, and then they want you to change, too. You don't know, but I do. Look, you don't remember your grandmother. Rustico remembers her as a saint. And she was, at least, towards him. But she had a temper, and do you know who was the object of her temper? Not Rustico, but me," Leo clarified.

"Now, I am an old man, too old for change. I need one good reason to put myself through that again. Give me one," He probed.

"For her soup," Gianni quipped.

Leo shook his head and remarked, "You and your father are such practical men."

Two days later, at dawn, the Gulf waters cold and dark, Ariosto was waiting at the galley with a crew of fourteen men as Rustico and Gianni walked to greet them. All wore leather coats and woolen mittens to remain warm against the cold. "Only fourteen men?" Rustico frowned.

"That's enough for a trial run," Ariosto argued. "As I'm sure you're aware, most of the fishermen are out in the gulf. We'll place these men as needed, maybe every other bench, and move them as needed. You'll find oars at each bench."

Rustico and Gianni climbed into the galley, which was ninety feet long and twenty-five feet wide at the center, tapering toward the bow and stern. Ariosto led the men in pushing the galley off the beach into the gulf and Rustico and Gianni helped pull them aboard from the surf. Planking around the perimeter of the hull provided bench seating for the oarsmen; below this planking was a partially covered hold, now empty except for some ropes.

Sailing south on the Gulf of Venice, Ariosto, stationed at the stern, observed the crew rowing briskly. He was aware that most of them had previous experience rowing in Roman galleys - called dromons by the Greeks - and knew how to do so efficiently. Rustico and Gianni walked along the upper deck, noting the crew and occasionally repositioning them to different benches.

After an hour, Rustico turned the boat west toward the Rivo Alto, a cluster of small flat islands in the middle of the lagoon that barely rose above the high tide. As the wind stiffened, Rustico instructed Gianni to raise the two lateen masts, one just behind the bow and the other amidship—and they sailed without rowing. Rustico and Ariosto took positions on either side of a ten-foot square flat covered area behind the prow, each watching how the galley responded and staying alert for any problems. Ariosto's foreman, Julian, steered as necessary by way of a large paddle that extended down along the stern into the water.

Small wooden houses, some farms, and larger, two-story warehouses were visible on the edge of the Rivo Alto islands. Most of these warehouses, as well as various stone structures, including a chapel, had doors that opened directly onto a boat moorage on the gulf. Rustico scanned the surroundings, searching for the planned location of the Doge's palace. He finally spotted what appeared to be a construction site a short distance back from the waters of the lagoon. In a few days, he was to ferry a load of lumber there, ordered by the Doge, for the galley's first commercial trip.

Ariosto approached Rustico. "She responds well, don't you think?" He added. "You are aware that you will need more ballast in the open seas?"

Ignoring Ariosto, Rustico replied, "I've been on the sea many times. I'll take it out with a full load soon, possibly next week. Can you get the crew back?"

"I think I can. Some need to fish and make a living, you know," Ariosto responded. He added with a nod, "Gianni looks like a real sailor."

Rustico nodded. "Yes, he does well, particularly with setting the sails," as he continued to move the galley further into shallow water. "Let's see what it will take to loosen the galley when stuck."

"It will be different with a fully loaded ship," Ariosto repeated.

#####

Four days later Rustico brought the galley under sail to Ariosto's boatworks located on the northern shore of the lagoon. The builder, together with Julian and two more of his workers, closely watched the galley approach, curious to know how this new project had done on the open sea. Ariosto greeted Rustico with, "Good Morning, Signore. I see she still floats."

Rustico smiled. "She's pretty much just as I asked. But I'd like you to check its bottom once more. We will sail soon, and I want to start loading cargo."

"Of course," Ariosto said as he directed his workers to draw the galley up on the shore and turn it on its side for an inspection under the supervision of both the owner and the builder.

As the workers were restoring the galley to the gulf waters, Rustico presented a bag to Ariosto and said, "I've brought my last payment for you." After Ariosto took the bag, Rustico continued, "I know I've been demanding and that building this galley just as I wanted it was difficult, but I don't see that anyone could have built it any better."

Ariosto nodded and replied, "You explained what you wanted and why, and I appreciate that in a client."

"You know, of course, that if it performs well, others will want one like it," Rustico said.

"That thought has crossed my mind. I do appreciate your allowing me the chance to build such a boat. The lateen masts are going to prove invaluable," Ariosto acknowledged.

"You'll be the first to know if there are problems," Rustico said as the two started walking back to the galley.

"Oh, I already figured that out," Ariosto replied, chuckling.

#####

When Rustico entered the house, he found Gianni and Leo huddled around the fire pit for warmth.

Leo asked, "Did you settle with the builder?"

Rustico answered, "Yes, and I had them examine the galley's bottom once more. What's our dinner tonight?"

"Fish. I bought some today and still have enough to salt for later. You probably want to take some on your journey." Leo said. Rustico remained silent but, recognizing that his father had finally accepted his planned trip and would no longer complain, felt relieved.

Leo had cut chunks of fish and now spit them on blackened sticks and positioned them over the fire. "I gave some to Signora Luchesse also. I told her how much you two enjoy her soup."

Gianni and Rustico courteously murmured noises of appreciation.

"When do you plan on sailing? What route?" Leo asked

Rustico responded, "Possibly in six weeks. I have only half a load so far, but more pelts should arrive soon from upriver. How much salt is there available?"

"There will be plenty for you. How many men will you need?" Leo questioned.

Rustico began to explain, "Twenty, I should think. The sails should move us pretty well, better than I anticipated actually. Gianni is really quite adept at managing them. We'll sail along the east coast primarily. There are the Croat pirates to be concerned with but there are also many safe moorages for spending the night. And we'll stop at some of the ports to sell or buy supplies."

Leo reached for a spit and gingerly removed one of the chunks of fish. He checked it, determined that it was done, and handed portions to his son and grandson, who nodded their thanks.

"I know it is not as tasty as the Signora's soup, but it is warm, and there is bread to eat with it," Leo remarked.

Ignoring Leo's subtle gibe, Rustico asked "Shall I arrange for more help for you while we are gone?"

"Don't worry about that. I'll probably have to hire workers to harvest the salt, but not that often. I still need to make money at it," Leo assured.

"And in the house?" Rustico probed.

"I'll be all right." Leo paused, then added, "The Signora will move in after you leave."

"What do you mean?" Rustico, astonished, asked.

"We will marry in a month, God willing," Leo placidly responded.

"I have to say I am surprised," Rustico said, observing his father. "You've been so reluctant to even consider it."

"You two can leave without having to worry about me. She has told me she likes me as I am, and I am taking her word for it," Leo replied.

###

On a cloudy day marked by intermittent gusts of wind across the gulf, Rustico brought his galley up to moorage at the Rivo Alto islands with a load of lumber. Signore Giustiniano Participazio, recently named Doge of Venice, was waiting on the mole for the galley's arrival and greeted Rustico. "Good day, Rustico!" he shouted. "Punctual as usual."

Rustico shrugged and maneuvered the galley against the mole and tossed a rope towards the Doge, who retrieved it and held the ship steady while Rustico and his crew disembarked. "I'll have my men unload the lumber here, and your workers can move it to the site."

Doge Giustiniano nodded in approval. "Can you stay a while? I'd like to show you what we have done so far in the new palace. And there's someone I'd like you to meet."

After instructing his crew, Rustico and the Doge started walking. Doge Giustiniano glanced back at the ship and remarked, "We've heard a lot about your new galley. Very nice, and I can see you've mastered it."

Rustico replied, "My son and I have taken her out on a daily basis and have even run her out at night. I'm pretty confident she'll do well in the Mediterranean Sea."

"When do you plan to sail?" the Doge asked.

"Early spring as the weather permits. I am still lining up a full cargo. We need to sell a lot in order to pay for this trip," Rustico answered.

"I fully expect that you'll do well on many future voyages also. Constantinople is still your main destination?" the Doge questioned.

Rustico explained, "Yes, but we will make inquiries all down the Adriatic and east towards Crete."

"You expect to be gone two-three months?" the Doge probed.

"God willing, yes," Rustico replied.

"Would you entertain a passenger?" the Doge inquired.

"I'd consider it. A paying passenger, I imagine," Rustico clarified.

"Some agreement could be reached, I'm sure. Here's the new palace site." The two paused to watch a small group of laborers setting out markers for the foundation of a large rectangular structure. "As you can see, it'll be bigger and much more grand than the last," the Doge explained.

"I imagine so. Out here, though, far from the shore," Rustico responded.

"Purposively. This last war with the Franks has shown that our safety is best served by distancing ourselves from the mainland." The Doge continued, "As I'm sure you'll recall, my father and predecessor, Doge Agnello, really began this movement away from the shore, including building up some of the outer islands into breakwaters."

"Of course. And your family has bought a great deal of land out here, too," Rustico wryly noted.

"I won't deny that our family has been financially involved with the development of the Rivo Alto," the Doge countered heatedly. "But someone had to begin it. We have offered the property on which we're building the new palace to the city of Venice at no cost."

"I meant no offence, Doge. But you must know that many people are aware that your family stands to gain from this move. I, myself, don't object. It looks like a good business move to me," Rustico countered.

"You fought the Franks," the Doge continued, his tone softening. "You of all people must be aware that our settlement was saved from the Franks by our being on the water, in boats, or on the islands. I still laugh when I imagine the anger of Charlemagne's son, Pepin, at not being able to fight us his way on land."

"True. But is it enough to get people to move?" Rustico mused. "That war was twenty years ago, and we've made peace with the Franks. I myself wonder more about the Romans in Constantinople or even the Arabs. Both might like some control over the gulf. And they can sail."

"You're correct, of course," the Doge agreed. "We must be ready to deal with many potential enemies, and so we must be strong enough to deter any thoughts of taking us on. The Franks, for now, have other problems with the Moors in Spain. And I believe they have probably learned their lesson."

Rustico nodded and replied, "I hope you are right. I'm a merchant, and war, unless quickly won, is bad for business."

"Come this way," the Doge invited, leading him. "There's a chapel we use for planning and supervision of construction."

The two walked a short distance toward a small stone chapel marked by a cross above the door. The Doge opened the door and they entered. Inside was a rough wooden table covered with drawings of the proposed palace. On a bench in a corner sat a tall, thin man with a sallow face, long brown hair, and a mustache and goatee. He appeared to be about 35 years old, and he sat with his legs crossed and leaned against the wall. Turning to Rustico, the Doge introduced, "Here's someone I'd like you to meet. This is Signore Bono of Malamocco. Signore Bono, this is Rustico from Torcello, the merchant who will sail to Constantinople soon." The two nodded, eyeing each other cautiously.

The Doge retrieved a bottle of wine and three cups, setting them on the table. "Shall we toast to new friends?" he proposed.

Bono and Rustico each took a cup from the Doge and slowly sipped while the Doge emptied his glass, wiping his mouth. Addressing Rustico, he explained, "Signore Bono has recently returned to Italy from Spain, where he was involved in some delicate discussions with the Moors. He was there for some time—three years, wasn't it, Signore Bono?" Bono nodded, and he continued, "As you can imagine, Signore Bono learned many things about the Moors, including how to speak Arabic, a talent which I believe shall be most valuable in the future."

Rustico responded agreeably, "I have no doubt about it."

"Signore Bono has offered his services for the benefit of Venice. He grew up here and shares my belief in the promise of a city situated here," the Doge declared proudly.

Bono stood, smiling at the Doge. "It's good to be back. Spain is beautiful in its own way; a bit hot, though, for someone who grew up in the lagoon."

"What were you doing there?" Rustico inquired.

"Actually Agnello, the previous doge, originally asked me to go on his behalf, inquiring about business opportunities," Bono explained. "Mining in Spain has always presented opportunities for profit; for instance, the ore often requires transportation by sea. I stayed longer of my own accord because it became obvious to me that the Islamists are here to stay and in control of much of the lands of the old Roman empire; they represent a formidable force, both militarily and economically.

"They are now determined to make their way over the mountains in the north of Spain into the land of the Franks. But they're also interested in locations closer to us, Sicily, for instance, Cyprus, Crete and perhaps even southern Italy. They would then be able to keep us blocked off the Mediterranean and from any access to Constantinople."

"That would pose a problem for the businesses of Venice," Rustico murmured thoughtfully.

The Doge interjected, "I am determined to make this settlement one to be reckoned with by any and all potential enemies. I am aware, however, that we don't presently have the necessary fighting power. We know we can win a defensive war here in the lagoon, but we need to be able to aggressively meet any challenges before they get here."

"You'll need a navy," Rustico pointed out.

"Precisely," the Doge agreed. "And that requires a lot of money and time. I won't ask you how much your galley cost but imagine scores of them, bigger and rigged for fighting. That's what we will need. But we have to deal with our immediate threats first and that involves, to my way of thinking, making a deal with the Romans."

"What about the Saracens? They seem to be winning more often than the Romans," Rustico noted.

Bono explained, "It's true the Moors are running over the Mediterranean lands with little opposition. But that's why they presently have no concern with in a small, trading city located up at the top of the Adriatic. Why should they? We offer no threat to them. And what can we offer them?

"But the Romans are in a different position from us; they're challenged by the Islamists in many ways. Specifically, they need to concentrate their defenses in the east and really can't afford to police the Adriatic and the Gulf any longer. The Doge and I believe that the Romans might be interested in our providing an armed deterrent to both the Moslems and the pirates here in the Adriatic. They know that we beat back the Franks."

"On behalf of Venice," the Doge stated, "I'm interested in offering some sort of naval assistance to the Romans in exchange for money, know-how in building warships and weapons, and perhaps trade concessions. I am proposing to send Signore Bono as an envoy to Constantinople to open discussions. That's where you come in. Bono needs to get there safely first of all; and he would need help from a merchant in negotiating appropriate trade concessions."

A silence fell over the trio. Eventually, Rustico asked, "How long will you need to be in Constantinople?"

Bono responded, "I don't know. It depends on how quickly they will see me. And then how long they take to consider our proposal."

"I can't be gone long. I have a business to run," Rustico said emphatically and sat his cup down. "I understand what you're trying to do. But I also have heard how long it takes to get anything done there. Then there's the question of whether they can be trusted. Think of all the times the Greeks have suddenly turned on each other.

"I can give you two weeks there, maybe three, but if you can't reach a deal, you'll either have to leave with me or stay and return some other way," he concluded.

Bono and the Doge looked at each other. After a pause, the Doge proposed, "We would pay you well if you would agree to four weeks."

Rustico, rising to leave, responded, "I'll think about it."

As the Doge escorted Rustico to the door, he emphasized, "Remember this, Rustico: we need to be a powerful force in order for merchants like you to be able to safely trade throughout the Mediterranean."

After Rustico left, Bono sat and watched silently as the Doge paced the room. Finally, the Doge muttered, "He's a difficult one, that Rustico. Pigheaded."

"He does make a valid point, though," Bono acknowledged. "Merchants don't make any money, just cooling their heels waiting for a decision of some mid-level Roman official.

"And I'm sure he's not the first Venetian to notice your family's financial involvement in the development of this part of the gulf. He may be the first to openly mention it to your face."

"Oh, I know that," the Doge conceded. "I also know that he was not fond of my father and some of his doings."

"And neither were you on occasion," Bono replied wryly.

"Of course, of course. But I'm not to blame for his overreach, am I?" the Doge defended.

Bono shook his head briefly. "I'll see him alone and try to smooth things over. I doubt he holds you responsible for Doge Agnello's foibles. Rustico appears to me to be a serious man. He's ambitious- absolutely. But above all, reliable. And we are in need of reliable men. I want him with me, not against me."

####

That night, after dinner, Rustico silently sat with his father and son around the fire pit, each holding a cup of wine.

"The Doge may be a scoundrel, just like the rest of his family, but he's right," Leo finally conceded.

"Why do you think so?" Gianni inquired curiously.

Leo began to explain, "It's been many years, but people still remember when the Romans here in Italy ruled the whole of the Mediterranean, even up beyond the Frankish lands. They did so with strength, and people knew that they would suffer if they resisted. But the result was much wealth coming into Italy, some from conquests, but also much from trade.

"Pirates and thieves knew that they could expect a horrible death if they were caught. Crucifixion, possibly, or death in the games.

"Nowadays, a merchant ship on its own is an easy target for brigands. Who in the lagoon is going to provide protection now? No one. Those so-called Romans in Constantinople do little to help us, so we must fend for ourselves."

"I understand what you are saying," Rustico answered. "I'm concerned that the Romans will drag things out and still refuse to help. We could be stuck in Constantinople for weeks and for what? We have a lot of money riding on this trip, and I don't want to jeopardize it."

"What did you think of this Bono of Malamocco? The Doge must trust him greatly," Leo inquired.

"He is subtle and closed-mouthed, from what I could see," Rustico replied.

"He sounds like the right kind of man to send on a mission like this," Leo remarked approvingly.

"Perhaps," Rustico mused. "At any rate, they are offering a large sum to take him there. I think I can demand some demonstration that the negotiations are proceeding, or else I'll leave with him or without."

"Good," Leo responded with a nod. "Now it's time for sleep. I have to meet with the priest tomorrow about the marriage."

CHAPTER 2

eo's wedding was scheduled for the last Friday of February, to be held in a small chapel on Torcello with the local priest, Paolo, officiating. It was to be a small affair. Of course, Rustico and Gianni would be there. The bride — Angela was her given name - had two surviving daughters, Claudia, a childless widow with whom she lived, and Maria, who lived nearby on the mainland with her husband and two children, who also would be there. Angela assumed responsibility for the wedding preparations since Leo was going to be busy at the salt works - he insisted on dealing directly with the boatmen who would conduct the family business up the Po River in the meantime.

Late one afternoon, a small boat landed in front of the saltworks. A tall, gangly man emerged and came to the door.

"Yes?" Leo asked.

"Ah, Signore Leo, I imagine."

"Yes. And who are you?"

"My name is Bono, from the island of Malamocco. Your son may have mentioned my name."

"Ah, Signore Bono. Of course, come in. My son should be home any minute."

They sat on benches in front of the fire after Leo served them each a cup of wine. "I understand you are soon to be married. To the widow Luchesse."

"Yes. I'm surprised that you've heard of our betrothal." Leo answered.

"The Doge somehow knew about it and mentioned it to me. I hope you don't mind. I only meant to offer my good wishes." Bono said, hoping he didn't seem impertinent.

"Oh it's no problem." Changing the subject, Leo asked, "Are you staying in Malamocco with your family?"

"No. Much of my family died in the Frankish invasion and most of the others from disease. I'm staying at Rivo Alto until we sail. I wanted to discuss some matters with Rustico and hoped to find him free."

"He's still obtaining goods for the trip. Gianni, my grandson, is working at the salt works. He is also sailing with you. Have you met him?"

"No. I'd like to, but I don't wish to disturb him at work."

"It's time for his midday meal anyway. We'll go find him."

The weather was overcast but unseasonably warm and muggy as they made their way towards the salt works. Gianni was letting seawater into the first trenches and when he saw them, he wiped his face and moved to greet them.

"This is Signore Bono. You remember he is accompanying you on the galley's sailing to Constantinople."

"Glad to meet you," Gianni said, wiping his hands.

"It's a pleasure to meet you."

Leo said to Gianni, "It's time for your meal. Let's go home."

They sat before the fire pit. Gianni hungrily started eating bread along with Signora's soup, while Bono accepted only a small piece of bread.

"I'm looking forward to sailing in your new galley," Bono said. "I had a chance to see it briefly when I met your father at Rivo Alto. I understand you've become quite a hand at the use of lateen sails."

"I've worked them a great deal in order to learn. We are trying to sail with a limited number of oarsmen. We need to keep the costs of the voyage down."

"Of course. As you may know, I spent some time in Spain with the Moors and was impressed with their sailing techniques."

"Let me know if you notice anything that I should try."

"I'm sure you'll be fine. I have congratulated your grandfather on his upcoming marriage to Signora Lucchese. A fine woman, I hear."

"An excellent cook. I don't know how she manages to make her food so tasty."

Bono replied, "I've been told that many of the local women have been trying to learn to prepare meals like they did in Rome and Milan many, many years ago. Using herbs and spices when they can get them. I gather some of them are particularly trying to make garum again, a sauce the old Romans used a lot."

"Really? I wonder if my father knows anything about these spices."

At the same time, the door opened, and Rustico entered, asking, "Knows anything about what?"

Leo responded, "Spices! Ah, Here you are. You, of course, remember Signore Bono. He came by to see you and has met Gianni. They were just speaking of the Signora's cooking and why it is so much more tasty than mine."

Gianni exclaimed, "That's not true. We like your food too; it's just different from the Signora's."

Shaking his head at Leo's words, Bono chuckled and clapped him on the back. He then rose and greeted Rustico. "I hope that my visit is not inconvenient. I know you must be very busy getting ready."

"No, this is fine. I hoped to discuss some matters with you also. Perhaps we could walk towards the galley." Rustico grabbed a piece of bread as he and Bono left.

They commented idly on the weather as they made their way to the galley, now lying in the surf, partially loaded. Rustico showed Bono the hold and described its contents primarily as pelts, lumber, and bags of salt.

Bono began, "I wanted to speak with you without Doge around. I understand you have concerns which Doge may not appear to recognize as significant. I am also aware that some members of the Participazio family have a checkered history of pursuing power at all costs, which many Venetians find unacceptable.

"I have agreed to perform what I believe is an important mission on behalf of the settlements here, but that doesn't mean I can't see your points. Let me start with this: I have reason to believe that the Romans, or Greeks if you like, are quite likely to be receptive to our offer. I have had tentative contacts with some members of the government and have been told that they are aware of their predicament. They are met on all sides with enemies and can no longer adequately defend large portions of what was once their territory. This is particularly true here in Italy and the Adriatic.

"The Saracens control much of the south, and there is piracy up and down the coasts of the Adriatic. Those knowledgeable believe that Italy, particularly the lagoons, must be protected and that we are the most likely protectors. After all, we Venetians have the most to lose."

Bono weighed his words before continuing. "The emperor may not yet understand this danger completely, but I am sure many of his advisors do. If the emperor presided over the collapse of authority in the Adriatic, the army might involve itself, much to the emperor's discomfort. I assume you understand my meaning. We Venetians have a strong position in this matter and can demand much.

"I know that trade is your business and that you have to compete with many. Goods are coming into Constantinople from as far away as China. Jewish merchants have been able to do well, living among the Moslems and bringing in goods from the south, even Africa. But these business rivals of yours cannot add to the empire's defense like we can. And so the empire should pay for our services and provide knowledge. For example, many of our sailors would really like to understand how this Greek fireworks. How do they manage to create a fire on the sea and damage their enemy's boats?

"And the empire ought to grant our traders privileges, perhaps in the form of reduced taxes and expenses or convenient access to the city. I am not telling you we will get all of these now or even soon. But I will say if we can make the Venetians indispensable, good things will come our way."

Rustico nodded. "How long will this take?"

"I will give them a deadline. Two weeks. Certain advisors are already aware of our plans, so it should come as no surprise. And if the army sees us as an ally and not a foe, the emperor must agree."

"What do you need from me other than transport?"

"Broadly speaking, let me know what you believe the empire could use that we can routinely provide at a profit. Advise me as to what might make a Venetian merchant's job easier, and I'll see what can be done.

"Consider this an extended opportunity to look at all the business opportunities Constantinople has to offer, and they are vast. Goods and spices from all over the world - India, China - find their way there. See what the Romans want that you and other Venetian traders can provide. I'm quite sure your two weeks in Constantinople will be well spent.

"On board, I understand you are in control. I have no desire to undercut you in any way. Refer to me as a fellow merchant. If asked, say I have business contacts to the west and north whom I represent;

understand that I can take it from there. You have no reason to distrust me; we are on the same side for different purposes.”

“All right. I’ll introduce you to my crew as a merchant representing interests other than mine. Just to be clear, all orders come from me; if you want something you ask me first.”

“Agreed.” The two shook hands and Bono left for his boat.

####

Later that night, Leo inquired, “How did your discussion go with Signore Bono?”

“Very well. I believe we can work together. He seems to understand that Venice stands to do well in expanding our trade over the Mediterranean to the east. What did you think of Signore Bono, Gianni?”

“I think he understands people quite well.”

Leo added, nodding, “He certainly seems capable of knowing how to get what he wants.”

###

Five days later, on an early afternoon of a dark, dreary day, the Doge, in his temporary office on the Rivo Alto along with Bono, greeted Rustico as he entered and said, “Signore Bono here tells me that you feel the weather’s soon going to be good enough to sail. Do you have a date?”

“Two weeks, most likely. I would like a blessing from the Bishop if possible.”

“Let me see what I can do,” the Doge replied.

“How is the palace construction coming along?” Rustico inquired.

“It should be available for partial use by the time you return. Even better, we’re going ahead with building a church, or more precisely a chapel, nearby. As you might imagine, our new church will be a grand structure like the new palace.”

34

The Doge paused for a moment, leaning back with a cup of wine in his hand, and added, "I've been concerned about ways to increase the prestige of Venice in the eyes of the world. And I think we need to have a more impressive patron saint."

"What's wrong with St. Zacharius?" Bono asked.

"What do you know about him? Or better, what does the average Venetian know? A city of any consequence needs relics of consequence."

"Perhaps. Some people more or less 'find' their relics. Some churches will pay well for them," added Rustico.

"So I gather. The Dalmatians have many, I believe. I'm not sure that any are particularly important."

"I understand some merchants from Venice sold some relics they acquired in Constantinople to Kotor some years ago," Rustico told, then added, "I believe the locals were going to build a church around it."

"Are you planning on stopping at Kotor?"

"Most likely. The moorage there is quite well protected."

"You might look into it. I hate to buy these relics, but we must improve on what we have." The three men then began discussing what additional goods would be appropriate and available for the galley's sailing.

###

On the following Friday, Leo and Angela were married as planned. After the ceremony, the bride and groom, together with Rustico, Gianni, and Angela's daughter, Claudia, walked to the men's home, where the newlyweds were toasted and given best wishes. Angela, gazing around at the living area, said, "Leo, of course, will remain here with you until you sail. I will stay with my daughter until then, perhaps bringing some items over in the meantime. I hope that is satisfactory."

"That sounds fine," Rustico replied. "We want to accommodate you as much as possible." He added with a small smile.

"Thank you. Leo and I have discussed a few changes. I think it's appropriate for Leo and I to have some form of a barrier around our sleeping area. Do you agree?"

"Most definitely. Whatever your modesty requires."

"I would also like to improve the fire pit area a bit. Perhaps a larger hearth and a new table for food preparation and eating." Leo nervously glanced at Angela and then at Rustico.

"I'm sure that will be fine too. Let me know if you need anything before we leave."

Angela smiled and nodded. "Leo and I will miss you, of course, and will look forward to your safe return. We may add some additional trenching capacity at the salt works in the meantime."

"We'll see," said Leo uneasily.

###

The Doge was able to persuade Bishop Venerius Trasmondo to come from Aquileia, and not merely for the galley's blessing, for the Bishop also wished to discuss the new church to be sited adjacent to the palace under construction. He and two acolytes arrived on an unusually warm and sunny morning to find the Doge and Bono waiting for him. Greetings were exchanged, and the Bishop said, "I'd like to see where you intend to locate this new church. Do you have any plans?"

"I have a concept in mind from a church in Constantinople which impressed me as a young man. Please come this way."

Upon seeing the ongoing construction of the Doge's palace, the Bishop commented, "It's certainly going to be impressive. How many levels will it have?" eyeing the construction sight.

"Two levels at least, your worship. Of course, there is only so much flat land, so the new building will have to go up. As you can see, the church is being constructed immediately to the west, forming a side of central square."

"I see. You expect great things for your settlements. However, you do understand that your church will be under the control of Aquileia."

The Doge paused before replying: "I don't understand why that would be so. In my view, this new development will prove more defensible than Grado or Aquileia. You know perfectly well what the Franks are capable of on land. I'm sure you remember what they did to those cities some twenty years ago."

"Oh, true, true. But we have made peace with them. They would like us to adopt more of the customs of the western churches and we must accommodate them on certain doctrinal points. A lot of nonsense to my mind. But who's to say whether the Eastern churches have a clearer vision of Christianity? I understand some of you Venetians prefer the Eastern ways, but what can Constantinople do for us now? Isn't it better to look to the west, towards Rome, for guidance as it used to be many years ago?"

"I don't believe you understand our attitude towards the Franks," the Doge argued. "Not too long ago, they attempted to bring us under their yoke and failed. I see no reason why we should accord them any sovereignty over our affairs, religious, commercial, or military."

"Do you really believe the Greeks in Constantinople are going to protect you?"

"No, I don't. But I envision a city of such import and strength that could never control us. Don't get me wrong. I won't go out of my way to irritate the Franks. We will continue to strive to have good relations with them. And I hope they will understand that a strong, independent Venice is really in their interest."

"Perhaps what you envision will become a reality," the Bishop said. "but I must say a city built on these tiny islands, with no surrounding lands, doesn't seem likely."

"Ah, your worship, you underestimate what we are capable of in this lagoon. But perhaps we should return to the moorage for the blessing of this new galley."

####

The galley, fully loaded, had been oared to the Rivo Alto moorage by a crew of eighteen men. Rustico and Gianni were standing beside the ship when the Doge, Bono and the Bishop and his entourage arrived. The Bishop surveyed the vessel. "She is beautiful."

Rustico smiled broadly and replied, "Thank you." The Bishop began to intone in Latin as the acolytes swung censers about the galley. After completing the ceremony, the Bishop, accompanied by the Doge and his acolytes, walked back towards the construction site, leaving Bono with Rustico.

"I'm afraid I don't understand the old language," Rustico said to Bono.

Bono replied, "The bishop wished us and the galley a safe journey and that we be conducted back home under the guidance of God."

"Amen to that. We will leave in two days, at dawn. You might bring your belongings early for stowing."

"Thank you, but you will see I have learned to travel light."

Rustico smiled and replied, "A man after my own heart."

####

That night, Leo sat in front of the fire, warming his hands while Gianni was soundly asleep and Rustico did some final packing. Leo sighed and said, "I wish I could go with you."

"Listen," Rustico answered, "This trip will be difficult, with many long days on the water and sleeping and eating where we can."

"I know. And the work will be hard too. Too much for an old man."

"We need you here to run our business. The salt works have to be kept busy, and our trading up the river has to be maintained. You know we need to have you here." Rustico added, "And then there's your new bride."

"Yes, I know, but...."

"But what?"

"I haven't been with a woman since your mother died."

"Papa, I don't think they've changed."

Leo laughed. "That's what I mean. They usually want... you know ... things."

"Oh I see," murmured Rustico. "Angela seems to be a wonderful woman, and I'm sure she'll understand. She's also been a widow for a long time. Whatever you do, don't worry about it."

Leo rose, put his hands on Rustico's shoulders and said, "I won't. I'll be thinking of you and Gianni, wondering where you are and when you'll be back."

"And that's as soon as we can, rich as Croesus."

CHAPTER 3

Slipping out at dawn, one cold and overcast, onto the misty waters of the Gulf of Venice, the galley moved east and then south along the coast of the Adriatic. Usually, ten men were at their oars while another ten rested. The crew had been divided into two groups by Rustico, and the men determined to name their groups after the colors of the boat: the reds and the blacks. The reds were led by a lean, young, hawk-nosed Venetian fisherman named Filipo, and the blacks were led by Carlo, older and quieter than Filipo and a man who had accompanied Rustico on many previous trading trips up the Po River.

After a long day, their first night out was spent on shore in a snug moorage located next to a small village. After eating, Bono found Rustico and Gianni sitting in front of a fire wrapped in blankets and asked, "May I join you?"

"Signore Bono, please sit," replied Rustico, pointing to a place in the sand in front of the fire. "How did you find our first day of sailing?"

"Fine. I've spent much time on galleys, particularly in the Western Mediterranean. And as a native Malamoccon, I know the lagoon by boat."

"Of course. Has your family been on Malamocco long?"

"My father related to me that our lineage left Verona for the gulf with the first invasion of Italy by the Lombards and opted to stay there. That was many years ago now, maybe two hundred years or so, but the family has never been fond of the Lombards since. I assume your family has a similar story."

Rustico nodded. "My father, Leo, is a bit vague on the details, but based on what he heard as a child, he feels our family left Ravenna for the same reasons."

"You fought in the defense of the islands when Charlemagne's son, Pepin, attempted to seize control, I believe."

"Yes. I was a young man then but I was there," Rustico responded. "And you?"

"I was still a boy at that time, thirteen or so. My mother and I were actually staying in Rome, where I was studying. She wanted her youngest son to be a priest. My father and two older brothers remained in Malamocco and were there when the Lombards arrived. My father was a man of some consequence in Malamocco and was asked to parley with the invaders and they were to discuss Pepin's claim to the islands. He took my two older brothers as well as my uncle; they insisted on denying that the Lombards had any excuse to be there. For their candor, they were all strangled. My mother and I returned immediately upon hearing this news, but by the time we arrived most of the residents of Malamocco had withdrawn to the Rivo Alto. And that's where I first met Agnello Participazio, the father and predecessor of our current Doge."

Bono considered for a moment before continuing. "I know all about the shenanigans of the Participazio clan and their unbridled need for power. But, during the war, Doge Agnello was an outstanding leader in defending Venice. He led the efforts to block all possible water routes that the Lombards might have used to reach the islands and urged all Venetians to resist. For this reason alone, I have been grateful to them. In a sense, Doge Agnello became a second father to me, particularly after my mother died from the miasma of the lagoon."

Rustico nodded silently and finally said, "Yes, I can see that." He paused and added, "Perhaps you've been told that my relations with the Doge and his clan have been often difficult."

"I understand your feelings about the family," Bono replied. "Constant backbiting and feuding. But one thing is true about both the Participazio doges: they were and are still adamant about Venice being in control of its own affairs and not in the thrall of what they now call the 'Holy Roman Empire' located somewhere in Germany."

All three men laughed at that notion, and Rustico added, "I assure you that we are firmly in agreement with that."

Gianni inquired of Bono, "How did you end up in Spain?"

"Doge Agnello again. After my mother died and I was left basically without a family, I gave up the idea of becoming a priest. That was mainly to please her anyway, as I had no interest in such a life. Anyway, Doge Agnello started sending me to various places in Italy in an effort to see how other duchies viewed Venice - did we have any enemies or competitors? How were these governments run? How did they prosper? So, I essentially became something of a cross between an envoy and a spy.

"The Doge, needless to say, was aware of the spread of Islamists throughout the Mediterranean and became concerned about their intentions in Italy. So he asked me to travel there ostensibly to suggest using Venetian ships for transportation but mainly to see if they were likely to become our enemy and how formidable an adversary they might be. I remained there for three years and learned to speak and read Arabic, as well as the basics of the Islamic religion. I had no family in Italy anyway and didn't mind the trip. In fact, I grew to enjoy it.

"When the Doge became aware of his declining health, he asked me to return. He wanted me to be available to lend whatever assistance I could to any new Doge, who was most likely to be one of his sons. I had been able to stay clear of the family fights by remaining in Spain and so no one objected to this proviso.

"I remain on good terms with Doge Giustiniano, so he entrusted me with this mission to Constantinople. And I am pleased to have you two men working with me on it." He ended with a smile.

Rustico responded. "I appreciate your candor. I am a blunt man, as I'm sure you have noticed. But I do appreciate how caution and subtlety - diplomacy if you like - are often necessary and why you've been so employed."

Gianni added, "We're glad you are here."

#####

At dawn the next day, the Venetians pushed the galley into the Adriatic Sea. Working hard, Gianni adjusted the masts to catch the late winter's breezes and they made good time sailing south. The galley was now on the water from sun up to late afternoon and drawn up on isolated beaches or near small fishing villages before dark. As a rule, Rustico stood on the platform in front at the stern, watching the sea and occasionally glancing east towards the coast of what he had once been told had been called Illyria by the Romans.

Bono sat at the aft deck watching the sea for other vessels. They passed many smaller fishing boats and hailed them if within earshot and occasionally stopped and bought fish from them. Bono would ask if they had met or heard of pirates in the area. Usually, the fishermen responded that pirates generally didn't bother fishermen; they were after rich merchant crafts. Bono asked one, "Do you know any pirates?"

The fisherman shrugged and responded, "I know many sailors. How am I to know what a ship is up to? They don't bother me, and I don't bother them."

"Very wise," Bono coolly responded.

"At any rate, it is still too early in the year for many, including pirates. The sea, the winds, can be rough as you know. Pirates are most likely to

43

be out later in spring or summer. That's when the merchants are moving their goods about. Nevertheless, I would keep an eye open if I were you."

"Thanks," said Rustico. "We can probably outrun them."

"Perhaps. Yet it is better to avoid problems."

"Of course, you're right."

##

On Torcello that evening, Leo and Angela lay in their new bed, naked under a rough cover, his arm around her and her head on his chest. The remains of the fire glowed red across the dark room. "Happy?" she asked.

"Mmm," Leo responded. "I didn't think I could still do this. It's been many years."

"Yes. Me too." After a moment, Leo started chuckling, and Angela asked, "What's so funny?"

"I was just thinking of Gianni. He said I should marry you, and when I asked why, he said 'for her soup.'" They both chuckled for a moment.

"Did you really ask him why you should marry me?"

"It was only a joke. I was just working up my nerve to ask you."

"So long as it's only a joke."

"You needn't worry. I've been without a woman for many years and wasn't sure, well ...you know what I mean."

"I suppose I do. But we women have our own ideas of what to do."

"I know now, but I wasn't sure."

"I was."

"How so?"

"You haven't noticed, but there is something I've added to your meals."

"Really? What is it?"

44

"Let's just say it's my secret and that you don't have to worry about anything."

"Good. Was it in the soup?" She said and they both laughed.

"Maybe. I'll never tell. Just take life as it comes, is all I say."

The next day, Claudia came by to see her mother and asked how things were going. "Fine," said Angela. "It took some coaxing, but it all came together last night." Claudia looked at her mother, startled. "Don't worry. There's nothing wrong in an old married couple still enjoying life."

"No, of course not." Claudia paused and then asked, "So how did you manage it?"

"I told him I put a special ingredient in his meal to give him strength."

"And it did? What is this 'magic' ingredient?"

"Nothing special, really," Angela gaily responded. "But he doesn't have to know that, does he?" Both women laughed.

###

Three days later, midmorning, the galley stopped about two hundred yards from the eastern shore. "This should be the entrance to the bay of Kotor." Rustico gestured for Bono toward a narrow inlet. "I propose we stay here for at least two or three days. I'd like to speak to some merchants and the crew could use a day of rest as well as something different to eat."

"Fine. I'll find out what I can about their relics," Bono replied

Rustico guided the galley into the narrow inlet and had the full complement of men row around a long promontory and then south to the town of Kotor. After docking the ship, some of the men were allowed off and strode into the town, leaving a small contingent to watch over the galley.

After seeking directions, Bono walked to the town center where he found St. Tryphon's Church. He pushed the great wooden door open and, seeing a young priest busy sweeping the floor below the crucifix, entered and said, "Good day, padre."

"Good day to you, also. I don't believe I know you. Have you recently arrived?"

"Our galley docked here earlier today. We are from the islands of Venice and on our way to Constantinople."

"You are sailing early in the year."

"True, we haven't seen many boats other than those of fishermen. We'll stop at many places and have much merchandise to sell." Bono looked around at the church. "This church looks quite new and beautiful, too."

"Thank you. And thanks also to some of our townspeople who raised the money necessary to construct it. It is the home of the remains of St. Tryphon, as you may know."

"So I've heard. We were told that the relics were brought here some years ago by merchants from the gulf, Venetians like us. They were returning from Constantinople, I understand."

"You're well informed. Indeed, a local man, Signore Saracenis, purchased the holy relics from them and led the efforts to build this church to hold them. We are very proud to have such an illustrious protector here in Kotor." The priest then quickly added, "It's also true; we are still protected by St. George as well."

"Can one see this relic?"

"I would have to obtain permission from Father Gregorius. You understand that the bones are interred in a casket, and rarely does he allow it to be opened. We're concerned that it's possible that its powers might become diluted."

"Of course. I ask because the Bishop of Grado inquired if we might see it. He has heard much about it. I am sure he would authorize a donation for a viewing."

The young priest paused, thinking, and then asked, "Are you able to return tomorrow? I will speak with him tonight and ask what he might wish."

"Certainly. Understand there are two of us who wish to view it. Rustico, the owner of the galley, is also very much interested."

"Can I find you at the dock?"

"You will recognize a new ship, I believe, painted red and black. It's a galley but also outfitted with two lateen sails. By the way, my name is Bono, from Malamocco in the lagoon."

"I will look for you tomorrow morning, Signore Bono."

###

Rustico found his way to an area near the dock filled with various shops and was greeted with a cautious nod from an older merchant who sat on a bench outside a small shop. He was plump, about forty-five years old, with a red nose, mustache, and beard, and wore a dark vest above a well-worn tunic. Rustico greeted him, "Good day. What do you sell? Or are in the market to buy?"

"I'm called Angelo," answered the merchant, sizing Rustico. He rose and said "Good day to you, Signore. It depends on what is available. And you're from where?"

"Venice, north of Kotor. You know of it?"

"Yes, of course. Venetians have stopped here before. I heard that a galley from the Gulf arrived today. Is that you?"

Rustico nodded. "My name is Rustico, and I have a cargo for sale. Pelts from the north, some lumber, as well as salt, if you are buying. We're stopping here for a couple of days as I'm interested in establishing

47

a yearly trade practice following this side of the Adriatic and continuing east to Constantinople."

"Safe and reliable transportation into the Mediterranean would most likely attract attention from many of our merchants," Angelo thoughtfully replied. "However, we probably sell many of the things that you do, particularly lumber. It is somewhat harder for us since there is no river route inland and, therefore, such goods are expensive.

"And then there are the pirates to deal with. Perhaps it's unpleasant, but acquiring some of the people from inland, particularly Slavs, to be sold as slaves seems to be a good business. The Arabs are always in the market for slave labor."

"Slaves can often be sold profitably," Rustico shrugged. "Getting good, healthy ones for a fair price is another question."

Angelo cautiously continued, "Some people believe that selling fellow Christians as slaves, and particularly to the Moslems, is a sin to be avoided."

"Yes, I've heard much the same," Rustico replied. "I've also heard that many people in these hills are not truly Christians but heretics and that selling them is no sin."

"Yes, I've heard that too. Indeed, I've heard that selling heretics to proper Christians is a good thing, to be encouraged since their souls may be saved by being proximate to the knowledge of the true faith."

"I suppose, if necessary, one could speak to a priest for guidance about these questions," countered an uninterested Rustico. Considering the idea for a moment longer, Rustico asked, "Is there a supplier of slaves in the area? Or a market for selling slaves?"

"As far as I know, there's not a continual supply of slaves locally. Occasionally a ship will arrive, and the word gets out that slaves can be had.

"However, I gather that the Saracens are the most likely purchasers around the Mediterranean, so chances are that one might find a permanent market in an Arab port town."

Rustico slowly added, "I'm sure that there are plenty of Italian towns where slaves can be bought, including some on the Adriatic."

Angelo concluded his business with Rustico by agreeing to trade dried fish, wine and bread for a bag of salt, adding that "a salt works in Kotor would do well." He suggested that Rustico come back next year and, in the meantime, he would go about obtaining lumber for him for sale in Constantinople.

##

The next morning, the young padre arrived at the dock and located the galley. He called for Signore Bono, who emerged and answered, "Good morning."

"Good morning to you. I spoke with Father Gregorius, and he has agreed to show you the remains of the saint. Would you care to follow me back to the church?"

"Of course. Let me call Signore Rustico."

The Venetians, led by the padre, made their way to the church. Inside it, they found an older priest, about fifty years old, with a long grey beard and dressed in a brown cassock which stretched across an ample girth. He rose and greeted his visitors with a nod as they gave their names.

"I understand from Father Michael here that you have arrived from the islands of Venice and are on your way to Constantinople," to which Bono and Rustico nodded. "And that you would like to view the relics we possess of St. Tryphon. I'm happy to oblige you. You do understand that constructing and maintaining this church that is honored to hold such relics is an expensive pursuit."

Bono replied, "Of course. I have brought a financial token from our Bishop Trasmondo, which I trust will be sufficient," and drew a bag of coins from his tunic.

Father Gregorius, faintly smiling, accepted the bag, merely weighing its contents in his hand. "Thank you for your contribution to our cause. Follow me." He led them into a small room in the rear of the church and to a table with an unadorned wooden box, approximately twenty inches wide and deep and twelve inches high. He gently removed its lid so that all could see a skull placed on a piece of fabric together with five small bones. Rustico and Bono leaned forward to inspect the skull; Rustico looked up and raised his hands, "May I...?"

Father Gregorius shook his head. "I'm sorry, but these relics are, of course, hundreds of years old and quite fragile. They are only rarely cleaned, and then only with the most care.

"We are proud to house them, of course. They are of extreme importance to Kotor. Many people wish to see the remains of the saint. They know how powerful he is and how he protects Kotor and its citizens. Once a year we process with them through the town so that all can see who our protector is. As I am sure you are aware the greater the saint, or martyr, the greater safety to its home."

Bono peered closely, noticing small flecks of what appeared to be dried skin upon it. "Do you know its history?"

"We know that church authorities in Constantinople verified its authenticity before releasing it to your fellow Venetians, who brought it here almost twenty years ago. We will construct a finer, more permanent reliquary in the future. Dependent, of course, on the goodwill and contributions of individuals like you who understand the great value of these relics." The two Venetians stood admiring them for some time before Father Gregorius indicated that they needed to be put away as he had other duties to perform.

On the way back to the galley, Rustico said, "Interesting. I'd like to know more about where those relics came from originally and what they paid for them."

Bono absent-mindedly nodded, responding, "Did you notice the eye sockets? I had the eerie feeling that the saint was looking back at me. I've seen relics before but never had such a feeling."

"Perhaps you're particularly receptive to the power of these relics."

"Maybe so."

They walked on towards the dock, where they found Gianni sitting with another young man. He appeared to be around the same age as Gianni, was very thin, and had worn clothes on - rags really, but clean. His thick black hair was long and unkempt and swept down across blue eyes and a sunburnt complexion. Gianni stood up to greet his father and Bono and encouraged the young man to stand also. "Father, this is Boris. He and his sister made their way here from the land of the Bulgars, where they fled from slavers."

"I see," said Rustico. "How did you get here?"

"We walked, Irene and I, or occasionally rode on wagons when they were available. Our parents died some time ago and no one was willing to take us in. So we left figuring if we could get to the coast away from the Bulgars, we'd be safe and could find work."

"What can you do?"

"I'd like to work on the sea, but I'll do what I must," answered Boris. "So will Irene. She's older than me by two years. We were afraid the slavers would try to take us both, or our neighbors would offer us to them to avoid being taken themselves."

"What do you know about sailing?" Rustico asked.

"Not much, I know," admitted Boris. "I've spoken with many fishermen and heard about the great sea, many stories. I know I'm thin, but I'm a good worker and want to learn. My sister, too. She learned much about running a house before my mother died and might have been married by now, except that many young unmarried men who might have been interested have died or fled in the fighting of the Bulgars and Romans."

"I could use help with the sails," Gianni volunteered.

Rustico glanced at Gianni and then asked, "What about your sister? Can she stay here? I don't know about a young woman on the sea."

"I won't leave her alone here."

The men fell silent until Bono inquired, "Are you Christians?"

"Our village follows the Greek church as I understand it. I don't know much about that sort of thing."

Rustico, looking doubtfully, said, "I'll think about it."

He looked questioningly at Bono, who shrugged. "It's up to you, of course, but it would be nice to have another hand at the masts. Two masts appear to be difficult for Gianni to handle alone. The girl, that's another story."

As they spoke, a young woman cautiously approached Boris, who greeted her with a smile. She was tall and striking, with a fair complexion and long black hair, which she covered with a worn blue scarf. She wore a well-worn wool dress that stopped just above her sandals, cinched snugly at the waist, and had wrapped a green blanket around her shoulders against the cold. Her face was reddened by the sun and elements with the result that her large, cobalt blue eyes were accentuated and were now boldly staring back at the three male strangers talking to her brother, who pointed to her and said, "This is Irene."

"What have you been talking about?" Irene asked of Boris while looking suspiciously at the others.

Gianni interjected, "Boris and I would like him to sail with us to Constantinople. My father," looking at Rustico, "has said he is considering this idea." Rustico glanced at Gianni but said nothing.

"He's a good boy, and a hard worker. But we can make something of a life here in Kotor. There are many fishing boats looking for workers, and I can find something that provides us a roof over our heads. Come with me, Boris."

Boris looked at Irene, surprised. "Irene, wait...." He paused and said, "This is something I'd like to do. And think of going to Constantinople! A great city."

"You should listen to your sister," Rustico advised. "Who knows what we'll run into on the sea. I cannot promise great comfort or much pay, for that matter."

"But, father," Gianni implored, "I really could use the help. And she could come too."

"There are over twenty men on this ship and no women to be with for days on end. A young girl like this would find it difficult to fend them off."

"I assure you, Signore," Irene countered. "I can take care of myself."

"But you just said you could do all right here," Rustico countered. "Did I misunderstand?"

"No." Irene hesitated. "It's true we could do all right here...." Irene paused as in mid sentence and stood looking at the ground for a moment. "But if it's something Boris wants, he should go...I want him to have his chance to do what he wants. I can take care of myself. We haven't got this far and avoided becoming slaves only by luck."

"I won't leave you, Irene," Boris replied firmly.

"I do understand and meant no insult," Rustico broke in."Boris has said he won't leave you here alone. My son wants Boris to come and help with the sails, and Boris has said he'd like to work on a boat. So what am I to do?"

The group fell silent until Bono asked Irene, "What would you be capable of doing on the ship? Rowing is difficult work enough for men, and they are tired by evening. There's a need in managing our provisions and preparing meals. Are you willing to do that kind of work?"

Irene responded, "Yes. I can do that."

Bono paused and then continued, "Just a question, what languages do you speak, Irene?"

"The languages of the Slavs of course. I speak Greek fairly well, and a little Latin. And I can read."

Bono, surprised, asked, "Can you read all those languages?"

"Yes, pretty much."

Bono looked at Rustico and said, "Let's take a walk," and the two of them walked off, leaving Gianni with Boris and Irene, who looked from one to another silently.

Boris finally shaking his head, said, "I don't want to remain here. We've been here for more than thirty days, and I don't trust most of the people we've met. Perhaps we could go to Venice."

Gianni said, "You could work in our salt business, perhaps. My grandfather is old and needs help. We also sail up the Po River to trade. You could learn much about boats in that way."

At that moment Rustico, with Bono, returned and said, "This is what I propose. You can both sail with us; Boris will work with Gianni and Irene can manage the provisions and the feeding of the crew until we get past Crete. If it doesn't work out, we'll leave one of you, or both for that matter, on the mainland, where you can head north and return to Bulgaria or go somewhere else. Think it over and if you want, be here ready to leave tomorrow at dawn."

That night, lying on the ship wrapped in his bedding, Bono woke suddenly, startled by a cool breeze in the moonlit night. Looking up he saw grey clouds scudding across an inky black sky, seemingly forming two black eyes which were staring at him. He sat up on his arms and stared back, watching the clouds slowly moving away and waiting for others to form the eyes again. He thought *those eyes looked so familiar*. He then lay back and arms crossed under his head. He felt the morning dew settle on his face and arms and eventually fell back asleep but dreamt of the staring eyes.

CHAPTER 4

Karol from the galley's red team was up out of bed before dawn in order to relieve himself over the galley's side into the bay. While returning, he looked down at where the galley was tied up to the dock and saw two figures sitting back to back, each wrapped up in bedding with a large bag beside each of them. Karol surveyed the deserted dock, leaned over, and hailed them. "It's late. What are you doing there?" The two figures stirred, stood, and, in the dim light, appeared to be two young men.

"I'm Boris. We're here to sail with you. Just ask Signore Rustico," one of them announced confidently.

Karol stood for a moment, looking from one figure to the other, and instructed, "Wait here," before walking away. A few moments later, Rustico and Bono arrived, each with a torch, and stepped off onto the dock. Rustico lifted his torch in order to see the closer of the two faces and recognized Boris, who greeted him with, "Good morning, Signore."

Rustico then moved the lantern to Boris's companion. There stood Irene, her long black hair now shorn, a sheathed dagger at her belt, and she stared back at him. "Ah, I see you're both here and ready for life on a galley," Rustico observed. "Put your things on board so they can be stored, and I'll call Gianni. No doubt he'll be happy to see you."

Bono said to Rustico after the galley left the Kotor dock for the Adriatic, "It seems we have the protection of more than the saints."

On their first day out from Kotor, the weather was cool but sunny, with white clouds racing across the sky. There were such sufficient winds that Gianni had ample opportunity to show Boris how best to use the lateen masts. Boris proved to be an apt student and, by the end of the day, was able to manage the sails without Gianni's constant attention. Also, Boris was unbothered by seasickness, unlike Irene, who kept her head over the galley's side for much of the day and appeared to be wan and feverish. The crew made up of men who basically spent their entire lives on the water, observed Irene with a mix of pity and amusement, yet kept their distance from her.

That evening, as the crew sat on a beach in front of a fire, Gianni found Irene and Boris eating together and speaking to each other in their Slavic tongue. "May I join you?" he asked tentatively.

"Please do," Irene replied, managing a smile. "I'm afraid I made a bit of a fool of myself with sea sickness and all. I'm still not very hungry."

"Don't worry. Most of us started out seasick on our first trips out, particularly on the open sea. You should get better; if necessary, there's a plant which, when eaten, helps." Gianni paused and then asked curiously, "So tell me, are you happy with your decision to sail with us?"

"I am. I love being on a boat like this," answered Boris, who looked at Irene questioningly.

"It's fine," Irene responded warmly. "I'm sure we could have made a life in Kotor. But I, too, have often dreamed about seeing Constantinople. I may not be much of a sailor yet, but we're happy to be with you." She paused, then asked, "You've been sailing since you were very young, I gather."

"Yes, but mainly upriver into the mainland or around the islands in the Gulf. This will be new to many of us," Gianni shared. The conversation then drifted into Gianni's childhood and what it was like to live at the top of a gulf full of islands. The firelight cast a pink glow on their faces as they reclined against their bags. Finally, thinking that he shouldn't be talking about himself so much, Gianni shifted the conversation, asking, "Tell me about what sort of lives you've had and how you came to Kotor."

Irene looked at Boris, who shrugged as if to say, 'Go on,' and she began, "We lived in a small town called Ohrid not far from the Greek homeland and often under the control of the Bulgarian Empire. Boris and I are Slavs, you see, and not Bulgars; there are lots of Slavs in Ohrid, probably as many as there are Bulgars.

"Generally, we all got along; that is, until the wars of the Bulgars and Romans flared up, which regularly happens. Then, people tend to take sides. Generally, my father and mother favored the Romans, like a lot of Slavs, and the local Bulgars supported the Bulgarian Empire. As you might guess, those were hard times.

"We had a small plot of land on which we grew food to eat. My father often worked for some of the larger landowners to make ends meet, and consequently, often, he'd be gone for weeks at a time during harvest.

"Boris and I were lucky to have a mother who originally wanted to be a nun and could read and write not only our Slavic language but also some Greek and Latin, which she taught us."

"You mean you, don't you?" Boris interjected with a grin. "I didn't get much out of all that."

Irene laughed and teased, "Maybe you didn't try much."

"Possibly," Boris conceded. "But starting young I was working for the most part."

"Of course," Irene replied soothingly. "And you were tired in the evenings when Mother and I talked." Turning back to Gianni, Irene went on. "We were getting by all right until about three years ago when our father was run over by a horse-drawn wagon in a farming accident and had to be brought home. Mother tended to him for five months, during which he was bedridden, only sporadically conscious, and finally died.

"Afterwards, Mother had to live and work with some distant relatives. I was seventeen then and had to take care of myself and Boris until Mother could return. However, she stayed on for over a year, and then we received word that not only Mother but the entire household died during a recurrence of the plague.

"After news of her death reached our village, our neighbors, the Bulgar ones particularly, started treating us differently. They didn't seem as friendly or as helpful, or so it seemed to us. At this time, there was a lot of fighting going on with the Romans, and consequently there were some soldiers staying in Ohrid from the Bulgar Empire. They kept looking at me – appraisingly, shall I say. It was generally known that these soldiers weren't always paid and would, if the opportunity arose, find and sell isolated local Slavs into slavery.

"So we decided it was best to quietly pack up and leave Ohrid. There really wasn't that much to keep us there, so we opted to try our luck on the coast of the Adriatic, where there were lots of other Slavs. That's how we came to Kotor."

Gianni, slowly absorbing their story, could only say, "I see," and a thoughtful silence fell over the group.

After a moment, Boris started the conversation again. "But it wasn't all so bad. We had some good times, didn't we?".

Irene responded, "We were fortunate in many ways. Our parents loved us and provided as well as they were able." She and Boris then began bantering back and forth, reminiscing about incidents from their early childhoods.

Gianni, tired from the day's journey and still reflecting on their story, lay back and listened to their easy-going chatter without interrupting. He began to think-

So this is what it must be like to have a brother or sister to grow up with, to share reminiscences, and to complete the other's stories.

He heard Irene exclaim, "That's not true! I distinctly remember Mother telling you to stay away from that house, but you wouldn't listen."

"I did try! But..."

"But what?"

"Oh, you know what I mean."

"Oh, I sure do know," Irene laughed along with her brother.

Maybe, but perhaps it's because Irene is older and feels a need to take care of Boris. Or maybe this is just what it's like to have a woman to be close to. I wonder what it would have been like having a mother or sister, a woman in the family. Leo and Rustico were fine, really, but It's nice seeing Irene and Boris like this.

"Oh, Irene, you know perfectly well what I mean...." he heard Boris chuckle.

Gianni gazed once more at Irene, saw her laughing, with her long legs stretched out on the sand next to him, her oval face pink in the firelight, with high cheekbones and large blue eyes and thought, *someday, I'd like a woman like this* before he drifted off to sleep.

######

The next days were blustery, with wind-blown rain angling into the galley from all directions. It was at first difficult for Irene, but by the third day out she felt somewhat at ease on the galley. She was finally able to examine the ship's food and wine provisions and oversee an evening meal. Three days later, the galley entered the open waters of the Mediterranean Sea and turned east, following the coast.

After spending the night beached on the southern shore of the Peloponnese, the galley continued eastward, threading through small, sparsely inhabited islands that fronted the Greek mainland.

The blacks were rowing, with Gianni and Boris stationed respectively at the front and middle masts. Bono walked back to the galley's stern looked up at the sky, and asked Rustico, "How long until we arrive at Athens?"

"Two days possibly, but three more likely," Rustico replied. "The winds are not likely to be as much in our favor once we turn north. The crew will have to work harder."

Bono squinted at the Greek coast. "Not many settlements to stop at from what I can see."

Rustico shrugged and said, "Once we get north of Athens, there'll be more."

"Boris seems to be a born sailor. He's almost as good as Gianni with the masts after only a few days," Bono observed.

"The crew likes him too. And Irene seems to have been accepted, although I understand she felt it necessary to pull her knife on someone on the black team," Rustico noted.

"Yes, Karol, I believe," Bono responded. "I gather he was only trying to give Irene a hand, and she took it wrong."

Rustico, staring at a distant point, straightened suddenly and remarked, "It looks like we have some company," and pointed to a speck on the sea perhaps a half mile away.

"Is it trouble?" Bono asked"

"I'm not sure, but let's get both teams ready for rowing, " muttered Rustico, who then called for Filipo and Carlo. Rustico pointed at the distant speck, and Carlo, after observing, nodded, "It's a galley of some sort, most likely not a merchant ship, for it's moving fast."

Filipo said, "I'll go get my crew prepared to row," and quickly walked away from the other men, all of whom had shaded their eyes with their hands and were watching the approaching boat.

Carlo remained staring at the speck and noted, "It's definitely outfitted for fighting and coming at us at full speed."

"It looks that way to me, too," Rustico agreed. "Get both teams rowing hard, and we'll see if we can outrun him." He then directed Bono, "Go to Gianni and Boris at the masts and tell them we need all the speed we can get." Bono sprinted away while Rustico steered the galley closer to the shore. The galley leaped forward when Filipo's crew settled in among the blacks, all hands rowing as hard as they could.

Boris was handling the lateen mast at midships when he yelled to Rustico, "Look behind you, both sides." Rustico turned to see two more boats, each about a half mile behind him but coming up quickly. He saw men lining the sides of both boats, some armed with what appeared to be bows and arrows.

Rustico adjusted the direction of the galley away from the shore at an angle, aiming to slip behind a rocky outcrop and force the leading boat to alter its course. But as he brought the galley around the islet, there facing him in the east were two more boats, both filled with armed men positioned less than five hundred yards ahead. Rustico quickly changed course to running due south; the oarsmen were yelling at one another to pull as hard as they could.

An arrow struck the stern of the boat, missing Rustico by no more than two feet. Another arrow struck Filipo in his left shoulder as he stood urging the rowers; he winced in pain as a crew member tried to extract it. More arrows were now coming at them from the boats in front. "They are Saracen boats, pirates probably, at least five of them," Bono said. "I don't see how we can get away from them as they have surrounded us."

Rustico glanced angrily at the attackers and declared, "Let's go right at the closest ship and see if we can hold the rest off."

"They are perfectly capable of killing us all, even at this distance, and there is nothing we can do about it," Bono said grimly. "Let me talk to them. I speak their language and can at least find out what they hope to get from us." He paused, adding somberly, "They will kill everyone, including Gianni."

Rustico mutely stood, looking at the attacking boats and finally said, "All right. What should I do? Stop?"

"It's our only chance of surviving," Bono asserted. "I'll stand on the bow and ask for a parley in Arabic. If they ignore me, then we'll do as you wish."

"All right," Rustico yelled to the crew to cease oaring, and the galley slowed to a stop. Bono found a red cloth, climbed to the base of the mast at the bow, and began to wave and shout in Arabic. The arrows stopped coming, but the pirate boats soon surrounded the galley within fifty yards. A turbaned pirate stood at the front of the closest pirate ship and began speaking with Bono, who soon returned to confer with Rustico.

"They are sending a small boat to pick me up," Bono explained. "I'll go with them, and assuming they have no reason to keep me, I'll be back with whatever demands they have. They will probably want to search the galley, and you'll have to let them." He turned as a small skiff was approaching the galley for him. As the skiff was moving away from the galley, Bono turned and looked solemnly at Rustico for a moment. Then, he turned back and looked towards the pirate ship.

Gianni and Carlo joined Rustico and stood silently beside him, all looking at the Arab warship. Finally, Gianni, frustrated, said, "There must be something we can do?"

"I'm not sure what can be done," Rustico admitted. "We'd likely all be killed if we tried to escape. We'll have to wait and hope that Signore Bono convinces them we're worth more alive."

Half an hour later, Rustico watched as Bono returned in the skiff. Meanwhile, two pirate ships began backing towards the galley. Meeting

Bono as he climbed onto the deck, Rustico asked, "They didn't kill you, I see. Are they going to let us go?"

"Not this time. They are from Crete. Apparently, a large group of Arabs left Alexandria and landed there not long ago; they have now taken control of most of the island, as well as this part of the sea. They plan to take us back to Crete and let their Emir decide our fate. Many of them are from the Al-Andalus, in Spain. I told them that's where I learned to speak Arabic." They looked around upon hearing Saracen voices speaking to each other and watched as pirates attached the galley to two of their ships by ropes. Bono added, "They expect us to begin rowing as they want to get to Crete by late afternoon."

CHAPTER 5

Several hours later, the boats arrived at the port of Rabdh el-Khandaq, where the galley's crew disembarked and, guarded closely, walked into the city, crossing over a large moat by way of a retractable bridge. Filipo, pale, with his shoulder crudely bandaged with filthy rags from the galley, walked slowly with the assistance of Karol. They were led to a large, recently constructed one-story hall, at which point all the crew but for Rustico, Gianni and Bono were led off to an auxiliary building where they were allowed to sit.

When Rustico looked at Bono questioningly, Bono explained, "All I told them was that we three are the galley's owners and that you," nodding to Rustico, "were its captain." Shortly the three Venetians were led by two Arabs to a large room at the rear of the hall. Bono spoke to them in Arabic and, upon their departure, said to Rustico and Gianni, "We'll be kept here while the Emir considers whether he wishes to hear us speak."

Rustico asked, "What are you going to say?"

"We are merely Venetian merchants on our way to Constantinople, selling goods at various stops. We're not combatants in any dispute they may have with Romans and are not interested in getting involved. In fact, they may be interested in doing business with us. We'll see how things go. The Emir will know that I was in Al-Andalus and I'm not sure whether that may work in our favor or not. Don't worry. I'll make no agreement without your knowledge." Shortly, two guards brought in olives, bread and figs, which they ate before settling into an unsettled sleep.

Next day, they were roused early and told to get prepared to appear before the Emir. Soon the pirate captain appeared and brought with him a short, bald man of around thirty years old. He introduced himself in Greek as Nikolas, a native Greek Cretan, who said he had been pressed into the service of the emirate because he knew a smattering of Arabic. "I was told of your capture yesterday. I'm sorry, but you're not the first. The Emir is basically allowing Arab pirates free reign over the sea between Crete and Greece. We assume they are paying the emirate for its protection."

Bono asked, "Have you met the Emir? What can we expect?"

"It's hard to know. Sometimes, he's abrupt and couldn't care less. Then, most of the captive men would be killed, and the women kept or sold as slaves.

"On the other hand, I have seen him on occasion, if not generous, at least not cruel. It depends somewhat on what the Arabs get from them in booty."

"We have one woman with us; the rest are Venetians, for the most part, fishermen."

"The pirates don't care. They'll sell anyone who moves. But they need to keep the Emir happy." A guard appeared and signaled that the five men were to follow him.

Abu Hafs Umar al-Iqritishi, usually known as Abu Hafs, obese and dressed in a white robe and turban, sat on a large chair on a raised platform in the center of the hall. He was swarthy and wore a beard, black with some grey, and appeared to be forty years old or so. "I am informed that your galley carries a cargo destined for Constantinople. And you are from...?"

"We are from Venice, islands off of Italy," Bono replied. "We had not heard that Crete was now an Emirate. I gather since Crete had been a possession of the Romans that there are some difficulties between you and them."

"Difficulties? That's one way of putting it. Your Arabic is quite good, I notice."

"Thank you, your worship. I spent some years in Al-Andalus and recall that you were there then also. Of course, I never met you, but I was aware of your reputation for valor and wisdom amongst the Moors."

"Were you in Cordoba during the reign of Emir al-Hakam?"

"Alas, I spent some time there and knew of some unpleasantness which involved some faithful followers being required to leave. I understood many of these people were grossly misunderstood."

Grimacing, Abu responded, "Yes, many of us had to leave, I for Alexandria where I again had difficulties and had to leave. So we came here where there is no one to please but myself."

"You are a fortunate man then."

"Yes, I suppose so. However, I hated to leave Alexandria and still have unfinished business there." Abu Hafs waved a servant holding a tray to him, picked up a date, and began eating it in silence. "It has not escaped my attention that you have the gift of a golden tongue."

Bono bowed, "You flatter me, your worship. But I only say what I believe to be true."

"No doubt. It remains to be seen whether you can be trusted. Nevertheless, it would be a pity to sell you off, perhaps to someone who did not value your gifts.

"I have the need for an articulate man. Thieves and killers I have plenty of, and I have made use of them, perhaps too often. But I've urgent matters I must deal with now, matters that apparently require persuasion, not force. I'm going to consider further what to do with you and your colleagues. By the way, I have been told that your crew includes a young woman, a Slav perhaps. Such a woman would sell quickly in Alexandria, and I'll deal with her separately."

Bono asked, "May I tell my colleagues what you have decided?"

Eating a second date, Abu Hafs shrugged. "Of course."

Bono turned to Rustico and Gianni and said, "He hasn't decided what he's going to do with us. It sounds like he might require some kind of service. He plans on keeping Irene and selling her as a slave."

"No," Gianni exclaimed. Bono and Rustico peered at hm, as he blurted out, "Tell him she's my wife."

"I doubt if that will mean much to him," Bono responded. To Rustico, he asked, "What do you think?"

"She understood what she was getting into when she came to us. But say what you can."

Turning to Abu Hafs, Bono bowed. "Please accept my apologies. Perhaps you were not completely informed but the girl, Irene, is the wife of Gianni." He paused for this information to sink in and then continued, "I understand the Koran contains many rules honoring the state of marriage."

"But not for infidels," the emir responded. "You are Christians, aren't you all?

"Yes, but we are people of the book and honor the state of marriage much as you do."

"Hmm. I don't immediately have the services of an authority on this matter." Then Abu Hafs turned to his guards and said, "Take them back. I'll see them again tomorrow."

The three Venetians sat on the floor of their locked room and looked from one to another. Bono said to Gianni, "What will Irene say if they ask if you're her husband"?

"I don't know. I doubt that she understands much Arabic."

"Still to be caught in a lie might be a problem for all of us. We might have to deny knowing anything about it. What do you think, Rustico?"

"I won't call my son a liar. I can say he hadn't told me."

"Okay. That will have to do," Bono concluded. "It's possible he'll order something different for each of us. He might let you go and keep me, at least for a while. If that happens, just leave. I'll figure some way out. I don't know that there's anything we can do for Irene. Or, for that matter, any of us."

###

The next afternoon, the three men were told that Abu Hafs would see them again shortly. Soon, two guards entered and the Venetians rose and followed them back into the hall where Abu Hafs again sat. He said in greeting, "Signore Bono - I gather that is an appropriate way of addressing you. I have someone I'd like you to meet." He turned and waved forward a thin man of medium height, about twenty-five years old. He wore a white robe like the other Arabs but had on a black brimless hat instead of a turban and was mustached with no beard. "This is my nephew, Mustafa. Like you he is proficient in various languages, including Greek and the Latin that is spoken in Italy."

Mustafa and Bono bowed to one another, and Bono said, "It's a pleasure to meet you."

"As for me. I am told that not only are you fluent in Arabic but that you spent some time in the Al-Andalus and are familiar with Saracens and Islam as well."

"I did have that privilege."

Abu Hafs said to Bono, "I have considered your situation and believe you and your crew can perform two services for me in return for your freedom. I understand you are only merchants from some islands off the coast of Italy and are, therefore, not under the control of either the Romans in Constantinople or the Franks. In fact, I understand you have

69

had your own 'misunderstandings' with both those Christian peoples as I have had with my fellow Islamists in Spain and in Africa.

"Currently, we are not on friendly terms with the Romans, who are upset that Crete is now an Islamic emirate. I would like to come to an understanding with them and propose to send Mustafa with you to Constantinople, where you will assist him in finding the right people to speak to. Mustafa is perfectly capable of conducting these conversations himself, without help from you. He will have two of our ships for the trip, but he will enter the harbor under your auspices. Once his business is completed, he will return here."

Bono, expressionless, relayed this to Rustico and Gianni, who looked silently at one another before Rustico said, "Is that all?"

Bono said, "I doubt it. It's much too easy." He turned back to Abu Hafs and said, "We would be pleased to perform this service for you. As we would be pleased to do business with you in the future should you have any needs."

"That's one item of business. There is a second. After your dealings with the Romans, you will then leave Constantinople for Alexandria, in Egypt, where you will deliver two slaves for me to the commander of the Arab garrison there. Two of our boats will accompany you, carrying these two slaves with their guards. Once you arrive, you are to tell the commander at Alexandria that I can deliver many more such slaves to him at good prices. You will tell him I have no desire to return to Alexandria at this time but would merely like to establish some type of a business relationship with the merchants there."

Bono silently absorbed Abu Hafs' words and replied, "Alexandria is a great distance from Venice and I cannot tell you how long such a trip would take."

"So you say. One other thing. To make sure you comply I will keep Gianni and his 'wife' here with me, as my guests, if you will. I will expect you back here within, say, sixty days; if you're not back by then, I shall dispose of these two as I see fit."

Bono translated this second requirement to Rustico and Gianni. "I don't see how this is possible in sixty days. And I need Gianni," Rustico immediately said.

Gianni, after a moment's silence, looking at the floor slowly said, "So it has to be." Turning towards his father, he added "Boris can take my place on the galley. Sixty days is not enough; ask for one hundred and twenty, but take what you can get. It's probably the best we could hope."

Bono turned back to Abu Hafs, "How can we be sure that you'll let us go when we return."

"It occurs to me that you're in no position to demand 'assurances," Abu Hafs replied. "Take it or not - I doubt if you would prefer the alternative. But I will say this. If they take my offer for more slaves in Alexandria, I'll possibly need some way of getting them there. That might encourage you to argue my case forcefully." Abu glanced at Mustafa, who nodded his approval.

"When do we leave?" Bono asked.

Mustafa leaned forward and asked Abu Hafs, "May I?" to which he nodded. "We will leave in two days. As the emir has said, I'll take two dhows. You will be reunited with your crew later today and allowed, under supervision, to board your galley and have any repairs made and stores replenished.

"I want to be clear on one thing: this trip and your participation in it must appear to all others as a normal, routine action of Venetian merchants. It is important that you and your crew act in your dealings with all others as if you are under no compulsion or constraints by the Emir. Specifically, if asked about the necessity for a return to Crete, you may say that two of your crew are staying here as the guests of Abu Hafs."

Two hours later, Gianni was ushered into a small building behind the hall, where he found Irene pacing. "Are you all right?" he asked.

"Yes. But I'm worried about being separated from Boris and the others. What does it mean?"

"My father and the rest of the crew are going to be allowed to sail to Constantinople in two days. Boris will be going with them. As part of the terms of their release, they are then to sail to Alexandria, in Egypt and finally return here. You and I are to remain here until they return."

"I see. Why you and me?"

"I told them you were my wife. Otherwise, they were going to sell you as a slave. As it is, two other captives are to be taken to Alexandria instead."

Irene stood quietly, trying to comprehend Gianni's words, and said, "And if they don't come back?"

"I don't know. My guess is we will both be sold."

Irene silently sat down, overwhelmed by her predicament, before adding, "I guess we'll be spending a lot of time together."

###

Rustico and Bono were led into a fenced courtyard, where they found the crew waiting. Carlo, with a questioning look, approached them, followed by Boris. Rustico said in a loud voice, "We're being allowed to leave here in two days. In the meantime, we'll pull the galley out of the water and check its bottom. We'll refill our supplies and be accompanied by two dhows to Constantinople."

Carlo looked at Rustico and said, "God has heard our prayers."

"Where's Irene?" Boris asked.

"I'm afraid she and Gianni are being kept here to guarantee that we come back. You'll need to take over Gianni's jobs." Turning to Carlo, Rustico asked, "Where's Filipo?"

"We tried to clean his wound when we got here, but it started suppurating, and he's found himself too weak to walk. I don't know if he'll survive the voyage to Constantinople."

"I don't know if he'll survive here either. We'll have to take him and, if need be, leave him somewhere else."

CHAPTER 6

Rustico and Bono were awake early the next morning when Carlo entered to say, "Signore, excuse me, but I have to tell you that Filipo died last night."

"What happened?" Rustico asked.

Carlo explained, "We had him sleeping in a separate room but always attended by one or two of us. The smell from his wound was bad, very bad. Stefano and Karol were sitting with him but fell asleep. When they woke, Filipo was gone."

"Do the Saracens know?" Bono asked quickly.

Carlo nodded, "Yes. We called the guards, and they took the body out. I don't know where."

"I'll see what I can find out," Bono said, "The Moslems like to deal with the dead very quickly." With that, he left swiftly.

Rustico stood silently, considering while Carlo waited. "Do you have any idea who can take his place?"

"Giacomo is a good sailor," Carlo suggested. "A bit older and not much of a talker, he's respected. Most of the crew would probably approve of him."

Rustico nodded, "Send him to me when he has a moment. We're going to be down two sailors with Gianni staying." As Carlo turned to leave, he passed Boris, who was waiting to speak.

Boris stepped forward and said, "Signore, excuse me. But I need to stay with my sister. I got her into this by insisting on sailing with you."

Rustico responded firmly, "Your staying is not possible. The emir has made it clear that Gianni and Irene must stay, and I'm not going to ask him to let you stay. Understand that the Arabs were going to sell Irene into slavery and that Gianni told the Emir that Irene was his wife in an effort to keep her safe."

"His wife!" Boris exclaimed.

Rustico answered, "That's right. And now Filipo is dead, and I need all the men I can get. You and Irene both knew that there could be trouble."

"Yes, I know..." Boris replied reluctantly.

"You're going to have to do more now that we're a man down on the red team. I'm expecting you'll do your share of oaring. Also, I'm going to want you to look for someone else to help handle the masts, in case something happens to you. Look, I know there's a lot going on now, so there's no hurry about that; just keep it in mind." They walked out together, and Rustico continued, "I must see to a burial for Filipo. Prepare yourself for a long journey, and, God willing, you'll see Irene back here this summer or possibly in the fall."

###

Rustico walked towards the room where the crew had been staying and found Bono and Nikolas speaking. Bono said, "Nikolas has asked for permission to take Filipo's body to the Greek section of town where there is a cemetery and a local priest who will give him a Christian funeral."

Rustico nodded to Nikolas who said in turn, "The words will be Greek, but the sentiment remains Christian."

"Thank you for doing this for me," Rustico said gratefully. "I don't suppose you know any Cretan sailors here who would want to leave with us. And who the emir would let go."

Nikolas shook his head. "None that come to mind. Most of the Cretans who are sailors are fishermen with families here that they need to provide for. And frankly, many probably suspect you won't return."

Rustico assured him firmly, "We will be back by autumn; be assured of that. I ask that you look after Gianni and Irene as best you can. I know that the Arabs will be watching them both; I will reward you for anything you do."

Nikolas responded, "I will do all that I can. I also have a son, younger than yours but very dear to me."

"I must see to the galley now."

"Perhaps I can help. I used to be a fisherman and know this area of the Mediterranean quite well," Nikolas offered.

"I'd like that. I assume you can speak with the Arabs about our needs?"

"Of course."

Bono, meanwhile, was speaking intently with Mustafa about their voyage to Constantinople. Mustafa made it clear to Bono that his dhows would be manned by armed and seasoned sailors and that, at all times, the Venetians would be watched for any signs of treachery. "Understand, please, " Mustafa said placatingly, "I don't believe you or your crew would do anything foolish. But my uncle insists that I take all precautions."

Later that afternoon, Rustico asked to see Gianni and was taken to the younger man's room. Upon entering, he embraced his son and said, "Do what you can to stay out of Abu Hafs' way, and that is true for Irene, too. Don't draw attention to yourselves; we will be back as quickly as we can. Nikolas has promised to help as much as he can, and we must rely on him."

Gianni replied, "Yes. We will be here waiting and praying for your safe sailing."

###

The next morning, shortly after the dawn of a gusty spring day, the three boats set sail into the Mediterranean Sea, with the two smaller Arab dhows on either side of the galley. They headed north towards the Cyclades and then followed closely along the Greek shoreline. The dhow in which Mustafa sailed carried a slave, a Slavic woman named Flora, who had dark hair streaked with grey. She was perhaps thirty years old and missing most of her teeth. Her fifteen-year-old daughter, Nina, was being transported in the second dhow.

The boats were brought ashore at dusk, sometimes near a small village, mostly in uninhabited spots. They greeted passing boats with a courteous wave and conversed when hailed. With Mustafa paying careful attention to all that was said, Bono asked about the weather, the currents, and what the fishing was like. One captain, eyeing the silent armed men in the dhows, asked, "What are you Venetians carrying—jewels perhaps?"

Chuckling, Bono responded, "No jewels. But we have some valuable pelts. Are you interested?" The captain merely smiled, nodded and waved his crew to move on.

One evening, as the galley and dhows were drawn up on an empty shore for the evening, Bono found Rustico alone, leaning against the galley's hull and staring forlornly at the sea, and greeted him with "Are you okay?"

Startled, Rustico quickly said, "I'm okay." He shook his head and said, "Not really. I'm worried about all the things we have to do to get my son back."

"I can imagine," Bono replied.

Rustico, changing the subject, asked, "Where's Mustafa?"

"Tending to his slaves," Bono replied. "The daughter does not like being separated from her mother. Apparently, her guards expected some form of sexual satisfaction from her, and she wanted to say no. Now she is crying and won't eat."

Bono sighed and continued "We have to proceed in the belief that Gianni and Irene will be there when we return to Crete, waiting for us. I did tell Abu Hafs that Irene could speak, and even read, many languages in the hope that he knows the value of those talents."

"I know you're right," Rustico said. "My concern is will he give them up? Why should he?"

"There's that possibility. It would be nice to have something Abu wants or needs. We need to find something. Maybe he will need us in transporting slaves, but it would be better to have something else." Bono fell silent and then remarked, mainly to himself, "The wine-dark sea. See how quickly its colors change."

"Wine dark sea? What does that mean?" Rustico echoed.

"It's just an expression from an ancient Greek poet that seems to match my mood, Bono responded. "Anyway, It's time to get some sleep," Bono added, yawning.

##

On the fifth day, the boats entered the Marmara Sea and sailed east past the vast walls of Constantinople. The masts were not used much since the galley was sailing directly into the wind, and Boris did what he could with them alone. Mustafa had his dhow pulled up alongside the galley and said, "I suspect that the Romans would wonder what these two dhows would be doing trying to sail into the Golden Horn."

Bono, looking at the enormity of the city walls, observed, "I understand that not far from here there's a harbor at the Gate of St. Aemilianus, outside the city's walls, and perhaps not as vigilantly guarded as the others closer to the Palace. I suggest you come with us and leave the two dhows there. Your crew would have to stay on board, of course, but I assume there is enough water and food aboard to meet all needs."

Mustafa nodded in agreement, "I'll take Abdul with me as security. He doesn't speak Greek but I'll do all the talking. And perhaps someone from your crew should stay with them. Someone who knows a little Greek or Latin. Just in case."

Bono relayed the request to Rustico. "We can leave Boris. He can get by in Greek, and Slavs are common enough here, I imagine." Mustafa agreed, and he, along with Abdul, boarded the galley. Although Boris was initially unhappy, he relented when Rustico explained, "You're the best choice. No Roman guard is going to worry about a young Slav seaman, and you know how the lateen masts work. Try and see if the Arabs have anything to teach you about their boats and what's been going on in Crete."

Upon arriving at the Gate of St. Aemilianus, the two dhows were tied together and left in a relatively secluded section of the harbor. The galley continued moving under oar power around the eastern tip of the city into the Golden Horn. The galley was cursorily examined by Roman guards and then allowed to dock at the Neorian Harbor.

Giacomo and Carlo were summoned by Rustico, who stood with Bono and Mustafa and announced, "We will be here at least a week, most likely two or more. The three of us are going into the city to arrange different things. Signore Mustafa will be staying there at night mostly. Possibly also Signore Bono. I plan on returning to the galley each day and may sleep here, too. In the meantime, you two are in command of the galley.

"You may let two or three men off at a time for a day. It is important that they not get too drunk or talk indiscreetly about why we're here. They may find a woman if they like, but anyone who causes any trouble or doesn't return, we'll hunt down, and I'll turn them over to Mustafa's crew."

Giacomo and Carlo looked from one to another before asking. "May one of us leave the galley with the crew members?"

"That's probably wise," Rustico responded. "It's up to you to make sure that the entire crew is here when we are ready to leave. I'll leave only a small amount of money with you for them; they won't get their pay until we get back to Venice." After Giacomo and Carlo left, Rustico said to Bono, "We have a lot to accomplish in the next couple of weeks."

Bono replied, "Tomorrow, I'll present myself at the Palace. I've been given the name of a contact there by the Doge, Claudius Eugenides. He is probably expecting me, but not Mustafa, obviously. I'll ask what he might be able to do for Mustafa and tell him that it's important for us that he has his opportunity. He may need to have a present offered to him sometime," Bono said looking at Mustafa.

"I assume so too. I have some discretionary funds available," advised Mustafa.

Rustico declared, "I'll be looking up a Jewish merchant named Jacob, located in a market near the Gate of Perama. I understand he has some connection to silk goods available here. At any rate, let's meet at the galley tomorrow at dusk so that we all know how things are going. And where we can each be found."

###

Rustico left the galley soon after dawn the next day on foot and reached the market within thirty minutes. The street was crowded and noisy even at this early hour. He asked in Greek for directions and was informed that he could not miss the entrance to the market for it was marked by a large arched roof over heavy doors which were then open for shopping, as they were every day, sometimes even including the Sabbath. Outside these doors stood the stands of money changers as well as some representatives of the city office of the Eparch, that entity responsible for governing commerce in the city.

Rustico entered and found a narrow passageway winding its way through shops on either side. Each shop had windows as well as a doorway which stood open for shoppers, and outside of which Rustico found some goods on display. Several shops displayed large open bags of spices, such as pepper, cloves, nutmeg and paprika, while others sold glassware, bronze or iron pots, pans and other items for the kitchen. Rustico inquired for directions to a shop owned by a man called Jacob, who sold silk items and was directed to a shop about a five-minute walk away.

Jacob's shop had a few items outside the door, but its open windows were filled with items of silken clothing such as dresses, tunics, cloaks, hats and vests. Rustico entered and found a man sitting in front of the table folding a cloak; he looked to be about fifty-five or sixty, had a substantial paunch, and wore a long grey beard falling midway to his chest as well as a black brimless cap over a balding head. "I'm looking for a man called Jacob. Is that you?" Rustico inquired, looking around the shop.

The man turned and squinted at Rustico, replying, "That is my name. And who are you?"

"My name is Rustico," he introduced himself. "I'm from Venice, here to trade, and was told by some merchants from Ravenna that you might be interested in doing business."

"I see," Jacob responded, gesturing towards a seat. "Come and sit and tell me what you have to sell and what you wish to buy. But first, would you like some tea?"

"Yes, thank you," Rustico accepted, smiling. "It smells wonderful."

"'Honey, I believe, is indispensable in making tea," Jacob said, leaning back and stirring his tea. "Tell me how you got here and what sort of cargo you have for sale."

"My father and I in the past have sailed up the rivers into northern Italy," Rustico began, "Trading with Lombards as well as some Franks, usually for timber, animal pelts and some metals. In return we offer them salt—we have our own salt works—dried fish and glassware, things readily available in Venice. Since the wars have ended, there is now more money available, and they are asking for more and different items. Specifically, they want spices to go with our salt and nicer, more colorful clothes. These are things which we currently have little access to, but we do know how to sail and how to trade."

Jacob, sipping his tea, listened intently as Rustico continued. "I have had a galley specially built for long-distance sailing, using some new boat-building techniques. And I plan on having other galleys built in order to obtain these desired items."

"You have come to the right place, Signore," Jacob affirmed. "You can find most things in Constantinople. We have spices from all over India and China, for example. I, myself, operate a workshop where silk garments are made. I should be happy to show it to you, and you'll see what beautiful cloth we make. You must understand there are some things the Eparch will not allow to be sold without approval from the emperor. In Constantinople all trading here is done under the supervision of the Eparch. I, of course, know how its permission is obtained, and we could discuss what a business relationship might look like."

"I'd very much like to visit your workshop," Rustico expressed with interest. "Can one purchase raw silk from your export?"

"The Eparch probably wouldn't agree to such a sale," Jacob cautioned. "You see, we used to have to purchase silk from China at exorbitant prices as they wouldn't allow us access to the secret of its production. We did finally 'obtain' this knowledge, but, again, the Eparch does not want others in turn to have this knowledge."

"When could I see your workshop?" Rustico asked.

"In two days when I have some time," Jacob replied. "And when might I see your cargo?"

"At your convenience," Rustico offered. "We are docked not too far from here at the Neorion Harbor."

"Can I send someone over to inspect it tomorrow morning so he can report to me before your visit?" Jacob questioned.

"All right, sure. My galley is black and red. I'll make sure that I will be there tomorrow morning. Assuming you are still interested, you can let me know when I should return."

"Then let us toast to our potential business relationship," and the two men lifted their cups to one another and drank with pleasure the honeyed tea.

###

Bono, together with Mustafa who wore no head covering, left after Rustico for the imperial palace. They walked along the Severion Wall towards the Great Palace, each absorbed in their thoughts as well as by the swell of people and the smells and sights of the city. They turned east and entered the palace, walking through a concreted square courtyard bounded by porticoes at the Chalke Gate. The entrance doors, twenty feet high as well as wide, were wooden and ornamented with bronze and iron artifacts and opened outwards from a large, high-ceilinged foyer. Here, they were met by Roman guards dressed in tunics and armed with swords.

"We're here to see Claudius Eugenides. I am Signore Bono from Venice and am here with an Arab emissary from Crete."

"You may sit on the divans while we see if Claudius Eugenides is available to speak with you," the guard politely instructed.

Bono and Mustafa moved towards an area by the wall lit with sunlight coming from a window high in the wall. "Hopefully, we'll be at least seen today," said Bono. "Pardon me, but I just want to be clear. I'll introduce you in Greek as an emissary from an Arab settlement in Crete but not refer to it as an emirate." Mustafa nodded.

"There appears to be nothing gained by an immediate confrontation," replied Mustafa.

"If required, I think that I must say that members of our entourage are still in Crete as the guests of Abu Hafs. I'll leave it at that, although I don't doubt that he will understand what that means."

"No doubt. I believe the use of 'guests' in order to encourage commitment to a promise ought to be well understood by the Romans," said Mustafa and continued, "Recall, however, that this does not change what I said about behaving in a normal fashion - that is, not under any duress."

"Of course," Bono nodded.

They waited for an hour when a guard walked up to them. "Claudius Eugenides will see you now for a brief meeting when you can describe how the empire might be interested," and he led them through a series of anterooms into a small room furnished with three divans on one of which Bono and Mustafa sat.

Some ten minutes later, a tall, florid middle-aged man wearing a toga and sandals entered. His hair was brown, streaked with grey and was receding over an oval, clean-shaven face with wide-set brown eyes. "Welcome, gentlemen. I hope I haven't kept you waiting too long. I assume you must be Signore Bono from our friends in Venice."

Bono bowed. "I am here as an emissary from the Doge. I believe you've been informed that I was coming to discuss trade, among other matters."

"Certainly. I have been looking forward to meeting you. Your Greek is quite good but I can also speak the Latin of Italy and some Arabic."

"We were required to stop at Crete where we asked by Abu Hafs, a Saracen noble who you may have heard of, to bring his nephew, Mustafa, with us when we were able to proceed here to conduct our business."

Mustafa bowed to Eugenedies and stated, "I can speak Greek reasonably well and have been tasked by my uncle to discuss with appropriate members of the Roman government on what terms we might be able to coexist."

Eugenides paused to consider Mustafa and then responded, "I see. And your uncle is expecting the Venetians to return to Crete after their business here is completed?"

"There are two members of their crew remaining as my uncle's guests," Mustafa smoothly responded. "One is the son of Signore Rustico, the galley's captain, and the other a Slav woman from Bulgaria. They were described to us as husband and wife and will be allowed to return to the galley upon my safe return."

"With or without an understanding?"

"I believe so. However, we are not assuming that the Roman government has much interest in this arrangement. My task here is to suggest to you that we are in Crete and plan on remaining there. We'd like to know if there is an honorable way for both the Emirate of Crete and the Christians of Constantinople to share in that part of the Mediterranean. I suppose I should add to that the Venetians."

"The Venetians are under the protection of the Roman empire, as you know," Eugenedies replied.

"Perhaps. But the Adriatic Sea and the Gulf of Venice is a long way from this city and its navy."

Bono interrupted, "As you can see, we, Mustafa and I, would like to confer with you about a variety of issues as soon as practicable. And not together. I am sure Mustafa would like a private meeting to discuss Crete while I am here to talk about Venice and our relations."

"Where can I find you?" Eugenides asked.

"Our galley is docked at the Neorian Harbor. Sheik Mustafa and I may take separate lodgings in the city and we let you know where we each can be found. But messages can be left with the galley."

"I see. I'll have to discuss this with the Emperor's advisors and then arrange appropriate meetings," Eugenides replied. "You'll most probably be talking to me about trade matters."

"Signore Rustico should also be involved in discussions on business issues. He is a merchant and the captain of the galley and is presently in the city looking at trade opportunities." Eugendies stood, nodded, and ushered them to a waiting guard.

"I understand you have a limited amount of time here in Constantinople. You will most likely hear from me within the next two days. But, please, enjoy your stay here. I believe there's a race scheduled this week for the Hippodrome. You wouldn't want to miss it."

##

After their return to the galley, Mustafa said, "Abdul and I are going to find lodgings ashore. I'll send a message to Sheik Eugenides; but we will be keeping in touch with the dhows and you, of course."

Bono stopped and turned to Mustafa, "I don't believe we need to be at cross purposes. We Venetians are merchants, not empire builders. It's in our interest to maintain relations with the Greeks and Arabs as well."

"I understand and don't see any reason for animosity between us at this time. Signore Rustico understandably wants his son back. I won't deny that Abu Hafs is a warrior and can be unpredictable. But he is now attempting something different, seeing if he can find a way where he can rule on Crete and not be constantly at war. I see no reason why he shouldn't honor his word."

####

That night, Bono and Rustico were sitting on the banks of the Golden Horn after relating to one another the events of the day. "We need to keep Mustafa with us for the voyage to Alexandria," Rustico began. "That's the only way I can see keeping Gianni safe."

Bono nodded. "I see what you mean. Mustafa has a better chance there of getting Abu Hafs what he wants. He should know who is in control and can allow what Abu wants. We should try and return to Crete first after we're done here and suggest that to Abu."

"If we let Mustafa get back on land at Crete, how can we be sure he'll return?"

"I think I can convince Mustafa that he should come with us. He's

clearly enjoying his prestige as a negotiator for Abu, and he's likely to have more chance of success in dealing with his fellow Islamists than with the Greeks. It's impossible to see the Greeks agreeing to allow continued piracy coming from Crete. It'll soon choke off much of the Roman trade by sea."

Rustico nodded in agreement and added grimly, "I'll do what I can to cut Mustafa's throat if something happens to Gianni."

"And your crew, what will they do? They'll know that we'll all die then at the hands of the Arabs. It's best to keep that to yourself for the time being."

"I know, I know."

"Our situation is difficult, no doubt. But we must proceed with the idea that Abu Hafs has nothing to gain by harming Gianni and Irene.

"There's a chariot race tomorrow afternoon at the Hippodrome," Bono said. "Let's go and see what Constantinople has to offer. There aren't many races there these days.

CHAPTER 7

The crew was breakfasting the next morning when a messenger from Eugenides arrived requesting that Bono, together with Rustico, appear after the lunch hour the next day at the palace. When asked, the messenger said he had no message for Mustafa at that time. Shortly after the messenger left, two men arrived, one young, about eighteen, thin, dark and Slavic in appearance, and the other chubby with curly hair, closer to thirty, and said they had been sent by Jacob to inspect the galley's inventory. "Climb aboard," Rustico said," and I'll show you."

Rustico opened the hold, stepped down into it, and removed the heavy leather skin tarp that covered the trade goods. Both Jacob's men stepped down into the galley and closely examined first the timber and then the pelts, peering at each one. "Okay. You have salt, I'm told."

"Yes, I have five bags." They opened each one and checked to make sure there was only salt in them.

"Everything looks okay?" Rustico asked.

The older man only grunted and said, "We'll let Jacob know and he'll get back to you about what he might be interested in," and then they left.

Irene, up before dawn, was sitting at a table, moodily eating a meal of orange and flatbread, when Gianni yawned and stood up. "You're up early," he said, sitting down across from her, examining a fig.

"I didn't sleep well," she glumly replied, and then looked up and asked, "And you?" Gianni merely yawned and shrugged. Irene crossed her arms in front of her, stood up and continued. "I've been thinking about what might persuade the Emir to keep us here until the galley returns. Both of us could probably be easily sold in Africa."

"True," Gianni replied. You're concerned that he won't keep his word. I am too."

Pacing back and forth, Irene responded, "I'm also worried that your father might be slow in getting back here."

"I know, but what can we do? If we managed to leave here on this island, the Arabs could easily hunt us down. Neither of us know anything about Crete, such as where we could hide and survive. We couldn't ask for help from the local Greeks - they couldn't help for fear of retribution. Then the Emir would then be able to say that he was justified in getting rid of us."

"I know. But they might think twice if somehow our value as slaves was temporarily diminished."

"How so?"

Irene paused. "What if I were pregnant?" For at least nine months, buyers would be put off by being worried that I might not survive. Nor the child."

"And me?"

"We'd say that you would be needed to take care of me during the pregnancy and then afterwards. It may or may not be completely persuasive, but it would buy us some time."

Gianni, still toying with the fig, responded, "We're not married."

"But they have been told we are."

Gianni studied Irene's face silently and confided, "I've never been with a woman before. What about you?"

"I've done enough to know what to do."

"Okay, if you're sure about it."

"Don't worry, I'll manage that part. You might even enjoy it."

###

Around noon, Rustico and Bono left the galley on a warm and beautiful spring day. They walked by the entrance to the palace and continued towards the Hippodrome where they entered it at a gate at its south end. Inside they found a U-shaped raceway following its perimeter; the center spine was lined with dilapidated statues of ancient pagan gods and some emperors. They moved slowly along the two-hundred-yard eastern leg toward the starting gate and Rustico, glancing up at the concrete tiers, said, "I don't believe I've ever seen so many people in one place. There must be fifteen or twenty thousand here, and it's not close to being filled." Ornamenting some of the higher tiers were tapestries, flags and other hangings, usually purple, the imperial color.

Bono looked towards the starting gates, above which, glinting in the sun, stood four large statues of horses made from gilded copper and said, "I see three chariots are racing today." The chariots were each pulled by four horses and were of different colors: one blue, another green, and the third white.

About halfway along the leg of the raceway they started to climb the stairs into the lower seating tiers, looking for a place to stop along the flat concrete platforms. They sat near a group of three men who greeted them in Greek. Bono nodded to them and, responding in Greek, said, "Good afternoon." He then turned and spoke to Rustico in Venetian Latin, saying, "We should be able to see the race well enough here."

Upon hearing this, one of the men addressed Bono. "You speak a dialect from Italy, I see. My name is Benedetto, originally from Rome but more recently from Genoa." Both Bono and Rustico turned with interest to examine Benedetto, who was clean-shaven, a little stout, of medium height and dark wavy hair, wearing a tunic of blue and white.

"How long have you been here, Signore?" asked Bono.

"Three weeks. I return to Italy next week."

"What brings you here?"

"Business. I represent a Genoese trading firm."

"What do you trade?"

"Generally, we bring amphoras of Italian wine and olive oil. We like to return with spices and household implements. Things that are hard to find in northern Italy."

"Have you been coming here long?" Rustico asked.

"This is my fourth trip, and I like it here. It's a fascinating city, so crowded, so much to see and do. The church here, the Hagia Sophia, is like nothing you'll ever see, even in Rome. The services are different from ours in Italy, and in Greek of course, but still worth seeing. What brings you here?"

"We're from Venice and primarily bring lumber and salt for sale," Rustico replied.

Benedetto chuckled, "Traders too! And from Venice of all places, a bunch of damp islands. I thought Venetians were primarily involved with trading inland. I guess that's where the lumber comes from. Who are you dealing with here in Constantinople?"

Bono glanced at Rustico and intervened, "We've had some general discussions with some low-level administrators." Changing the subject, Bono asked, "Have you been to races here before?"

"Once only. They are not held very often nowadays." Benedetto looked at the Venetians appraisingly and then continued. "It's not like it was in years past. You can see that this structure is old and not well maintained. I understand two hundred years ago, there were races all the time, and this place would be filled with up to a hundred thousand people if you can imagine that. The teams then, particularly the blues and the greens, would really go at it; lots of fights and drinking. Some really bad riots even, depending on whether your team won or lost. It's settled down somewhat today, and not as many people come."

"What can we expect?"

"The emperor, Michael II, will probably appear. The palace opens into the Hippodrome up there." He pointed to the eastern end of the track. "He'll emerge from what they call the Kathisma and greet his public. He may make some public announcements but I doubt it."

Suddenly, trumpets blared and the crowd rose to its feet. Moments later, Emperor Michael II did emerge amid a crowd of soldiers and dignitaries dressed in togas. He stood on a balcony extending from the palace, waved, and said, "Let the best team win." He waved again, then retreated back into the palace along with his retinue.

Benedetto sat and said, "Not much to say today. I've heard he hasn't been well."

The three chariots moved onto a starting line across the track, with the white lining up on the inside lane, the blue in the middle, and the green on the outside. The charioteers had to keep reining their teams of horses in as they exchanged gibes with one another. Finally, a woman, middle-aged and glittering with jewels in her hair and dress, emerged and, after looking over each chariot, yelled, "Go." The charioteers relaxed their grips on the reins and brought down their whips, snapping at the backs of their horses. The white and green teams lurched out simultaneously while the blue's horses reared up onto the hind legs before rushing into the track.

The white team took a narrow lead over the green, while the blue remained about twenty-five feet off the lead. The white team at first extended its lead but slowed as it approached the curved southern end; the blue charioteer, on the other hand, started whipping his team more fiercely and quickly brought his chariot abreast of the white halfway through the turn. The green chariot, on the outside, maintained its speed but soon, by the end of the turn, was still fifteen feet off the lead of the other chariots.

The chariots came charging up the eastern leg of the Hippodrome when the white chariot brushed against the outside wall, slowed almost to a stop, and was jerked back into the raceway, but now behind the blue. The blue charioteer looked behind briefly at his white competitor and began whipping his team harder, springing well ahead of the white as well as the green. The green charioteer also began whipping his team harder but finished eight feet behind the blue, yet still well ahead of the white.

The noise of the crowd, largely standing since the teams went through the one hundred and eighty-degree turn, was from the screaming of the blue supporters, as the followers of the white and the green either sat in silence or walked, disgruntled, towards an exit. In the meantime, a group of acrobats and a dancing black bear came out onto the race track, performing various feats in front of a disappearing crowd.

Rustico and Bono said goodbye and safe voyage to Benedetto, who thanked them and gazed after them speculatively as they left by the same gate they entered. Outside people were milling about, discussing the race and its outcome, some eating food from the stalls in front of the Hippodrome. They came across a group of young men, some wearing blue and others green, taunting one another with accusations of cheating or playing it too safe. Rustico and Bono walked back slowly towards the galley, taking the time to look closely at some of the statues lining the streets. Stopped by the smell coming from an outdoor fire, they bought a small pastry, which, huddled together, they hungrily shared.

"Quite a city," said Bono.

"Yes. But I can't imagine living in such a small area with so many people," answered Rustico.

"Al Andalus has many beautiful towns but not on this scale. I suppose Rome was once like this. Alexandria is reputed to still be beautiful and the home of people of many different nationalities, but it is much smaller now, much of it in ruins." Bono paused and added, "I guess we'll soon find out what it looks like."

Bono looked around and went on. "I'd like to attend a service at the Hagia Sophia, and the Doge asked that I inspect the defensive walls. I doubt anything like them would work for Venice, but he wants to know the secret of Constantinople's security."

"I'll go with you to the cathedral. Do you know why I've been specifically asked to attend your next meeting at the palace?"

"I did mention you as the owner and designer of the galley. They are undoubtedly aware that you were involved in the war with the Franks. And they will want to know how Venice can defend itself, and the empire for that matter." The two men continued their slow walk to the galley, arriving before the evening meal.

They checked with Carlo, who reported that all the crew had been allowed ashore for at least four hours and they all returned with no one suspected of considering trying to leave. They were talking about where and how to unload the galley's cargo when Mustafa, together with Abdul, arrived. After a brief greeting, Mustafa announced, "Today I received an invitation to return to the palace early in the morning in three days."

"Do you know who you're meeting with?" Bono inquired.

"No. And you? What about you?"

"Both Signore Rustico and I have a meeting scheduled for tomorrow afternoon. I imagine it will involve discussions of trade and doing business here. I doubt whether they are going to involve us in what happens in Crete." In reply, Mustafa only nodded. "Do you need anything from us?"

"Are you going to discuss why you're going to Alexandria?"

"They'll no doubt ask and I'll tell them we are delivering two slaves and a brief message from Abu Hafs. In my opinion, it would be unwise to not be open and honest."

"No doubt."

Rustico paused and then commented, "Signore Bono and I have been discussing this matter, and we are concerned about whether we can be successful in pursuing your uncle's request. We think that such a message would be better received if delivered by someone in Abu Hafs' inner circle."

Mustafa looked at Rustico and then Bono. "What are you saying? That I go too?"

"Look at it from the perspective of your co-religionists in Africa," Bono interjected. "What do they know of us? We are merchants only. How can we make promises on behalf of Abu Hafs? What do we know of his plans? Or ambitions?

"But you do. You're obviously close to your uncle, a confidante. They are much more likely to be persuaded by you than us. We would be there, of course, and would provide whatever assistance you might need. Not that I think you'll need any."

Rustico, who had been nodding in agreement as Bono spoke, added, "In all honesty, you're more likely to be able to gain something for Abu Hafs in Alexandria than here with the Romans. You've been tasked with a difficult job in getting much from them."

Mustafa looked at the two Venetians skeptically and muttered, "Perhaps."

###

The next morning, Rustico and Carlo were examining the hold for any leakage when they heard someone hailing "Signore Rustico. Are you there?"

Rustico emerged and found Jacob and the older of his two workers waiting by the galley's side. "May we come aboard?"

"Yes. Of course."

With a push from his assistant, Jacob arrived unsteadily on deck. "Thank you for seeing us. I have heard reports about your cargo and would just like to see for myself."

"Certainly, Carlo, show this man the contents of our hold," Rustico replied and watched Jacob gingerly lower himself with some help from Carlo into the galley. A few minutes later, they returned to the deck.

Jacob, out of breath, wiped his brow and asked, "I'd like to discuss our business with you a bit further. Can we step off your galley and walk down the quay and sit and talk?" The two men disembarked and walked to a bench fronting the harbor.

"Your timber is of a satisfactory quality. And the pelts and salt are acceptable too."

Rustico silently crossed his arms in front of him, maintaining a noncommittal expression. Chuckling and shaking his head, Jacob said, "We're both merchants, so there's no need for such talk, I suppose. I wish to make a deal with you. You'd like a selection of silk products, and I'd like the timber and pelts. I also happen to have recently acquired a selection of very high-quality salted pork. I can't sell it all, as many of my customers don't eat pork, so I'm willing to offer it to you at an attractive price."

"What about the glassware?"

"The glassware is acceptable. We do have a lot of glass available here, though, and I can't pay much. How about a variety of spices?"

Rustico nodded. "Yes, I want a selection of spices, and I'd like to see the pork as well as the silk garments before settling on the relative amounts. I'd still like to see your silk workshop as you offered."

"We understand each other. I believe we can do business in the future. Why not come to my shop this afternoon, inspect the pork, and then I'll take you to my factory."

"I expect your crew will transport the goods to and from this dock."

Jacob shrugged, "All right. By the way, I've spoken to the Eparch about this sale and obtained its approval. Through friends in the Eparch, I have come to understand you and your partner are to meet with a representative of the palace later this week. You will be expected to discuss any future business arrangements at that meeting."

"I imagine so. Thanks for letting me know.

Leo pushed the door open to his house and found Angela stooped over a kettle on the fire pit. She asked, "What happened to you? You're wet and muddy."

"I know. I'm sorry to make such a mess. I slipped in the mud and fell."

"Are you hurt?"

"No, just my pride."

"We need to hire someone to help. The work is too hard for you."

"I can still manage. Don't worry."

"We can afford help, you know. You used to have Gianni to help."

"I've got to get out of these clothes," Leo replied, ignoring Angela.

They sat eating in silence until Angela said, "I worry about you, you know. You're no longer a young man."

"I had asked for help from a young man in the village, but he didn't appear. I don't know why."

"I see."

"Perhaps I am too demanding and have a reputation as such."

"Maybe so," Angela murmured. "I can ask my son-in-law if he would help."

"If you like. I can't afford much."

"You also can't afford to hurt yourself and not be able to do anything."

"Very true. I'll also go back to the village and see if any of the fishermen are not out on the gulf and might be willing to help out."

"Okay. I'll feel better then. Don't you have a river boat due back here soon up the Po River?"

Leo sat silently for a moment and said, "They are late in returning. Again. Just like the last one."

"Didn't they explain that the weather slowed them done?"

"Yes, yes. It's always something with these boatmen."

"It's always something because it's not Rustico or Gianni."

"Possibly," answered Leo. "We need this part of the business to be successful. In case this new venture doesn't prove as successful as Rustico anticipates."

Angela nodded. "I understand that. I do. But don't you see you can't continue to take on all these responsibilities yourself.'" Leo moodily continued eating without commenting. Angela continued, "Leo, I know you're a proud man and have a right to be so. You and Rustico have built a thriving business and are admired by many. But now you're trying to do all the work that Rustico and Gianni did, as well as your own." Angela reached across the table to take hold of Leo's hand and said, "I should be part of this world of yours too. I want to be with you when the boat arrives and you review their transactions. Okay?"

Leo leaned back and said, "Of course, you're right. I sometimes forget about what you can do. I would like that."

"Thank you," Angela said, squeezing Leo's hand gently.

CHAPTER 8

Irene, naked under a blanket, rolled onto her side and looked inquisitively at Gianni. "Well?"

Gianni, on his back staring at the ceiling, turned towards her and said, "It all happened so fast. Did I do all that I was supposed to do?"

"You were fine. It'll get better." She moved closer to him and laid her head on his arm. "The pleasure will come, don't worry. I have a few ideas on what we can do, but right now, I'm more concerned about getting pregnant."

"Oh it was pleasant, all right." Gianni moved his hand down her side and pulled her closer and added, "I'm ready when you are."

Rustico walked with Jacob west on the Mese Road for twenty minutes until reaching a section of the city largely comprised of warehouses and workshops. Turning onto a side street, Rustico shortly found himself outside a large, unpainted, two-story structure with a set of stairs leading to a door into the second-story.

Jacob pushed the first-floor door open, and they entered a large room with fire pits up against two outside walls and filled with ten wooden looms. Each of these was tended by an operator, all of whom were older women dressed in shabby work clothes, with their heads covered with scarves. All of the looms were in use, its operator making silken fabrics of various designs and colors. Against the windowless walls were long tables on which were placed completed articles of clothing as well as large spools of silk thread. Children were going up and down the aisles, retrieving silk thread for the operators and taking the woven products to one of the two tables. A foreman sat at a desk in a corner, supervising the crew and noting what sort of product was next to be woven.

Rustico walked among the looms, watching the weaving process and then examined some of the completed items, carefully running his hand across the material. "These are beautiful, the colors are so brilliant."

"We produce a twill known as samite," Jacob explained. "It can be used for clothing or wall hangings or even bookbinding. As you can see, the main threads are hidden due to the patterning. Occasionally we receive an order for a specific weave - usually by wealthy people for formal clothing and the like. Mostly, we produce what we know is normally in demand. Seamstresses who actually complete the garments are our main customers." Rustico nodded appreciatively.

"I suggest you select a variety of weaves for your first purchase and see what your customers want. I'm quite sure you'll sell what you take. Purple, however, is not available."

"What's upstairs? Storage?"

"My home."

Rustico chuckled. "I understand all too well. I live next to our salt works."

"We're men of business, aren't we? And we do what we have to do" Jacob said as he followed Rustico to the door.

###

Early the next afternoon, Bono and Rustico entered the palace through the Chalke Gate. They had left early, bought food from a street vendor and sat in the ceremonial square fronting the Gate, watching the throngs of people going in and out of it and studying at the statues which ringed it.

"What do you expect from me in this meeting?" Rustico asked while eating a pastry sweetened with honey.

"I'll do most of the talking, but you are welcome to add what you feel is appropriate. I'm expecting them to ask what we might want in exchange for our security services. They may not come right out and ask in the hope that we might offer them for no cost. I'm guessing you have some idea of what Venetian merchants might want for such an obligation."

"It seems nothing happens here without the approval of the palace, including where and when you can conduct business," Rustico observed. "And I can see why having a permanent presence here would be beneficial. Then, orders could be sent overland or by boat without having to guess what might be available or needed."

"Anything else? What might be of benefit to our merchants?" Bono asked.

"I can't say how it might be achieved, but it would help businesses both here and in Venice if there was some way of conveying money without having to carry it in our boats."

Nodding, Bono replied, "I see what you mean. It's an interesting concept."

Inside the Gate, they told the guards they were expected by Claudius Eugenides, and they were soon led back to the same room where Bono and Mustafa had their initial palace interview.

Eugenides entered, followed by two men dressed in military fashion, one an older man, frowning, with short gray hair and large brown eyes. "May I introduce Leonides," Eugenides said to the two Venetians. "With the army. And his associate, here, is Justin and is with the Roman navy," he said, indicating to a short, muscular man with a sunburnt face and a full set of very white teeth.

Eugenides continued, "Please, everyone, have a seat. Would anyone like a glass of wine, watered, of course?" Everyone except Bono declined. "It looks like it's you and me," said Eugenides to Bono and signaled to a slave waiting outside the door for two glasses.

Seated, Eugenides began. "Thank you all for coming. Just to let you know, we will have a meeting with your acquaintance, Mustafa, tomorrow, but we felt we might be better served talking to you first.

"We understand you are in an awkward position. You have a son essentially held as a hostage by Abu Hafs, who styles himself as Emir of Crete. As you may or may not know, he's only been on Crete for no more than two or three years. Apparently, he was forced to flee Alexandria due to some subversive activities there and took his following to Crete where, undoubtedly for a percentage of their take, he seems to be encouraging Arab piracy in the surrounding sea." Bono and Rustico patiently nodded in understanding.

"We're presently in a difficult position militarily. We just successfully put down an uprising in Bulgaria but still need to keep an army there. Plus, we are constantly being harassed to our east by Saracens and need to have some military forces there. So, just now, we don't have the ability to remove Abu Hafs from this new emirate. He's a problem for us all."

Leonides cleared his throat and said, "We've been told by Cretan fishermen that Abu Hafs has several thousand Saracen followers, fighting men and their women and children, with him on Crete. He was able to seize the Greek port city of Heraklion and rename it. We know this city and are aware that it's surrounded by a large moat and is well protected. It would require a substantial armed force to remove Abu Hafs and his followers, and I don't know where we could find one at this time."

Justin waited for Leonides to stop and said, "We've already had several run-ins on the Mediterranean with pirates who use Crete as their base. We do all right against them one-on-one, but then they slip back into their harbor and wait for us to leave. To be successful, we'd have to have a flotilla of warships enter the bay and catch them by surprise. This all takes time and money."

"So you see," said Eugenides "there's not much we can do for your immediate problem."

"Mustafa is here to negotiate some sort of arrangement so that Abu Hafs can stay in Crete and not continually fight the empire," said Bono.

"Our response to Mustafa is going to be noncommittal. However, the Arabs must see that the empire cannot let Crete remain a haven for pirates," Eugenides replied. "I don't see what Mustafa can offer us that can allow us to look the other way. Abu Hafs doesn't appear to have any desire to restrain his pirates."

"Mustafa will probably offer on behalf of Abu Hafs some sort of payment."

"We are expecting that. But I doubt any such payment could be anywhere close to our costs in lost trade."

"I might also interject here that the army is already very unhappy with having a Saracen enemy so close to the city by sea," Leonides added.

Eugenides nodded. "Which leads us to the reason why you are here in the first place. The emperor is aware that we can't successfully fight all of our enemies at one time, and we need to make arrangements for help, particularly in keeping the Mediterranean open. Venice has shown that it has the ability to protect itself, particularly from enemies at sea. I know that Signore Rustico, here, was among those Venetians who fought against a Frankish army not too long ago, using boats and thumbing their noses at them from your islands."

Rustico shrugged and nodded, allowing, "I was one of many."

"We are hoping that an understanding could be reached where Venetian ships could protect the sea trade routes on our behalf in exchange for an annual sum of money together with weapons and help in shipbuilding."

"What about Greek fire?" Rustico asked.

"That is one weapon we'll never negotiate away, not even to our closest friends."

"We Venetians are primarily merchants," Rustico went on. "We don't have a lot of land, nor a lot of people. We <u>do</u> know how to sail and how to build boats. But we need to conduct business here and throughout the Mediterranean in order to pay for what you're asking.

"I've have come to Constantinople with a cargo of timber and pelts, items which you need. You have things we want, silk fabrics for example, spices also. However, I don't want to have to guess in the future whether the Eparch is going to allow these transactions. I believe you understand what I mean."

"I'm aware of your recent dealings and understand your concerns. I believe we can devise some way of eliminating much of this oversight."

"And then there are the duties imposed on us traders."

"Go on."

"At bottom, we need the opportunity to maintain a presence here and a clear understanding that we can sell what we have, purchase such items as textiles and spices in whatever quantities we wish, with no duties imposed."

Eugenides drew his breath in and said, "You ask for a lot."

"And so do you. It's likely to be fighting Venetians who are keeping up the value of these items if you can't protect the trade that gives them their value."

"I understand. Some of these things will take time to work out, such as where and how you might maintain a permanent trading post. I'll discuss this with the emperor's advisors, and I'll propose that I travel to

Venice sometime soon, maybe within the year, with the response of the emperor. In the meantime, I understand you're sailing south to Alexandria.'"

"First, we must return to Crete," replied Rustico disconsolately.

"I wish I had some way to help you in that regard," Eugenides slowly responded. He added, "I'll stress to Sheik Mustafa that the Emir must keep his word about his 'guests' if he wants to have any productive dealings with us in the future, or anybody else for that matter. However, I'm aware that that may not mean much to him given our present situation."

"Thank you," replied Rustico. "Perhaps you can add that we did try and persuade you to negotiate with the Emir."

"Of course."

####

The next day, after overseeing the unloading of much of the galley's cargo onto the quay, Rustico together with Bono, left for services at the Hagia Sophia. They arrived well before the scheduled service, walked into the nave and craned their heads to look up at the dome soaring to almost two hundred feet over a floor composed of a white marble that seemed to Rustico to resemble a shallow sea bottom.

Unexpectedly they were interrupted with "Signores, I see you have found your way here."

"Signore Benedetto!" Rustico, surprised, replied. "What a coincidence. We just arrived."

Benedetto, holding a hat in his hands, looked from side to side and said, "I come most days, particularly now that I am leaving soon. There is nothing in Italy to my knowledge to compare with this."

"True, at least for the time being," answered Bono. "I know Rome is almost a ruin now, but it also had many wonderful structures built by

Roman engineers. Our Doge has plans for a new chapel, which I'm sure will also be beautiful."

"You've seen Rome then?"

"Some years ago, I studied there with the thought of being a priest," Bono replied. "And you?"

"I was born and raised there, but as far as I'm concerned, Rome is the past. The pope is there, true, but the future of Italy lies in the north, cities like Genoa and Firenze. Milan."

"Venice, too, I suggest."

Benedetto shrugged. "Perhaps. Our future is on the seas, and Venice certainly is on the water. Even in the water, one might say."

"When do you leave?" said Rustico, smiling and ignoring the gibe.

"In a few days. I hope to return next year. And you?"

"We'll probably leave in a week. I'll be back next year too. Who knows—maybe we'll see each other again. We might even be business competitors."

"Maybe so," replied Benedetto. "I gather you have had some success in lining up business then. What have you been selling and buying?"

Bono replied "We've sold some lumber and salt, bought a few luxury items. Nothing much."

"The taxes and fees here are ridiculously high, don't you find?"

"I suppose so," Rustico hesitantly answered. "But we must leave for an appointment."

"With the Eparch, I would guess."

"Yes, of course, the Eparch. Anyway, goodbye and bon voyage."

Benedetto watched the Venetians hurrying away and mused.

Being a little vague, aren't you? I wonder if they have discussed any special 'arrangements' with these Greeks. Perhaps I'll make some inquiries at the palace. Genoa shouldn't be left out of any deal-making.

##

Over the next two days, Bono viewed the walls and defensive fortifications of Constantinople while Rustico supervised the stowing of the goods purchased from Jacob. He had the pork positioned below the carefully wrapped spices and silk goods. He and Jacob also visited a workshop of seamstresses where he watched the stitching of the woven silk fabrics into garments and wall hangings.

One evening, Bono and Rustico were sitting on the quay when Mustafa, followed by Abdul, arrived and greeted them.

"How are things on the dhows?" Bono asked.

"Abdul has gone there each day, and I've also checked with them three times. They are bored, as you might expect, and want to return to Crete. They can't communicate with Boris since he doesn't understand Arabic. Are you both done with your business here?"

"We're ready to leave," Rustico replied, as Bono nodded in agreement.

"And you?"

Mustafa indicated to Abdul that he could sit. "I had a meeting with two men who described themselves as advisors to the emperor."

"Perhaps they were," Bono said. "But maybe not. Is that what you mean?"

"Exactly. Sheik Eugenides was there early to meet with me for a short while, but he soon left, although only after accepting a small present. I then attempted to interest these two 'advisors' in negotiating some sort of territory sharing. But they kept saying that the piracy had to stop before they would even entertain any ideas. They wouldn't even talk of

109

money, odd coming from a Roman. They did stress that you asked them to meet to negotiate further."

"What do you want to do?" Rustico asked. "It doesn't seem likely that staying here is going to be productive."

"No," admitted Mustafa. The three men sat in silence.

Bono asked, "I assume you were with Abu Hafs in Alexandria?"

"Yes, I grew up in Africa. And my mother, Abu Hafs' sister, is still there."

"I understand Alexandria is very beautiful."

"It's still a Greek city, well located and laid out, with lots of beautiful white marble." They were silent again. "I have been thinking about what you said to me, the reasons why going there with you might be beneficial. I intend to mention this to my uncle. He's not going to be happy about what the Romans want. But reconnecting with the Arabs of Africa is probably more important to him."

"Can we leave in two days?"

"Yes. You do understand that you might have expressed concerns about this trip; however, my going with you is my idea alone."

"Of course," said Bono.

CHAPTER 9

Two mornings later, the galley left the Neorion Harbor with all hands rowing. The sun was already well above the horizon as the galley turned south towards the Marmara Sea, sailing into brisk winds. They entered the harbor abutting the Gate of St. Aumilianus and found the dhows loaded and waiting to sail. Mustafa and Abdul were on the same dhow, and Boris was allowed to rejoin the galley.

Rustico yelled to Mustafa, "We'll go as long as we can, but with these winds, it may not be very far."

"We'll use the sails as much as possible and suggest you also do the same. Let's go," responded Mustafa.

The winds changed direction mid-day. Stefano, a younger member of the black team, volunteered to work the sails with Boris. He told Boris that he had some earlier experience with sails on a small fishing boat in Venice and he indeed learned quickly. The galley made good time and managed to get past the outer wall of the city and into the Aegean Sea by dusk when they pulled the boats out of the water and settled in for the night.

Boris and Stefano sat together and discussed the sails for most of the evening. Mustafa, with Abdul behind him, sat glumly looking into the fire. The crew rose before dawn, ate a cold breakfast, and pushed off into a sunny, windless day.

Beached that night on a small island in the Cyclades, Mustafa approached Bono after the evening meal. "I'm going to send the faster dhow ahead of us tomorrow so that Abu Hafs won't be surprised when we arrive. We'll dock and I'll go ashore and talk to him alone."

"Can we see Gianni and the girl?"

"Probably. I will certainly try," responded Mustafa.

###

The next morning in Constantinople, Eugenides, in his palace office, was informed by a guard that a certain Genoese gentleman of his acquaintance, named Benedetto, had appeared and asked if he could have a few minutes of his time. "What's this about, I wonder?" Eugenides moodily asked.

The guard responded, "He didn't explain much, saying only that he'd had the pleasure of meeting two gentlemen from Venice and needed a moment of your time."

Eugenides sighed and said, "These damn Italians! Show him to my private conference room and I'll be there shortly."

Thirty minutes later, Eugenides entered the conference room smiling pleasantly and closed the door behind him. "Ah, Signore Benedetto, what brings you into these drab walls on such a nice day? I thought you were returning to Genoa, fully laden with our Greek money." He said.

Benedetto rose and bowed to Eugenides, "Thank you for seeing me on such short notice. I am about to leave as you say, but I couldn't depart without delivering to you an additional, and not inconsequential, token of Genoese regard." He then drew a small bag, jingling with coins, from his toga and casually placed it on the table beside the Roman. Eugenides nonchalantly picked up the bag, gently weighed it in his hand, and then placed it inside his toga.

He pleasantly nodded to Benedetto, who went on to say, "You continue to be helpful to our Genoese travelers who occasionally bring items for sale here, and I want you to know how much Genoa appreciates your friendship and help."

112

Eugenides smiled and asked, "Did you have anything further to discuss? I am a little pressed for time."

"Of course. I happened to meet two Venetians recently here in Constantinople who appear to be here on some sort of business. In fact it was initially at the Hippodrome that I spoke with them and then again at the cathedral. They were rather vague about their business but mentioned they've had some dealings with Roman officials. I know that you often recommend to visitors that they ought to see the chariot races and it came to my mind that perhaps they had spoken to you. Their names were Signores Bono and Rustico."

"Very clever of you, Signore Benedetto, I must say. I did happen to confer with these Venetian Signores, particularly about what Venice might do to reduce the incidence of piracy on the Adriatic. But what of it?"

"Perhaps something similar to what we do on the west coast of Italy?"

"Somewhat similar, perhaps. But not completely. We can only do so much for them on the Adriatic."

Benedetto responded, "You can only do so much for us, too, apparently."

"We do what we must, as you are aware."

"I assume certain terms were discussed. Perhaps payments to be made to Venice for various services; maybe unusual trade concessions."

"The Venetians made certain requests which we offered to take under consideration. Much of what they asked for they won't get any time soon. As I'm sure you can see, it is in both the interests of Venice and the Empire that maritime trade be protected in the eastern Mediterranean by someone, the Venetians or us. I should think you know this and, in fact, ought to be happy about it."

"Genoa supports any new levels of protection for trade on the sea. In fact, we believe that we are part of this effort," Benedetto argued. "And as a consequence, we feel we should be treated in the same manner as the Venetians and profoundly believe we're entitled to the same compensation as whatever Venice gets."

Eugenides stiffly responded, "I understand what you are saying. But it is likely that the Venetians will have more of a problem than Genoa does, particularly with Crete."

"The pirates of Crete have attempted to interfere with Genoese ships as well."

"I haven't heard that Genoa has sent warships to deal with the Cretan 'emirate.' Did I miss something?"

"No, not as yet," Benedetto allowed, but then pursued with, "All I'm saying is that we Genoans have reasons to view Venice as a business competitor, now and in the future, and we want the same treatment. Remember, our largesse is not unlimited. Thank you for your time."

Eugenides, now smiling again, followed Benedetto to the door. As he held the door open, he said, "My dear Signore Benedetto, I want you to know that Genoese traders are always welcome in Constantinople, and I shall do whatever I can to maintain our friendship."

"We're counting on you to do so," answered Benedetto. "I'll be back next year and look forward to hearing more from you on this matter."

"Of course."

####

One cool morning, early, Nikolas rapped on the door and called, "Signore Gianni?"

Irene opened it partially and said, "He's not here right now. How can I help you?"

"Thank you. May I come in?"

"Of course," replied Irene. "Please come in. I just didn't expect anyone."

Nikolas, nodding, entered and continued. "I've been meaning to see how you've been doing. Abu Hafs sent me to the south of the island on some fool's errand, and I can't say no, can I?"

"No, I suppose not." Irene nodded

"I imagine you're worried. I know I would be. But I doubt that you've crossed Abu Hafs' mind much recently. He's been expecting his nephew, Mustafa, for some time. He hasn't been gone that long, but—what can I say?"

Irene cautiously responded, "We're doing our best to stay out of his way."

"Good. That's fine. Is there anything I can do for you? Most of the local Greeks know about your situation. They'd like to help if they can—but they can only do so much without irritating the Arabs."

"There is one thing perhaps," Irene asked uncomfortably. "Are there any midwives available?"

Nikolas, surprised, said, "There are some knowledgeable women. Are you...?"

"I don't know for sure. I'm having some bad mornings."

"Do the Arabs know?"

"No."

"Gianni?"

"He's aware it's a possibility." Irene relaxing a bit confided, "He doesn't know much about women."

"I'll have a woman come by later this week. Miriam is her name."

"Thank you."

Later that morning, Gianni came in, and Irene shared her conversation with Nikolas.

"It's a bit early, isn't it?"

"Yes, but to be careful we'll want it out soon. If I don't get pregnant, I can say I lost it. This happens all the time, and no one will be surprised. I think it might be better if the Arabs hear about it first from the local Greeks, not us."

Gianni nodded. "I see."

Irene, relieved as though a difficult decision had been suddenly made, said, "In the meantime, you're my slave."

###

On a hot, humid summer afternoon, the sky a vivid blue, the galley, accompanied by an Arab dhow sailed into the harbor of Rabdh el-Khandaq. Mustafa and Abdul disembarked from the dhow and walked into the town. The two slave women were also taken off of it. The Arab guards indicated that the Venetians could tie up the galley but needed to stay on the quay until Mustafa returned.

Rustico paced rapidly up and down the mole in front of the galley. The crew sat in the heat for an hour until Bono asked if they could take shelter from the heat in a shaded gazebo facing the quay. After some discussions among the guards, they were allowed to move out of the sun.

Two hours later, Mustafa, dressed in white robes and a blue turban, appeared. "My uncle wants to see you now."

"Is he unhappy with us?" a concerned Bono asked.

"He was unhappy with me. But I believe he understands the wisdom of my continuing with you."

"What about Gianni?" Rustico asked. "Can I see him?"

"I'll see if you can see him tomorrow morning. I understand he's fine, as is his woman."

"Thank God," Rustico exclaimed.

The three men walked across the bridge over the moat and entered the palace. "Wait here," said Mustafa. "I'll see if there's water and something for you to eat while you wait."

Rustico sat, leaning forward with his hands on his knees, staring at the marble floor. "I don't know why we can't see him tonight." Bono, lost in his own thoughts, nodded in agreement and then indicated a need for silence with a nod of his head toward the presence of two Arabs waiting outside the door.

A jug of water, some cups and a plate of figs were brought, which they silently consumed. Mustafa appeared with two other armed guards and said, "Follow me, please."

The Venetians entered the large hall and found Abu Hafs seated on his throne again, now leaning to his left to hear the whispered words of a courtier, to which he nodded. "You're back unexpectedly," Abu Hafs began. "But no matter. My nephew told me of the Roman response to our proposal, and I'm not surprised. At any rate, Mustafa says he wishes to accompany you to Alexandria; I gather you understand why and have agreed to provide whatever assistance he might need."

Bono bowed and said, "Your nephew, I'm sure, did his best to reach some accommodation with the Romans. We were not in those meetings, of course, but I might add that we did not gain all we wanted from them either."

"Really?" Abu Hafs replied, unimpressed. "I expect better results with this venture to Africa."

"And rightly so. I imagine a steady, reliable supply of slaves ought to seem attractive to your associates there."

"You will leave the morning after for the port of Sitia. You'll stay there long enough to resupply and to take on more slaves. Our boats, carrying these slaves, will then accompany you to Alexandra. You're to follow Mustafa's instructions in all matters. In the meantime, you are free to meet with Signore Rustico's son, Gianni, and his wife tomorrow." Abu Hafs waved them away and they were led back to the galley. The guards, informed of their prolonged stay, led the crew, including Bono and Rustico, back to their respective rooms.

Bono and Rustico sat on benches in front of their room, still quite warm, and watched the evening come upon them. "So far, so good," Rustico said. "I wasn't sure how Abu Hafs would react."

"Me neither," Bono replied and then added. "We need to do all we can in the hope that Mustafa will be successful in Alexandria."

###

Bono left early the next morning to see how the crew had been treated. As he was leaving, he met and greeted Gianni, who had been brought to see his father, still in his room. Gianni was dressed in clothes provided by Nikolas: rope sandals, a green tunic and a matching cap, items which had been gotten by Nikolas as cast-offs from local Greek fishermen and farmers. The father and son embraced silently.

"How are you being treated?" asked Rustico, still holding Gianni's shoulders. "You look fine."

"All right. We don't have much dealings with the Arabs. It looks to us as if they are having Nikolas responsible for taking care of us."

"I see. Do you trust him?"

"I think so. But neither I nor Irene tell him much."

"He's probably reporting back to the Arabs about you."

"That's what Irene says, too." Gianni glanced around and continued in a low voice. "Irene is probably pregnant. By me. She feels she has a better chance of not being sold if she is with child."

Rustico, taken aback, thought for a moment and then added. "She's probably right. I certainly hope so."

The next morning, Gianni and Irene walked to the harbor and watched as the galley and a dhow were being prepared to sail. They found Nikolas there, speaking with the Arab guards, who seemed to know him well.

The dhow was equipped with three lateen masts and was to carry a small crew of Arab sailors who were then busy inspecting them. Nina was clinging to her mother in the dhow, glowering at her captors.

Rustico approached his son and Irene and embraced Gianni. "We will return as quickly as we can but it's likely to be several weeks. We'll do what we can to see that Abu Hafs gets what he wants. Be careful."

Nikolas walked back towards the Greek section with Gianni and Irene, all silently consumed with their thoughts. As Gianni and Irene stopped at their front door, Nikolas addressed Gianni. "Perhaps you could help us out. Most of the native Cretan men are out fishing now or tending to their sheep, and we need some help making cheese. It would give you something to do and you'd meet many of the older men. Of course, we'd provide you with additional food and clothing. I know the Arabs don't give you much. What do you think?"

Gianni anxiously looked at Irene, who nodded and said, "That sounds fine to me. It's up to you if you're interested."

"I'd like that. Something to do would be great," Gianni said.

"Fine. I'll come by for you tomorrow early, and take you to our cheese factory."

An hour later, on a cloudless, humid summer day, both boats were sailing east along the Cretan coast over calm turquoise waters. Mustafa found Bono and Rustico at the rear end of the galley. "My uncle was brief in his instructions, I know. Our sailors have crossed the open Mediterranean Sea many times, and I believe you haven't yet." He said.

"We normally would sail along the coast, it's true," Rustico replied. "But this galley should easily cross the sea. It undoubtedly will be faster."

"I'll make sure you have a Greek pilot. I don't want to take any chances. We'll pick up other boats in Sitia and sail due south towards Africa, then east to Alexandria. If the winds hold, we should be there in two or three days. We'll be stopped and inspected at the harbor, and again, we will say that we are sailing with you, carrying slaves as a gift from Abu Hafs."

##

Sitia proved to be an excellent port, controlled by a few Saracen guards but largely operated by native Cretan fishermen. After disembarking, Mustafa said to Bono and Rustico, "I'll be arranging our voyage to Alexandria, including finding a local to join you on the galley. The sailors here routinely sail all over the eastern Mediterranean Sea, and particularly south to Africa. We'll be loading on the dhows eighteen, perhaps nineteen, more slaves for our trip. Be ready to leave no later than mid-day tomorrow."

Bono and Rustico walked into the town and found a small inn where they sat outside, each with a glass of local white wine and some Cretan cheese, enjoying the relative cool in a nook shaded from the warm sun.

Rustico leaned back and said, "This would be a very satisfactory place for a business outpost. Some distance from Abu Hafs and the Saracens, it has a protected harbor and a good climate—certainly not as cold as Venice. It's close to the markets of not only Africa but also of the Holy Land."

Bono nodded meditatively. "Does it bother you doing business with the Moslems? Most likely, the Arabs are like taking Slavs who adhere to the Eastern church or some other version of Christianity for sale."

"The Bishop at Grado says that heretics need not be treated as true Christians." Rustico paused. "Perhaps they are some type of Christians; think about Nina and her daughter, for instance. What do you imagine their life was like? Somewhere west of Constantinople, in the Bulgar empire, most likely. An area constantly beset by wars with the Greeks, or other Slavs, or Hun-like people from the East. They had no father or husband to provide for them. What would happen to them? You know as well as I do. Is that any better than a life in an Arab harem?

"What about us Venetians? What would life be like if the Franks had won? We might as well be slaves, working for overlords. Our ancestors came to the lagoon running from the Huns first and then the Lombards. What would life be like for us if they had followed and were able to rule over the lagoon?

"We have a chance to control our own destiny, and to do that, we must do business in this world on the best terms we can. That's not just with the Italians and Greeks, but also the Arabs and Jews and whoever is out there." Rustico shrugged and added, "God has allowed his people to be slaves in the past as well as the present. I don't see that changing for my future. I'll leave the morality of it to the Doge and the bishops. Right now, I'm interested in ensuring that Abu Hafs understands that it is in his interest to keep his word regarding Gianni."

###

Midmorning the next day, the flotilla, consisting of the Venetian galley and four dhows, left Sitia heading south. Mustafa had arranged for a local Greek sailor to board the galley, where Rustico and Boris met him. Called Alexios, he said he thought he was twenty-nine years old. He was balding, short and lean, with bushy eyebrows over small black eyes and a shaven, weather-beaten face. After a brief inspection of the galley and crew, he nodded appreciatively and said, "We should do well. There are occasional late afternoon winds blowing north into the sea

121

from Africa, but they are not normally a problem at this time of year. I'll be looking specifically at the way to get the most out of your masts."

Rustico turned to Boris and said, "Boris, assisted by Stefano, is currently in charge of the masts." Rustico added, "I'm sure they will be happy to learn what they can from you." The flotilla headed due south, rowing into a gentle breeze while Boris and Alexios discussed tacking into the wind, which increased in the afternoon. Forty-eight hours later, they saw the coast of Africa and the boats turned east, following the coast.

They reached the eastern harbor of Alexandria, reserved for non-Arabs, before dawn two days later and waited for an hour as the sun rose over the sea for it to be opened for entrance. Bono pointed to a tall, dilapidated tower located on an island between the two harbors and said, "That might be the Pharos or whatever is left of the lighthouse of Alexandria."

A dhow carrying three Arab guards approached them, and Bono, watched carefully by Mustafa, said they were merchants from Venice and Crete and asked permission to dock. The dhow led them into the harbor to a section of the mole where they were instructed to tie up and prepare for a complete inspection of all boats. A team of five guards boarded each boat and inventoried what they were carrying. A senior guard asked for the owner of the galley, and Mustafa introduced Bono and Rustico as its owners.

The guard asked, "What are you bringing for sale? Slaves?"

"Twenty slaves," Bono replied, "But these are meant as a gift from Abu Hafs, Emir of Crete, for Abdallah ibn Tahir, the governor, or his representative if he isn't present. Most of the remaining items were purchased elsewhere and are being taken back to Venice. I do have some glass items and silk textiles we'll attempt to sell."

Mustafa interjected, "We'll pay an appropriate tax on whatever goods are taken off the boats and sold. We need to remove the slaves to appropriate quarters before I can present them to the governor."

"And the palettes of meat?"

"That's salted pork, brought from Constantinople," Bono responded.

"That's what I thought. We noticed it in the galley and avoided it as instructed by the Prophet." The guard turned to Mustafa and said, "I can lead you to a guarded structure for your slaves. You'll be responsible for their safety as well as the safety of the city."

The guard then turned to Bono and Rustico and said, "You and your crew may disembark. There are various inns for lodging immediately beyond the harbor area. You must keep us informed daily as to your whereabouts."

####

The next morning, Bono and Rustico were eating when Mustafa appeared. "The slaves are now in satisfactory quarters and are guarded by my sailors. I'm going to try and get an appointment with the acting governor within the next few days. It appears that Abdallah ibn Tahir continues to reside in Baghdad and that his lieutenant, Yusef al Mutaz, makes all decisions. You'll need to be present for this meeting, of course; the gift is from Abu Hafs but your services have been necessary and undoubtedly will remain so. Leave a message here where you'll be or if you move."

##

In Venice, at his temporary palace, Doge Giustiniano Participazio sat at his table together with his wife, Felicita, staring at his plate. "You're not hungry?" asked Felicita.

The Doge ran his hand over his face and leaned back. "Not particularly. I'm tired."

His wife studied his face for a moment and said, "You're tired a lot these days. You're working too hard trying to get the palace and church built."

"I suppose that's true."

"Others can do that work too."

"Perhaps, but will they get it done as quickly as me?"

"Is it worth your health to get it built so quickly? Why must it be done so fast?"

"Because I don't want either of the patriarchs of Grado and Aquileia to imagine they can demand control over the church here in Venice. Even as we sit here, both of them are eyeing Venice for expansion of their authority. They are actually competing with one another in order to see who can seize power here first. But I want us, living and working in Venice, to have complete autonomy over our affairs. The sooner the church is built - and a grand one it'll be - the safer we'll be."

"Why does it matter whether the Venetian church is controlled by some bishop from the mainland?"

"Because their power will not be limited to the minutia of theology. Inevitably, they will demand a say in how Venice is run. It's laws, how we do business and, most importantly, which emperors we would have to swear fealty to. I couldn't imagine being a puppet for the Roman government in Constantinople or for the Franks, either. As far as I'm concerned, even the pope in Rome should stay out of our affairs. The Doge of Venice should have complete control of Venetian affairs."

Felicita silently looked at her husband and said, "There will always be ambitious churchmen to be wary of. Your father before you knew that, and you also know this to be a fact. This church will be completed whether you're here or not. It may be completed next year, the year after that, or even later. But it will be. You, however, have your own life to consider. Just think about how you're spending it."

The Doge smiled and said, "Of course, you're right. And now I'll go to bed for some rest."

CHAPTER 10

On a hot and muggy afternoon on Crete, Irene, alone at home, heard a tapping on her door. She opened it just wide enough to see a short, middle-aged, heavy Greek woman wearing a light blue cotton shawl and a black scarf covering her grey head. "My name is Miriam. I'm a midwife. May I come in?" She paused and then added, "Nikolas asked me to look in on you."

Irene nodded, saying, "I see," and opened the door wider, allowing Miriam to enter.

"How are you doing?"

"Fine. But the mornings can be difficult."

Miriam looked around, made sure they were alone, and then took off her scarf and shawl, thereby revealing an apron beneath. "May I examine you?"

Irene looked apprehensive and said, "Is it necessary? I'm not sure yet."

"No, of course, it's not necessary. But it's good to be careful, in my experience. Your first?"

"Yes."

"Where's your husband?"

"Nikolas has asked him to help make cheese, and he won't be back until time for the evening meal."

"Good. Let's lock the door just in case." Miriam led Irene to the narrow bed and had her lie down and lift up her skirt. Miriam palpated Irene's abdomen and gently probed into her vagina, all the time looking to the side at the wall. Shortly, she withdrew her hands and drew Irene's skirts down. "Is there water for washing?" Irene pointed to a pitcher of water and a bucket, which Miriam used and began drying her hands on her apron. "Are you late?"

"A few weeks. I can't be sure."

"Are you trying?"

"Not especially, but not trying to avoid it. Things happen."

"Of course. You may be, but I'll have to check again in a week or so. Do the Arabs know?"

"I haven't said anything except to Nikolas. I don't know what he's said."

"Nikolas probably has made mention of it." The women eyed each other in silence. "You don't trust Nikolas?" Miriam suggested.

"We're worried. And we don't know what to think about him."

"Yes, I'm sure. It's true that Nikolas is likely to keep the Arabs informed. But you must understand how it is for us Cretans, particularly here in Chandax - we have to live under the constant observation of the Arabs. There doesn't appear to be much likelihood that the Constantinople Greeks are going to return any time soon. Not that they were much better than the Saracens, frankly." Irene nodded a bit impatiently.

"If the Saracens wanted, they could kill us, or sell us, or enslave us for themselves. As it is, we fish and grow crops, which the Arabs buy at low prices, but we are able to live reasonably normal lives."

"Someone like Nikolas is necessary, don't you see? He keeps the Arabs informed about what is necessary but not much more. And he tells us what the Arabs are worried about so we can watch out for problems. All the local Greeks know him and try to keep on his good side. Tell him what you want the Arabs to hear, but nothing more. He's not going to pry and I doubt if he has any reason to dislike you; nevertheless, keep on his good side. I'll be back next week. If you need anything more, have Nikolas tell me."

Irene told Gianni what Miriam said when he returned. Gianni asked, "Do you trust her?"

"Yes, I think I do. What she said made a lot of sense."

"So you are late."

"Yes, three weeks."

"Boy or girl?"`

Laughing, Irene replied, "Who knows? Maybe one of each."

###

Rustico and Alexios walked to the harbor, stopping at the galley. Rustico had arranged with Carlo to have two of his crew members watching the galley at all times; he reasoned he might be able to relax that number to one, particularly at night after he became comfortable with the security of the harbor. As they walked on, Alexios said, "As you can see, there are two harbors; the western one is for the use of Arabs only and is blocked off. Entering the eastern harbor can be a bit tricky if you aren't aware of a narrow spot. In between them is a mole which stretches out to connect to an island."

"I noticed it when we arrived," replied Rustico. "And that spire is the lighthouse?"

"What's left of it, I gather is only half of its original size. The top half collapsed many years ago during an earthquake, and the Arabs show no interest in repairing it. Occasionally they will light a pyre at its top to welcome some notable from Baghdad. Let's walk on and I'll show you where the merchants can be found. The Arabs are building a new town just north of here, Fustat. That's where you must go to deal with the city's rulers." They passed into the town from the harbor area into an area filled with shops and storage buildings.

"Where do the natives live? The Jews? Greeks?" Rustico asked.

"It's a bit odd here. There are Arab-only neighborhoods, even exclusive to the tribe level. And there are areas where the Copts, Egyptian natives I mean, live primarily, as well as neighborhoods for Jews and Greeks. Yet you'll find that occasionally, they live side by side. Don't get me wrong; that doesn't mean they get along. Alexandrians hate each other with a passion and argue constantly over ridiculous things. They always have, I gather. Yet you'll sometimes see a Jew living next to a Coptic Christian. Or an Arab in a shop run by a Greek. The Arabs tax non-Moslems more than their brother Moslems. Consequently, Jews, Copts, Greeks, and Melkite Catholics all have some reason for resentment. Particularly the Copts, who generally don't have much money or influence; in fact, some Copts are converting to Islam in order to avoid this taxation."

"Is that so?" said Rustico, surprised at the notion.

"Yes. I imagine they're finally coming to grips with the fact that the Arabs have been here for two hundred years now and aren't going away. And why not? What do the niceties of Christianity mean to the average person? Just a bunch of nonsense. Islam, on the other hand, is relatively easy to live with; the laws are laid out in the Koran. There are no arguments over who Mohammed was or how he is related to God. In Islam no one has to wonder over how many parts of God there are."

They continued walking east from the port area up a long boulevard bordered by large columns leading to the Eastern Gate. Rustico stopped and looked around, saying, "I have never seen a city street like this - broad and straight. Everything seems so bright."

"All this city is built with these white stone walls. As a result, the city almost seems to glow, particularly in the moonlight. Come on. I'll show you where the merchants can be found."

###

129

Bono sat on a bench outside a Melkite Eastern Orthodox church, enjoying the early morning sun rising into a hazy blue sky. He had waited at the inn for a message from Mustafa; none arriving, he decided to walk through the city before the afternoon heat fell on the city. As he looked at the church, its doors swung open, and a young priest, bearded and wearing a black cassock and hat, stepped out and began sweeping the steps. Bono rose and approached the priest and asked, "May I enter?"

"Of course. Father Benjamin is inside at the altar." Bono nodded and walked through the doorway out of the fierce sunlight into the dark cool of the church.

"Good morning," said an older priest, also dressed in a black cassock but tied with a gold sash. A large man of fifty, heavy and grey-bearded, with a furrowed forehead over bushy eyebrows, stood wiping a candle holder with a rag. "I don't believe I've seen you here before."

"No. I'm from Venice, here on a trading mission," Bono responded. "I'm Bono, from the island of Malamocco. Actually, we just came in from Constantinople, where I visited the Hagia Sophia."

"I haven't seen it, but I understand it is quite beautiful," the priest replied. "I am Father Benjamin. I assume you are not a follower of the Eastern tradition."

"No, we Venetians are generally ministered by the Bishop of Grado, who follows the Roman bishop. However, I am interested in all traditions of our holy faith,"

"Very wise of you." The priest nodded and said. "It's unfortunate that the Christian church today is torn into so many divisions. It is quite true that the Bishop of Rome appears to be quite ambitious, overly so we might say, over the extent of his authority. It has caused some resentment in these areas where Christ actually lived his ministry."

"I understand. I also spent some time in Spain among the Moslems and know that they too have differences of opinions."

Father Benjamin nodded, changing the subject. "Arab Moslems are our overlords here, and we try and keep on good terms with them. They generally let us be if we pay our taxes. I'm not sure how we would be treated in Rome."

"Even in Constantinople, perhaps. There are lots of arguments there over icons still," Bono added.

Father Benjamin merely held up his hands and shrugged. "I don't want to get dragged into that quagmire. We value icons but will follow the words of our Patriarch."

"I believe that there are Christian Alexandrians who follow yet another, perhaps older tradition."

"You refer to the Coptic Church, I assume." Bono nodded. Father Benjamin sighed and continued. "These Copts, Egyptian natives mostly, are a stiff-necked people. Many of them think of their ancestors who were converted hundreds of years ago and believe that they consequently have some special insight into the true religion. Some of these early Christians became monks and lived in the African desert, but there are none any longer there." Father Benjamin frowned as he concluded, "Worst of all, they are unwilling to acknowledge that Christ had a human dimension, which all true Christians accept.

"These Copts cause us all trouble because they don't get along with the Arabs. Earlier this year, they rioted here and would have thrown out the Arabs if they could and installed their own government. It was foolish, of course. The Arabs are too strong and too close. They are paying the price now because the Arabs are tearing down some churches in order to obtain marble and stones to build their own mosques here and in Fustat."

"I understand that there is still the church that St. Mark established."

"It is not too far from the port if you wish to see it. I can give you directions if you like."

"Yes, I would. Thank you."

Bono left just before the noon hour and, following the priest's directions, arrived at a glistening, white marble church with a rounded dome. He pushed open the door and entered. He called out "hello" and waited before moving into the apse to examine the wall decorations. Soon, a priest dressed in a simple white robe emerged from a room at the back of the church. He was beardless, tall and lean and was darkly complected. His hair was black but streaked with grey, and he looked tired and suspicious as he stopped in front of Bono. "Good day. How can I help you?"

Bono bowed, smiling, and said, "Good day to you. I was just passing and noticed your beautiful church. My name is Bono. I'm here from Venice on a trading voyage."

The priest bowed and looked at Bono silently. "We don't get many visitors at this church but welcome. I'm guessing you are not a Coptic believer."

"'No. But I am interested in the history of our faith."

"I see. My name is Father Theodore. We Copts trace our adherence to the true faith of our Lord Jesus Christ to almost eight hundred years ago when St. Mark arrived, well before the faith was adopted by the Romans and Greeks."

"So I understand. I was visiting a Melkite church prior to coming here. I gather there is some tension between you and them."

"No doubt they told you that we hold a different belief about the nature of Jesus Christ and that they, like all other true Christians, hold the correct belief."

"Something like that. I admit that I am not an expert in the intricacies of the faith and don't have an opinion."

"They probably also told you how it's our fault that Christian churches are being torn down so that the Arabs can build a new town east of here, Fustat. What they won't tell you is that the Arabs have been destroying churches for years and that they will eventually tear down the Melkite churches, too. They're not now because these Greek Melkites are paying the Arabs not to; they do have more money than we do. But it's only a matter of time.

"In the meantime, we are struggling to keep our congregations together and to preserve our precious relics. We have many right here, including the body of St. Mark himself."

"Might I see him?" Bono asked hopefully.

"Certainly. A monk named Stauracius venerates him and tends to his remains. Can you come back tomorrow, and I'll arrange it?"

"By all means yes. For me, the actual, physical remains of the saints, their relics, are much more important than some words among theologians." On his return, Bono found a message from Mustafa awaiting him, asking that both Bono and Rustico meet him for an evening meal at an Arab inn located a few minutes walk from their lodging.

###

Mustafa arrived and found the Venetians at a table drinking a sweet, warm tea. He pressed his two hands together in an expression of apology. "I'm late and I'm sorry."

"Don't worry," replied a tired Rustico. "I only just got back from meeting a variety of merchants myself."

"The governor's chief lieutenant in Egypt works in Fustat a bit of a distance from here. He has time to see us in two days. He has tentatively accepted the gift of the slaves we brought, thank God. But he is unsure of any future dealings with Abu Hafs. I believe we all expected that there might be such problems. You have only to say that you'll act as a middleman in any future dealings; this is probably the sort of business dealings you were hoping for, true?"

"Yes. And no," replied Rustico, grumpily. "The bishop of Rome is likely to be upset with any Italians doing business with what he thinks of as Arab infidels. We can explain one occasion as being a necessity due to Gianni's predicament. They also would be unhappy if practicing Christians - following Rome, that is - were to be sold as slaves to Moslems. I am prepared to run some risks in this regard, but only for adequate compensation. We may be required to hire non-Roman Catholics to perform some services."

Mustafa nodded unhappily. "Do you foresee any problems which can't be dealt with?"

"No, but there will be costs to be borne by Abu Hafs. Or whoever is in charge."

Mustafa, irritated, looked at Rustico for a moment. "I'm trying to get your son back."

"And why is he there now anyway?"

"Hold on, both of you," Bono intervened. "There'll be time to resolve these issues later. Right now, we will try and offer an arrangement that will satisfy the governor. And we fully expect cooperation with getting Gianni and Irene back. Let's take it one step at a time."

Mustafa frowned momentarily and then relented. He picked up a glass and said, "Here's to success for all of us. By the way, my mother will be there also, urging the governor to allow whatever her brother, my uncle, wants. She is a woman, but she's used to getting what she wants."

##

Later that evening, Rustico said to Bono, "I have to apologize for losing my temper with Mustafa earlier. I'm worried about my son, and

134

it's difficult for me to remember that Mustafa is only a functionary of Abu Hafs, just carrying out orders."

"Don't worry. I imagine Mustafa is also edgy. I have no doubt he's concerned about this meeting we have coming up. He has a lot riding on it." Pausing, Bono added, "Listen, I am returning tomorrow morning to the Coptic church to see the body of St. Mark. Why don't you come with me? We can watch their service too."

Rustico mused for a moment and said, "Yes. I'd think I'd like to."

The next morning, shortly after dawn, Rustico and Bono stood watching a Coptic mass, mysterious to them. Being performed in a language neither knew, they had to surmise what was said by comparing it to the Catholic mass which they knew. They stood aside at its conclusion, waiting for the congregants to file out into the cool Egyptian morning. Father Theodore had seen that they were present but didn't greet them. After the last parishioner left, he came up to Bono, who introduced him to Rustico as his business partner.

"If you'll follow me, Friar Stauracius is waiting for us with the saint's body," Father Theodore said. He turned and walked to a door at the rear end of the church, which opened into a narrow passageway that led to a series of doors. Father Theodore opened the last door and waved the Venetians into a large, cool room filled with narrow tables that were loosely covered with winding sheets. At the far end of the room stood an old man, short, with long grey hair and bearded, leaning on a staff and wearing a rough brown robe and worn sandals. He stood smiling expectantly beside a bed that was not covered with a sheet but rather held a wooden coffin beautifully decorated with silver ornamentation. Father Theodore approached the man reverently, touching his palms together, fingers up, in front of his chest. "Brother Stauracius, these are the two Italian merchants who wish to view the body of Saint Mark."

Friar Stauracius nodded and looked to Father Theodore. "I'm afraid my Greek is very limited, so bear with me. Father Theodore must occasionally translate for me. The bones of our first Christian bishop, the sainted Mark, are in here." He then carefully opened the coffin to reveal the skeleton of a man about five feet tall. What flesh there was on it was stiff and tough as sinew, but most of the bones were there.

"May I?" Bono asked as he leaned forward over the body. He peered intently at the body, scanning it from the toes and ankles up to the eyeless head. "Might I touch it? I'll be careful." Father Theodore looked expectantly at Stauracius, who nodded his approval. Gently, Bono lifted the skull from the box and caressed it while looking into the eye sockets. After a while, he held it out towards Rustico and asked, "Would you like to feel it?" Rustico carefully ran his finger over the skull, looking from it to Bono and back. "Just think this is the remains of one of the greatest church fathers. And also a martyr." Turning to Father Theodore, Bono continued, "It must have great power in this world."

Father Theodore gently removed the skull from Bono and handed it to Stauracius, who returned it to its coffin and said, "Of course. There is no greater relic than this." Stauracius nodded goodbye and the Venetians followed Father Theodore back through the passageway into the church, where the three men sat, lost in their thoughts.

"What's to happen to these relics?" Bono asked. "You say the Arabs are razing churches for their materials. Would you give them to a Melkite church?"

"Never."

"Then what?"

Father Theodore shook his head slowly back and forth before responding, "I don't know."

Bono thought for a moment and offered enthusiastically, "Then let us take them out of Egypt. For safe keeping in Italy."

"Italy? Why?"

"They'd be safe from the Moslems and from the Eastern Greek church. We just fought off the Franks, the most powerful land in Europe. There's no chance the Arabs would take us on."

"The Arabs here would never allow it. They watch us like hawks, wondering what we're up to," Father Theodore explained.

"Don't worry about them," Rustico added. "We're traveling with four of their boats. They'd never know anything about it."

"But outside of Alexandria, his home, his cathedral?"

Bono smoothly answered, "We'd return him when the Moslems are gone."

"I must think about it. Poor old Stauracius. Those relics are his mission in life."

"He could come with us and tend to them in Venice. You'd know the martyr was in good hands," Rustico added.

Father Theodore sat glumly, staring at the floor. "Let me think about this. And pray,"

"Yes, pray for guidance," said Bono. "We'll be back in three days for your answer."

"Yes, do that."

On their way back to their lodgings, Rustico said to Bono, "Offering to take back the relics of St. Mark! That was quick thinking."

Bono replied, "I'm sorry I didn't talk to you about it first. But I notice you chimed in quickly.

"I hadn't really thought about it until we were walking back into the church. And it just struck me an opportunity we couldn't pass up."

Rustico laughed. "Don't worry about not asking me. I'm just thinking how the Doge would be thrilled if we could really take those relics back with us to Venice. He'd be beside himself."

"Let's try talking the Copts into it again tomorrow. They obviously are aware of how precarious their position is here in a Moslem-controlled city."

CHAPTER 11

The next morning, Rustico told Carlo to take Stefano and Karol with him to the harbor and check the condition of the galley. He particularly wanted to determine how much room was left in the hold. Rustico added that if necessary he wanted its contents rearranged so as to make room for some possible valuable new acquisitions.

As they walked through the streets of Alexandria in the cool breeze of early morning, Stefano asked, "Have you any idea when we'll leave for Crete?"

"Soon, I hope," said Carlo.

"The sooner, the better," added Karol. "It will be close to a year when we get back to Venice. A lot longer than I expected."

"Who did?" Carlo responded. "I've no doubt Signore Rustico anticipated there might be problems with Croat pirates in the Adriatic. With them, we could have handled one boat at a time or maybe even two. But he hardly can be expected to have known that there were Saracens in control of Crete protecting an armada of Moslem pirates."

"No doubt," replied Karol defensively. "I'm not the only one to wonder; many of the crew are concerned about how long this is going to last."

Carlo stopped and said, "Perhaps what we are really talking about is how it is going to end."

"It all seems one and the same to me," interjected Stefano. "Everybody wants Gianni back and safe. There's no doubt about that. But can we really trust the Arabs to release him? What's to stop them from demanding more?"

"I'm guessing that Signores Bono and Rustico have considered what you're saying and are doing what they can to ensure Gianni's release," answered Carlo.

While nodding, Stefano looked at Karol and said, "We don't have enough men and weapons to get him back by force. And many would die in such an effort."

"I know. Look, we're part of this whether we like it or not. I've been with Signore Bono on many past trips and have seen him deal with lots of problems, including thieves. In reality, it could have been any of us kept as a hostage, and it happened to be Gianni. I'm confident that Signores Bono and Rustico will do whatever is necessary in order to get us back to Venice."

"Maybe," Stefano cautiously responded, slowly beginning to walk. "I understand what you're saying and hope it's true. I like Gianni, the whole crew does, and Irene too. But I need to get back to Venice. I have a wife and child there, living with my mother, and all depending on me."

"That's true for me too," Karol added. "Most of the crew have people expecting that we should probably be heading home now."

"I understand," Carlo replied. "But what can we do? We can't just leave here for home. As it is, I don't know any quicker way to get home than going back to Crete, and honoring our promise and expecting the emir to do the same. We all have people waiting for us."

Rustico was disappointed that they were not going to be able to take a canal boat to Fustat. The waters of the Nile were already too low to deliver enough water into the poorly maintained canal. Mercifully, Bono and Rustico were provided horses for the trip, while Mustafa rode a camel. They arrived at what appeared to be a large military encampment in the center of a city being quickly built around it and stopped before a large, palace-sized tent. Inside they were shown a place on a carpet where they sat waiting for the appearance of Yusef al Mutaz. Mustafa stood separately, talking and occasionally laughing with other Arabs.

Suddenly, loud voices could be heard as a group of young men entered, surrounding a huge woman, about forty-five, wearing a white robe, her head and face covered with a shawl and veil. She spoke angrily and constantly, appearing to be alternately complaining to or cajoling her entourage. Mustafa appeared briefly beside the Venetians and said, "My mother has made her appearance." He then moved towards the woman, greeted her politely, bowing, and then gently led her, still complaining, to two chairs sitting in the middle of the tent. They both sat close to what seemed to be a throne, where she held Mustafa's hand silently for the moment.

Five minutes later, Yusef al Mutaz, tall and lean, with a handsome mustached face and dressed in an immaculate white robe, entered from the rear door, followed by two advisors. He sat on the throne and signaled one of his advisors to draw near who then whispered in his ear. Yusef listened and nodded silently, indicating that he understood, then began. "We have been asked by members of Abu Hafs' family to reconsider the terms of his banishment from Africa and whether to allow him to return in some form. To start, many have counseled against it. I have reason to believe I know the feelings of the governor, now in Baghdad.

"My cousin Mustafa, on the other hand, has spoken on behalf of his uncle very eloquently, and I have seriously considered his request- to allow Abu Hafs to do business here with the idea that he might someday again be allowed to personally return." Yusef turned to Mustafa and asked, "Did I satisfactorily summarize your position?"

Mustafa arose, bowed, and said, "Yes, Sheik. Thank you."

Yusef continued, "And Abu Hafs sister, Sheikha Aisha, has also spoken in favor of allowing her brother to return. She states that her brother has been misunderstood and his services grievously underappreciated by the governor.

"I might add Abu Hafs has sent to the governor, as a token of his esteem, twenty slaves, which we do gratefully accept. He proposes to continue bringing slaves to Alexandria for sale and perhaps other items. He suggests that the Venetian traders present with us today would transport them initially. Presumably, therefore, Sheik Abu would like to bring slaves here himself at some point in the future." Yusef paused, allowing his words to sink in.

"While I accept these gifts and will not preclude the possibility that our Venetian friends might bring additional slaves here for sale, one thing must be made clear: Abu Hafs is an unrepentant rebel and would-be usurper and while I am in power, will never be allowed to return."

Suddenly, Mustafa's mother began crying and wailing, "Oh no. It cannot be. It's too unfair for all he has done."

Yusef sat, grimacing and staring at the floor, when he suddenly brought up his hand and yelled, "Stop. Enough of this. I have listened to you out of duty to the memory of your late husband, Sheik Omar, a man I revered. But this is too much."

Aisha, still crying, said, "How can you do this to your cousin, your own kin?"

"Abu Hafs maybe your brother, but he is of no blood relation to the late Sheik Omar or to me, for that matter."

Aisha kept moaning and saying over and over, "How could you do this?" until Yusef sighed and signaled for Aisha's entourage to take her away with "I've had enough." Leaving Mustafa behind, Aisha kept crying and imploring Yusef as she was led out of the tent. After she was gone, Yusef turned to Mustafa and said, "Well? Do you understand? Your uncle has been nothing but trouble all his life, not just here but in Spain too. We have no intention of interfering with his 'emirate' in Crete, but he will not be allowed to cause trouble here again."

Mustafa, now standing, said, "I appreciate your forthrightness in dealing with this difficult matter. Do I understand correctly that you will allow future sales here as long as Abu Hafs is not personally present?"

"I see no reason to prohibit such transactions. We have other suppliers of slaves, of course, from the south and west of Africa. It can become a problem if we find that they are Moslems. That's unlikely to be a problem with Slavs. Let me add this condition. We will allow the sale of no more than, say, twenty-five slaves a year from Abu Hafs. I know that's not a lot, but he'll have to find buyers elsewhere." Turning his attention to Bono and Rustico, Yusef asked "Are you prepared to work with Abu Hafs in this matter?"

Rustico was about to respond when Bono gently touched his arm and said, "We are merchants and transporting goods is something we do. However, we are unsure of what he might ask of us, Sheik, and request that you allow us to negotiate directly with him. Can we infer that you are requiring that we be preferred as the transporters of items for sale from the emirate of Crete?"

"That sounds reasonable enough. I'm sure my cousin Mustafa will prove helpful in these discussions.

"I can safely say that, like you, we Arabs are also merchants. Fighters too, and bearers of the truth of Islam. But our history is also one of long-distance trade. As long as you don't interfere with our plans and policies, you are welcome to come to Egypt to buy and sell."

##

"Your cousin?" Bono asked on the return trip to Alexandria.

Mustafa sighed, "Second cousins, really. My father, Sheik Omar, was Yusef's cousin and, in fact, was instrumental in Yusef's successful rise in the governor's service. My father was a highly respected man, intelligent, and a faithful friend. My mother was his first and primary wife; they were promised to each other when they were both very young.

This marriage was required as part of an agreement to end a tribal rivalry, which did, in fact, work.

"As you saw, my mother can be impulsive and demanding. My father had two other wives, and she made their lives miserable, making sure she maintained her role as the number-one wife." Bono shook his head from side to side. "What can I say - she's my mother. Her entire family, including her brother, are like that, and I do what I can for them."

##

That evening, Bono and Rustico walked to the harbor to check on the galley. They sat on its side, looking back at the city, luminously white, glowing under the light of a full moon. Looking west, they saw the ruins of its ancient western wall and many empty buildings, including residences. To the east stood the remains of the lighthouse; it had a pyre burning at its top, indicating the expected arrival of an important Arab ship.

Rustico sighed, "This city must have been a spectacular sight all those centuries ago."

Bono nodded, "Yes."

Rustico paused and said, "I've been thinking about the saint's remains."

"Me too. What about it?"

"They'd greatly expand the prestige of Venice I imagine. And, of course, the Doge would be very ecstatic to have them. Maybe we should offer to buy them."

"I doubt Father Theodore would respond to an offer of money. Something else perhaps," Bono thought briefly and replied.

"A new building maybe, but where?" Rustico countered. "The Arabs are not going to be happy with a new Christian church here."

"Constantinople perhaps."

Rustico countered, "You've seen what Father Theodore thinks of the Greek Orthodox church."

"Then why not the new church in Venice? It could be dedicated to the saint," Bono argued.

"We could offer to take both the priest and monk to serve in the new church," Rustico mused. "The bishop might be unhappy but a new church could have more than one priest."

"I think if we get the remains to Venice, we can solve any problem there."

Rustico fell silent for a moment. "What if he says no?"

"Just taking them? He'd raise all hell and the Arabs would get involved and cause us problems," Bono said.

"I understand, but I don't want to leave without them. One way or another.'"

"Nor do I."

##

The next morning, Rustico and Bono stood outside St. Mark's church and knocked on the locked door. Moments later, the door opened slightly and Father Theodore peered out. Recognizing the Venetians, he opened the doors and allowed them in.

"How are things?" Bono asked.

"I haven't been sleeping. There are so many rumors about."

"We understand," said Rustico, glancing at Bono. "What do you think about our offer?"

"I still don't know," the priest replied.

Bono, surveying Father Theodore, went on. "Let me add this - I can assure you that the Doge is building a magnificent new church, looking more Eastern than Catholic. The saint's relics would be prized, and I'm sure the church would be named after St. Mark. If you like, both you and the monk could come with us and see for yourself. I'm sure both of you would be allowed the responsibility for his care."

"And we could return here with the saint," the priest responded, "when it's safe again?"

"Yes, of course. When Alexandria is Christian again, that is," Rustico confirmed, looking at Bono for agreement.

Bono nodded and then added, "I think I should tell you what we recently heard." He glanced at Rustico. "We were at a meeting at Fustat with the acting governor, Yusef al Mutaz. He stated that they were going to redouble their building of Fustat and intended to tear down any Coptic church for construction materials. Not later, but very soon.

"You know they have no use for Christian relics. It's possible they might try and sell them; who knows? But it seems more likely they would destroy the bones of a Christian martyr. Either way, it's certain that you will soon lose possession of the saint."

Rustico turned and looked at Bono, then shook his head and said, "That would be tragic. Particularly if it could be avoided."

An ashen Father Theodore looked down and said, "You're undoubtedly right. When will you leave Alexandria?"

"Soon. When can you leave?" Rustico replied.

"I don't know. I have responsibilities to my church...."

Bono then added "You understand that the Arabs cannot know of this. You could say that we are taking you and the monk with us, perhaps as part of a trip to the Holy Land. No one would wonder about that."

"Yes," responded the priest decisively. "That's what I'll tell Friar Stauracius in fact. It's possible we could return, right? Can we leave within the week? That gives me time to get things in order."

Rustico responded, "I should think so. We will be boarded by Arab guards, so we'll have to explain to them why you're going to be aboard. And we'll have to smuggle the remains out at night and hide them on the galley."

"I see. But people will realize the body is gone from its resting place."

"You have many relics back there," Bono said after a brief pause. "You and the monk can replace the saint with the relics of others that you have back there. Who could tell the difference other than you and the monk?" Bono looked at Rustico again, "We'll put the saint under the stores of pork. We're pretty certain the Moslem guards won't touch them."

The three men looked at one another until Rustico said, "Are we agreed?" Bono and Father Theodore nodded their agreement.

Unexpectedly, Father Theodore embraced Rustico and said, "Thank you for doing this. It'll be hard, but I feel relieved that the saint will be safe somewhere. Come back in two days, in the evening and I'll have the body ready for you."

On the way back to the galley, Rustico said, "You know, if we get the remains, we could sail whenever we want. How could Father Theodore complain without compromising himself?"

"True, but we need someone to authenticate them. The monk alone would be enough; however, we need Father Theodore to translate for Stauracius."

As requested the Venetians arrived at the church pulling a wagon filled with fabrics and knocked. This time the door was opened by Stauracius with Father Theodore immediately behind him. They entered, and the four men formed a square, silently but expectantly facing each other. Father Theodore then locked the door and said," Friar Stauracius moved the saint into this smaller, unadorned box for his travel. It's not likely to attract much attention. I have told Friar Stauracius of our plans and he wants to know why not take us to Palestine and leave us there."

"I don't think that would be wise," Bono argued, "The Arabs control that area and they would be wondering where these remains came from; you'd have to say that you left Alexandria with no explanation or agreement with the Saracens. Second, there is a lot of fighting going on there between Christians and Moslems. I've heard, much to my sorrow, that Christians are looting the local churches for anything of value, including relics. As we said, the saint will be safe in Venice and venerated as he should be. It's by far the best choice you have."

Father Theodore explained Bono's response to Stauracius, who shook his head gravely. The priest added, "He's very unhappy about leaving Egypt, but he does understand why it's best for the saint."

"It's his choice if he wishes to stay," Rustico offered. "We would bring him back next year if he wanted, But I can't guarantee how safe it would be here for an itinerant Coptic monk."

In his halting Greek, Stauracius said, "I understand what this means to St. Mark, safety and much adoration. I will pray and decide whether I will go with you. Father Theodore will tell me when you are to leave; if I am there, I will go with you. If I am not, then leave," The four of them unloaded the wagon of its fabric, placed the new box in it, and covered it with the fabric.

When the wagon was loaded to the satisfaction of all, Rustico said, "We're going to return to the galley using a different route than we came on. If stopped, we'll say we are traders and have been showing goods to some local merchants." Rustico added, "We will load the saint onto the galley ourselves and hide him safely at the bottom of its hold."

"When we know, we will send word when to meet us for sailing."

Bono added. "We'll say, as necessary, to anyone who asks that we've been to church services here and have become acquainted with you both.

I don't want Mustafa to get concerned about a change in our travel plans to accommodate you. He could get suspicious when he sees you're going with us."

Bono concluded with, "If it seems necessary, we'll say that at your request, we may leave either of you at Sitia, where you can find a ship heading to the Holy Land. To Rustico, Bono added, "We should tell Mustafa ahead of time in a matter-of-fact manner that the priest has paid us for both his and the monk's trips to Sitia.

"We can later add that Father Theodore has decided to continue with us to Venice and that we understand he will probably return next year. He should understand why a Coptic priest may want to leave Alexandria."

The trip to the galley went smoothly, as no one stopped or questioned them. At the galley, they found Carlo and Karol guarding it. Rustico told them that they could go into the town for a meal, and to come back in an hour. They promptly left, and Rustico and Bono moved the remains of the saint into the galley's hold, hiding it temporarily by wrapping the box with tarps.

That night, over dinner, Rustico said, "I'm not happy about the monk. What if he changes his mind before we can leave? Maybe he'd say something to the church's congregants about the saint's relics being missing."

"I'm not happy either about him going with us. He might try to say something to Mustafa or another Arab. One good thing is that the sailing time with our Arab friends is not long. We'll probably lose most of them at Sitia. Mustafa will be aboard his dhow until Chandax. We'll have to make sure Father Theodore keeps an eye on him now and on the galley."

###

149

The next morning, Mustafa arrived at the Venetian's lodging and found them discussing what the galley might need for the trip back to Crete. "Good morning, gentlemen. I'm glad I found you together."

"Good day to you, Sheik Mustafa," answered Bono. "What brings you here?"

"It appears our business here is over, so I'd like to make plans to return to Crete within the week perhaps. I assume you wish to leave as soon as possible."

Both Venetians nodded warily. "We'd like to go home, of course. But we are aware that you may need more time to urge Abu Hafs' request."

"I believe you saw for yourselves that the acting governor is not going to change his mind. It's possible if we went overland to Baghdad and spoke directly with the governor, he might relent and override Sheik Al Mutz.

Rustico looked at Mustafa incredulously. "I assume you're joking."

"Of course. I don't see how your appearance in Baghdad would help our case."

"Nor do I," responded Rustico. "What do you have in mind for us?"

"We'll return to Chandax, and I'll report to Abu Hafs the response of the acting governor. I will say that Yusef al Mutaz was clear that he was not welcome here. You, on the other hand would be welcome, even carrying items belonging to Abu Hafs. But he is not, at least at this stage."

"You're quite optimistic if you think Sheik Yusef might relent. Are you concerned Abu Hafs might be unhappy with you?"

"He might. But I never guaranteed I would be successful in getting him put back in good graces in Africa. Anyway, to assure him I did my best, I am bringing my mother back with me to Crete. He can hear from her all the efforts which were made on his behalf."

"I see," said Rustico. "I assume she'll be traveling with you in the dhow."

"That's the only way she would travel. She doesn't care for western infidels."

"I'm heartbroken."

"You laugh. But I think you'll find she'll be an advocate for a quick release of your son and his woman."

"Why so?"

"My mother is a very complicated person, but one thing she is adamant about is family - taking care of family. I have told her of your predicament and also of how we have tried to work together to obtain our separate goals. And while she would never criticize her brother for taking Gianni as a hostage, she would complain bitterly if he failed to live up to his promise. So, combined with your agreement to take another group of slaves to Alexandria at a low cost, Abu Hafs should release Gianni and his woman to you."

Bono and Rustico looked at one another, and then Bono nodded. "We also will be taking someone back with us, Father Theodore, a Coptic priest, and perhaps a monk named Stauracius. They wish to go on a pilgrimage to the Holy Land and then return to Alexandria. I'm sure, as a Moslem, you understand how important such a trip might be to a Christian priest - it would be like a haj to Mecca for a Moslem. We are encouraging them to accompany us to Venice first and then we will find a way for their pilgrimage."

"I have no problem with that. We should keep them and my mother apart as best we can. She really hates Christian holy men."

Rustico stood and said, "Then it's all set. We leave in three days,"

###

On Torcello at dusk that day, Leo and Angela sat with glasses of wine mixed with water in chairs in front of their house, looking over the lagoon. Earlier they had supervised the unloading of a recently returned river boat, having the newly acquired pelts and lumber moved into the storage shed sited next to their house.

Angela began, "The pelts look satisfactory to me. What of the lumber?"

"From what I saw, the quality is good, but there was not enough of it," Leo replied.

"What did you think of Dominic's explanation that other buyers had already bought most of the acceptable timber available?"

"It happens. Quite often, really. We were late sending the boat up the river this year. That's the problem."

Angela responded, "We did what we could."

"Yes. In prior years, Rustico would have left earlier, but of course, he was busy with this new trip instead."

"But he may find new purchasers for lumber and at greater prices."

"That is the goal. Still, we did all right. It was good having you involved, I must say, having a second pair of eyes looking over what they brought. You knew what to look for in those pelts."

"Thank you. I think it all went fine. I'm not sure of the value of what you sent, but what Dominic brought should sell easily enough."

"True. What about the salt works?"

"You need to let me find another younger man to do the hard labor, including bagging and moving the salt. I know many of the families here who are good workers. It's just too much for you. It was hard for Gianni. Look, you can check on the salt and make sure it's acceptable; but I better supervise any new worker. We can manage the sales in the lagoon ourselves."

Leo sighed, "You're right, I know. It's hard for me to stay out of the salt works. It's been the better part of my working life."

"Don't worry. I'll keep you busy enough."

CHAPTER 12

The sirocco began the day before they were to leave Alexandria for Crete. A hot wind, it arose at the North African desert and swept northward across the Mediterranean Sea, picking up dirt and moisture, and blowing constantly at a steady fifteen miles per hour, with gusts of up to fifty. Rustico stood at the harbor squinting through the air, gritty with sand, at the choppy sea with Bono and Mustafa. "Perhaps it'll be over tomorrow. Or the next day, God willing."

"Perhaps," replied Mustafa. "Or it may last two or more weeks."

"What shall we do?"

"We'll wait a day or two to see if it eases. Either way, we'll have to sail east to cross it, then head north toward Crete. It won't be pleasant."

##

Miriam appeared the following week as she promised. As she examined Irene, she grumbled, "I hate this time of year- hot and muggy and sandy. I don't really want to leave the house." Standing back up, she said, "It seems pretty certain now. Are you happy about it?"

"Yes."

"And the father?"

"Yes, him too." Irene paused and, now confidant in Miriam, admitted, "We're hoping that it'll stop the Arabs from separating us if the galley doesn't return soon."

"Perhaps. You can never tell what Abu Hafs is up to on a given day, but it's worth a try. Young and pretty as you are, you'd easily end up in Africa or Arabia." Miriam momentarily mused, "Maybe even here. There are more Arab men than women here, and most Greek women want nothing to do with them. Who wants to be a second, or even third, wife?"

"Do you think I should tell Nikolas that it's confirmed?" Irene asked.

"I suppose so. Isn't that what you wanted?"

"I was hoping to be vague about it and see how much longer it was going to be for the galley to return."

"Of course. You won't be showing for a while, except maybe larger breasts. The mornings will remain hard for a time, but they will go away, and hopefully, by then, you'll be in Venice."

Irene looked down at her hands. "I'm a Slav, as you know. I've never been to Venice, or Italy for that matter."

"And you don't know what to expect," Miriam, musing, responded. "And the father, he's quite young, isn't he?"

"Yes, not quite 18."

Miriam sighed and said, "You'll have to make the best of it. I'm sure you will, but it won't be easy. As long as your husband doesn't drink and beat you, you'll manage. That's what women do."

"Thank you. You're very kind."

As Miriam left, she said, "I won't say anything to Nikolas now. We'll leave the matter up in the air for the time being. Let me know if you need anything."

That evening, their house still being hot and stuffy, Irene and Gianni sat outside, enjoying a brief respite from the heat and humidity. "Where do you suppose the galley is tonight?" Irene wondered.

"Who knows?" Gianni shook his head. "I wonder with this wind which way they're taking to return to Crete. If they sail up the coast of Palestine, it may take some time."

"Has Nikolas said anything about what might happen to us if they're late?"

"No, I doubt he knows. If he expects the worst, he hasn't said," Gianni responded.

"What do you suppose the worst might be?"

Gianni paused. "As Miriam said, it seems likely that you and the baby would be sold into a harem somewhere."

"And you?"

"Me? I think it's possible that Nikolas might try to have me kept here. The locals seem to like having me help with their work. And, of course, the Arabs depend on the labor of the Greeks here. If not that, I'd probably end up working in a mine or a ship someplace in Africa."

"We'd be separated, then."

"Yes." Gianni hurriedly added, "Of course, my father would definitely try and find a way to buy us - that's if he survives. I know he'd search for us. At any rate, it seems likely we presently are valuable."

"Just a little while ago, Boris and I were making plans for a life in Constantinople. I hope he, at least, gets there still. We'll just have to make the best of it."

The wind had been blowing for three days with no let-up when Mustafa said it was time to leave anyway. "There's no point in staying; it could blow like this for weeks. We are expected back by my uncle, and he'd not be happy if we delayed much longer." The crew, happy to be leaving but concerned about the weather, prepared for an early departure the next morning. Mustafa informed the port authorities and then advised Rustico, "The guards will search the galley, so be prepared to explain what your cargo is. They'll look at the dhows, but there's not much on them."

"When will this happen?" Rustico asked.

"First thing tomorrow."

Later that afternoon, after the crew had left the galley except for Carlo and Boris, Bono and Rustico appeared at the galley. "We will be taking two Copts back with us. I doubt they've sailed much, but at least one of them might prove capable as a rower," Rustico said. "I'm going to check the galley's hold one more time, and Signore Bono is going into town to make sure they're ready. You can have one last night in Alexandria, and I'll stay with the galley tonight." After Carlo and Boris left, Bono said, "I'm off to the church, but I'll return here tonight to make sure everything is all right."

"I'll make sure the saint is wrapped well, packed tightly under the pork and can't be seen by any Arab guards standing on the mole." Rustico continued explaining, "I've been thinking that a box might easily be seen as an item very apt to be searched by the guards, so I'm thinking of taking him out and wrapping him in an old cloak along with some pork."

Bono left and walked to church, where he found Father Theodore pacing. "It's tomorrow morning, for sure. The winds are still stiff, but we can wait no longer. Where's the monk?"

"He was here earlier and will be back. He said he was going."

"Good. We trust that he won't talk much, at least until we leave Crete for the Adriatic."

"As you've seen, his Greek is only so-so, and his Latin is even worse. His talking won't be a problem. He hates the idea of relinquishing the saint's remains and their leaving Africa. I've told him what you said about our church being torn down and added that the Melkites would probably want the saint then."

"Is that sufficient?"

"He dislikes the Melkites more than the Arabs. Speaking of which, a Melkite priest came by yesterday, saying he'd heard I was leaving for a while and asked if he could help. I told him the monk and I wanted to see the Holy Land and that I'd be back in a few months. I informed him that I'd arranged for another Coptic priest to lead the services. I don't know if he was sincere or just trying to find out my plans, but he appeared to take my word."

"I see. I'm sure you were convincing. You both need to be at the galley before dawn. The Arabs will be searching the galley, and they will undoubtedly want to know why you're going with us."

"Don't worry, I'll have him there."

At dawn the next morning, already hot and muggy, all five boats were ready to sail, and word was sent to the harbor master. Six Arab guards soon appeared one for each dhow and two at the galley. The dhows received perfunctory examinations, but the guards demanded that the galley's entire hold be exposed for a complete inventory. Rustico looked at the guards, grimaced and said, "All right," and ordered his crew to open the hold. The guards examined the silk items so closely that Rustico felt he had to remind them that they had been there when the galley arrived and that they had not found a buyer for any in Alexandria. As they approached the salted pork, both Rustico and Bono stood behind the guards.

"Once again, those items were on board when we entered," Rustico said. "I bought them in Constantinople as food for the crew for the trip home. You understand it's salted pork."

The guards looked uneasily at each other and bent down to peer at the slabs while not touching any of them. The older of the two stood up and, brushing his hands together, said, "There's some sort of a package below the pork."

Rustico replied, "I know. The galley will probably take on some water in these seas, so I wrapped some of the pork in it to keep it dry. I don't know how well it will work, but felt it should try it anyway." He paused, waiting for a response from the guards, who only looked at one another. He finally went on with," Would you like to help me get it out so you can go through it?" Rustico and Bono stood looking as the two guards talked; one was more animated, apparently unhappy at the thought of touching the pork, while the other remained undecided.

"Well, what do you want us to do?" asked Bono. "Do you want us to take the package out and let you go through it yourselves? After all, it's only salted pork."

The undecided guard gazed around at the dhows and saw Mustafa impatiently waiting to sail. He finally shook his head and said, "We're not allowed to touch it. Anyway, everything seems to be in order." The six guards stood on the quay and watched the boats sail out into the sea to the west.

The winds picked up in velocity throughout the day, blowing to the north mostly, with occasional gusts to the northeast. The sun, an unearthly orange from the grit in the humid air, bore down on the crew. Boris and Stefano worked constantly to get what they could from the masts. Both crews alternated working difficult one-hour shifts, with all hands drinking large quantities of water. Consequently, they had to go to shore early on the first day, where they ate a quick meal and quickly fell into a deep sleep. The guards were changed every two hours in order to ensure that whoever was on duty was alert. Dawn, the next day, found them sailing west again.

Father Theodore offered to row and did so for a while until his hands, unused to hard physical labor, were rough and bloody. Stauracius paced the deck, looking at the empty horizon, muttering to himself in Coptic.

Late the second day, the boats reached the point of the coast where they were to turn north directly to Crete, and they stopped for the night.

Mustafa found Rustico, Bono and Alexios silently sitting together and said, "Going north, we'll find it easier. At least we won't be sailing into the wind."

"Perhaps, but the seas are likely to be high," Alexios said. "The galley won't be able to keep up with your dhows. Usually, we sail across the open seas on well-lit nights and closely together."

"I understand," Mustafa responded. "There is a quarter moon tonight, although I don't know how much we'll see it with all the dirt in the air. We'll keep at least one dhow with the galley, and the others will sail together ahead. You know where we usually land. Just to let you know, if I get there before the galley, I won't wait for you, but will requisition horses, ride north to Chandax, and inform my uncle of what happened in Alexandria."

Rustico nodded uncertainly. "Perhaps Signore Bono could go with you."

"I thought that I would attend to the needs of the priest and the monk. They'll probably need help in getting a boat to the Holy Land from Sitia," responded a surprised Bono.

Mustafa looked at Rustico. "It will be better for your son if I get back soon."

"What about your mother?"

"She can't ride a horse that far, so she'll have to accompany you in the boats. In the meantime, just be pleasant to her and ignore her scorn for infidels."

##

The crew desperately needed another long night's sleep, and so the boats pushed off to the North late at midmorning. At first, it appeared that the sirocco was relenting, but after noon, its ferocity increased, whipping up the waters of the Mediterranean into frothy waves of up to three feet. Boris and Stefano had to constantly adjust the masts, concerned that they might rip under the severity of the wind's speed. The sky darkened more and more throughout the day until it seemed like dusk when it was only 3:00.

Night came early and with only a sliver of a moon to provide light. Stauracius still paced back and forth across the deck, now bowing up and down and praying in his native tongue. Rustico and Alexios had all they could handle in keeping the galley heading due north since the winds would unexpectedly blow across their path. Father Theodore, unable to row since his hands were still raw, distributed water continuously to the rowing crew.

By midnight, the sky was an inky black, and the wind howled. Alexios attempted to keep the galley steadily heading north, but the changing wind directions made that almost impossible. By two in the morning, the lateen sails began to become tattered, and their spread had to be drastically reduced in order to avoid further tearing. The monk now stood at the front of the galley, arms up in supplication and praying loudly as spray from the sea-soaked his clothes.

A sudden wind caught the galley at the crest of a wave and forcibly turned it sixty degrees. The masts swung wildly across the galley, and the rear one hit Stefano, then in the act of attempting to haul in the sheets in the back, sending him face down into the sea. Carlo rushed to the galley's side, grabbed a rope, and prepared to throw an end to Stefano, whose head and shoulders suddenly emerged from the sea.

"Stefano, Stefano," he cried, waving the end of the rope, which he then threw into the sea about fifteen feet from the galley. Boris and Bono joined Carlo as Stefano began to force himself through the water toward the rope and, at last, grabbed it. The three men began pulling the now taut rope back into the boat, dragging Stefano, who was struggling to keep his head above the waves.

When Stefano was within a yard of the galley, Boris leaned over the galley's side, holding his right arm out while clutching the boat with his left. Stefano was reaching for Boris' hand when the galley tilted up, and a rushing wave swept him hard head-first into the galley's side. He fell back, and his eyes closed. The rope slid out of his hand and he sank below the surface. Carlo and Boris stood leaning over the side of the boat, staring at the water, while Bono looked dumbly at the trailing rope. None of the three said anything as they sat down. Alexios, the galley having been maneuvered back on course, came over and asked, "He's gone?" Bono nodded yes, and Alexios grimaced and returned to the aft, where Rustico was guiding the ship.

Stauricius, oblivious to the loss of Stefano, was looking off the right side of the galley's prow, holding a cross in both hands, water splashing over him each time the galley plunged after crossing a wave. For Boris, exhausted and still recalling seeing Stefano slipping into the sea, time seemed to come to a standstill. The red of an early dawn at last appeared in the east, and the winds slowed to a brisk breeze. The silent crew stood as they watched a light creep westward across the horizon. There, about a half mile away, stood the shores of Crete, framed by steep, green coastal mountains.

###

Alexios didn't know precisely where they were, but there was a cove off to the east that seemed to offer a protected area where they could beach the galley. The entire crew now rowed the galley until it glided to a halt on a white sandy beach tucked behind the western entrance to the cove. They drew it up to a point where Alexios said it should not be in the water at a high tide, and the crew ate and, exhausted, slept.

Rustico roused a group of eight and told them to tilt the galley on one side and then the other while he and Alexios inspected its bottom. Alexios said, "It looks pretty good after such a storm."

"I had this galley built to withstand a lot. But last night was a test I hadn't anticipated."

"We had some luck. We didn't run onto any rocks."

"True, it's possible that the nearness of land might have forced the winds up and off the water," Rustico suggested.

"Possibly."

Bono, Father Theodore and Stauracius were standing nearby and watching. Stauracius started chuckling. Father Theodore asked, "What's so funny?"

"Those two," said the monk, gesturing at Rustico and Alexios.

"How so?"

"I gather they are talking about how we survived. But it was the saint that saved us. He soothed the wind and kept us from any rocks." Father Theodore and Bono looked at Stauracius quizzically. "I had him with me, and I felt his strength take hold of the boat."

"The saint is in the boat, I know," replied Father Theodore.

"Some of him. But I had a part of him, too. You see, when we first started preparing for this trip, I went back and took a small part of the knee. And I held that part in my palm next to the crucifix. It was the power of Saint Mark that saved us."

###

Mustafa and the four dhows arrived at Crete a few hours before the galley. They had experienced much of the storm but arrived before the final gales. The next morning, Mustafa took the dhows westward to a small fishing village and docked. While he was looking for three horses, he had them checked for leaks, and they were deemed safe enough to sail to Sitia. Mustafa told his mother, "You'll need to stay with the boats, and you'll get to Chandax a few days after me. Your boat and two others should go on as quickly as possible; I'll have one look for the galley."

"Why can't you get me a horse-drawn coach or wagon so I can go too?"

"Mother, look at those mountains. There are no roads for a wagon or coach. It would take you longer that way than to sail." Mustafa then ordered the boat he had been on, now to be led by Abdul, to search the coast for the galley and sent the other three on to Sitia. He and two others rode north through the mountains to Chandax.

###

The search dhow located the galley late that afternoon and anchored offshore. Abdul, together with an Arab sailor, took a boat to the shore, where he greeted Bono with a bow. "Sheik Mustafa has asked me to find you and accompany you to Sitia."

Bono replied, "He has left on horseback for Chandax, I imagine."

"It's a short distance across the island, but it is a mountainous route. Even so, he will be there several days before we arrive. Is your galley seaworthy?"

"Enough to get to Sitia. It'll be completely examined there, I imagine."

"We will make sure you get to Sitia, then we will push on. The Cretan pilot can help you get back to Chandax. We'll leave at first light tomorrow."

###

The dhow accompanied the slower galley as it moved eastward along the southern coast of Crete. The sirocco still blew but less intensely; there was less grit in the air, and the gusts were rare, so the galley's progress was slow but not awkward. Father Theodore and the monk Stauricius stood alone and quietly conversed. Bono approached them on one occasion and the two Copts were polite, yet did not admit him into their conversation. Rustico was preoccupied, only occasionally speaking to Alexios about the boat's progress. The crew, many of them thinking of the missing Stefano, rowed on in a somber silence.

Late that afternoon, they entered the harbor at Sitia and docked. Abdul, taking Alexios with him, went off to deal with the port authority while the Venetians disembarked. Happy to be on land, the crew strolled about the harbor. When Abdul returned, he said, "I've advised the guards here to take care of your needs and to allow you to leave when you can. You shouldn't be searched again. Alexios will remain here with you and will make sure to find your way to Chandax. I'm leaving early tomorrow."

That night, Rustico and Bono were sitting at a table outside an inn drinking wine when Alexios approached them. Rustico greeted him and offered him a chair and a glass of wine. "We've ordered a meal of fried octopus and rice. Would you like to join us?"

Alexios doffed his hat and sat. "Thanks. I'd like that. I've had enough salted pork."

Rustico leaned forward toward Alexios and said, "Maybe you can help us. I understand that the Norsemen have taken to arming their galleys with shields, which sit in grooves around the perimeter of the deck. That way, the ship's crew is protected from arrows. These shields can be taken down while sailing and perhaps used in hand-to-hand fighting on land."

Alexios, sipping his wine, said, "I can understand the value of such shields to such a fighting race."

"Do you know where I could have something like that added to my galley?"

Alexios paused, "Perhaps. I know of someone who could probably provide you with the shields. They'd have to be held by the crew for the time being while you figured out a way to attach them to the planking."

"I'd pay to have them quickly."

"I imagine so," replied Alexios. Shifting in his chair, he looked at Rustico and said, "You understand that I must live here with the Arabs after you leave for Venice. I can put you in touch with someone, but I can't get any more involved. You see that, don't you?"

"Of course. If you could provide us a name and location, we'd do the rest."

"Let me make some inquiries, and if I find someone, I'll let you know tomorrow. I know an old Greek gentleman who might have a supply of shields readily at hand."

"Thank you for this. Here comes our food."

Abdul sailed at dawn. Rustico had the crew check the condition of the cargo, supervised by Bono, who brought out the packaged pork himself with Father Theodore's help. At midmorning a messenger arrived who said he only had for them a Sitia address and a name, Demetrio. Bono gave him a Greek coin and turned to Rustico. "Let's leave Carlo in charge and go visit this Demetrio."

They asked directions from the innkeeper and were sent to a small shop a few streets back from the harbor. The shop had a shabby exterior, and appeared to need a thorough cleaning and definitely new paint. In the window, there were a few used items of pottery and clothing. They tried the door only to find it locked and then knocked. The door opened slowly, and a pale, moon-shaped face adorned with a thin mustache and arched bushy eyebrows appeared. "How can I help you?"

Bono bowed and said, "Are you Demetrio? A Cretan fisherman suggested we speak to you about some ornamentation for a galley."

The shopkeeper looked questioningly at Bono and then said, "Oh yes, ornamentation. Yes, I'm Demetrio." He craned his neck from side to side until assured no one else could hear. "I have a cache of old Roman defensive items which might serve your purpose. Come in, please."

The shop was full of ancient Roman and Greek implements, from pans and plates for cooking and eating to tools and clothing and even some pagan religious implements. Bono and Rustico browsed over the Cretan's merchandise. Demetrio explained, "People bring me items from ancient times and ask if I can sell them. The Arabs don't care about these things, and the native Cretans can't afford such useless items. Some of the pagan items barely escaped destruction by the Church, as you might guess. I say they are just items of ancient superstitions that can do us no harm now. Right?"

The Venetians nodded politely, and Rustico asked, "What about the shields?"

"They are in the back," Demetrio said as he led the Venetians to a dusty corner of his shop. There, in a pile, were nineteen rectangular, slightly curved shields approximately two and a half feet across, four feet high and three inches thick. They had once been painted but were largely made of bare wood strips bound across a metal frame. "I believe they were called scutums," Demetrio added as he picked one up and examined it.

"The wood seems to still be in good condition," Rustico said, running his hand across another one.

"I understand they come from a dry area of western Crete and were kept covered in a barn. The wood the Romans used had to be solid to survive in the areas where they were used."

"What do you want for them?" Rustico asked.

"I need to sell them. My wife wants me to change to selling things that a woman might like."

"Do you have any knives or daggers?"

"Some, older and perhaps not in the best of shape. I even have two short Roman swords, blades about a foot long." Demetrio went into a back room and returned with the two swords and an assortment of eight rusty knives and daggers. "I believe the sword was called a gladius and was mainly for thrusting by a block of soldiers. The Arabs like to fight on horseback and found no use for them."

Rustico examined them closely and said, "I'd like the two swords and the daggers as well. Can you clean and sharpen them?"

"I'll do what I can. But they will work well enough."

"I've got some silk fabrics from Constantinople. First rate material that I know will sell to Italian and Frankish women. I can give you a small selection of it and take these old items off your hands. I think that you'll find that you have buyers of what I provide. And I intend to return next year with more silk items for sale."

"I don't know," Demetrio equivocated.

"Look. No one here is going to buy these things. Ever. How long have you had them? I'd guess several years."

Demetrio paused and then said, "All right."

"Fine, clean and sharpen the blades and put them all in bags where the Arabs won't know what they are, and bring them to the dock this evening, and I'll have a selection of silk fabrics you can show to your wife."

Miriam, busy preparing her evening meal, answered a rapping on her door with "Who is it?"

"Me, Nikolas. Do you have a moment so I can speak with you?"

Miriam opened the door and pointed to a chair at her table, saying, "Please, sit."

"Thank you. I'm sorry to disturb you; I know it's late. But I wanted to speak to you about Gianni and Irene."

"Okay. I just saw Irene today."

"And how is she?"

"She's doing about as well as can be expected. She really doesn't know Gianni very well, as far as I can tell. And, of course she's worried about what will happen if the Venetians don't return soon."

"I can imagine. But is she carrying a baby?"

Miriam paused, weighing her response. "Possibly. Really, most likely. Tell me, is her pregnancy going to have any effect on what's going to happen to them?"

"The Arabs I've spoken to don't seem to know anything about what might happen to her, regardless of her condition."

"You've mentioned to them that she might be pregnant?"

"Yes. But I've only said it's a possibility," Nikolas clarified. "You see, I'm in an awkward position. The Arabs want to know what those two are up to. They'd undoubtedly begin to doubt my reliability if, in six months or so, she's obviously pregnant, and I hadn't told them."

"I see. But you don't want to disclose too much either, right?"

"Well, I'd like to believe that the native Cretans, as well as Gianni and Irene, don't think I relay too much information to the Arabs. I'm aware that many are suspicious of me and my relationship with Abu Hafs."

"I can only tell you what I think. And I believe you only tell them so much, but you have to tell them something."

"Exactly. Arab guards stop by every week, and one in particular wants to know about Irene. I do what I can to keep her out of what I report. But the fact is she's a lovely young woman who could easily end up with one of these Arabs someday.

"You know as well as I do that galleys are lost at sea all the time. And, who knows, maybe the crew will balk at returning to Crete in the distant hope of retrieving Gianni and Irene. They have their own lives to worry about. I'm sure that Irene understands this, and her becoming pregnant might be more than a coincidence."

Miriam sat pondering this and said, "As I said, I'm pretty confident she's pregnant, but she could still easily lose the baby. As you might guess, I've not pried into the circumstances of this pregnancy. I do know that both of them are cautious and trying not to draw attention to themselves."

"Good. Thank you for hearing me out. I'll try and figure out what I can tell the Arabs."

###

That night, after surreptitiously stowing the shields and blades in the hold, Bono and Rustico were discussing what else they might need when Father Theodore and Stauricius appeared. The priest began, "Signores, I hate to interrupt, but Friar Stauricius requires a word. Brother?"

"Thank you. I need to inform you that I'm not going with you to Venice. I wish to see the Holy Land before I die. I've made arrangements to leave on a boat heading to Beirut next week."

Bono said, "I thought you wished to tend to the relics of Saint Mark."

"And I did. But I realized after the storm that his power was so great that the small relic I retained was sufficient for my meager needs. And a visit to Jerusalem, and then perhaps Cyprus, would fulfill a long-held dream of mine."

"You understand that you are always welcome in Venice. But perhaps not in Alexandria."

"Yes, I know that. I would only return to Africa to live in the desert, but I fear I am too old for that sort of life."

Bono arose; he embraced Stauracius and said, "Very well. Do you need anything? Money?"

Friar Stauracius shook his head and said, "No. Thanks, but no. I'm used to getting by with little. And the saint will protect me."

"You're sure?" The monk nodded. "Ok. Then go with God."

CHAPTER 13

Mustafa arrived at Chandax at dusk after a day and a night of hard riding, changing horses twice, and went immediately to see his uncle, who received him in his private quarters. "How was your journey home?" his uncle asked.

"Very difficult. The winds of Africa were bad and the galley had a difficult time."

"But the Venetians are returning here as planned?"

"I can't be positive that they survived the storm, but if they did, they were supposed to sail to Sitia, accompanied by Adbul in one of our dhows. Presumably, any damage to the galley can be dealt with there. The other three dhows were to return directly here with no stops, and I expect them will arrive tomorrow or the next day, depending on the seas. I would expect the Venetians to arrive soon thereafter."

"I see. And how were you received in Alexandria?"

"The acting governor, Yusef al Mutaz, did see us in Fustat. The Signores Bono and Rustico were also present.

"He was quite adamant that you will not be allowed to return, I'm afraid. He basically described you as constantly rebellious and belligerent. He did say, however, that he appreciated the gift of the slaves and that you would be allowed to send each year up to twenty-five more slaves for sale in Alexandria. He seemed to insist our utilizing the Venetians as middlemen. The Venetians described themselves as merchants open to such transactions. I must add that they did what they could for your case."

Abu Hafs paused. "I see."

"Additionally, he said that if we wish to pursue this, you will have to send someone to Baghdad. I would guess that if some money changes hands, the governor might relent."

"That was the point of offering the slaves," Abu Hafs snapped.

Mustafa shrugged that he understood.

"Another thing: your sister, my mother, was there trying to win your favor."

"Oh, God. How did that go?"

"The acting governor was clearly unhappy. Her emotional suggestions that he was somehow related to you were not appreciated."

"No doubt."

"One more thing. She is coming here on one of the dhows and should be here soon."

"She sailed with you?"

"Yes, but not in my boat."

"Is she staying long?"

"She didn't say. And I didn't ask."

Abu Hafs sighed and said, "Thank you for telling me."

##

Three of the dhows arrived two days later, and Aisha was met by Mustafa. She needed to be helped to get off her boat by four young men he had brought with him and who bore the brunt of her tongue-lashing. However, she was gradually eased onto the quay and escorted to a set of rooms that Abu Hafs had set aside for her use. There, she rested for an hour, then bathed and changed from her traveling clothes and requested an audience with her brother.

Upon entering his brother's quarters, the two siblings stood and eyed each other cautiously.

"You've gotten fatter," Aisha started.

"And it's nice to see you, if only for a short visit."

"I assume Mustafa told you what happened at Fustat?"

"Yes. He mentioned that you were present."

"And unable to persuade Yusef that his family connection to ours ought to be sufficient."

"So it seems. Mustafa, I gather, prefers to advance his arguments more subtly."

"Of course he does; he's like his father that way. But sometimes people in power must be explicitly reminded of who helped them get there - just as Yusef was aided by my late husband."

"Omar was very helpful to many, including myself, I add."

Aisha paused, considering her words. "You know that much of that was due to my involvement, my persistence in convincing him of your capabilities."

"Of course, I know that. You've been my supporter all my life, even as a child."

Shaking her head from side to side, Aisha continued, "I think of how often I had to intervene with our father on your behalf, explaining that your aggressiveness was really a virtue and that you were destined to lead our clan to greatness. But then you had to have more - more power and more prestige. You had to push for more than what was available."

"Enough of this. I've made errors and I've had to pay the price."

"The rest of the family has paid this price too. Mustafa might have been acting governor by now, you know. Like Yusef. Yusef is certainly no shrewder than my son, but you forced him to choose between the governor or you, and he chose family."

"And I have rewarded him generously. I have let him act on my behalf for all of our interests."

"So you say. But it is also the case that you have required him to perform miracles by defending or explaining your rash choices. Just like I've done for you. Did you really think he was going to persuade the Romans to allow you to keep marauding through the Mediterranean? What chance did he have? Did you think he could get the governor to forget your attempt to usurp power from him in Alexandria?"

The brother and sister stared silently at one another before Abu Hafs asked, "How long are you staying in Crete?"

"I don't know. If you are not going to use Mustafa's talents appropriately, I will ask him to return to Alexandria with me. Perhaps we could go to Baghdad. I am sure that he would be appreciated there."

##

Aziz was seething. It was early morning and he was on his way to the native Cretan section of Chandax to meet Abdullah, a fellow guard. He was thinking about how his wife had angrily accused him of spending money visiting a Greek whorehouse the night before. Yes, he drank some wine, and yes, he did have a Cretan woman. But what of it? It was his money, and he'd do what he wanted with it. The women there were for one thing, and he didn't have to talk to them. But Amina insisted on crying loudly, scolding him, until he walked off, still hearing her wails. It was all he could do not to beat her.

He found Abdullah waiting for him and they began their slow progress through the neighborhood. Most of the men were already gone, either fishing, tending to goats or sheep, or making cheese. The few women they passed bowed submissively, averting their eyes but respectfully greeting them and then scurrying away. As on other days, the two Arabs stopped at the house of Nikolas, who asked them in.

Seated, Nikolas asked "Sheik Aziz and Sheik Abdullah, how are you today?"

"Tired of the sirocco," answered Abdullah. "I don't remember it continuing so long before."

"Yes, it is bad this year," replied Nikolas, shaking his head sorrowfully. He then proceeded with, "How can I help you, gentlemen?"

"Our usual inquiry. What do you hear from your fellow Greek Cretans? Are we likely to have any problems?" Abdullah asked.

"I have heard nothing unusual at all, Sheik Abdullah. As you might guess, there is some concern as to where the Venetians are. They're quite aware that the Arab dhows have returned, but the Venetians have not yet.

Nikolas stood and placatingly added, "Don't get me wrong. They don't misunderstand their situation and remain content with the government of Abu Hafs. Yet many have come to know and like Gianni and Irene. After all, Gianni has spent time with some of our fishermen. I believe he is helping with the making of our Cretan cheeses today."

Aziz said, "We haven't seen much of the woman, Irene."

"She has not been well and stays out of the heat. The woman Miriam visits her on occasion and says she is gracious. It's possible that she might join some of the native women at the laundry site on the creek today."

"When would that be?"

"There are usually women there from late morning on for a few hours."

The two Arabs exchanged a glance. Abdullah stood and said, "All right. Thank you for what you have provided us. Just a reminder to continue to keep us informed of any potential problems."

"Of course. If I learn of anything, I shall seek you out to tell you." The guards rose and left. As they walked away, Aziz said to Abdullah, "He didn't mention whether the Venetian's woman was pregnant."

"True, but he may not know. And what is the good of telling us something based only on rumors? And if she is, what of it?"

"I suspect that he doesn't tell us everything he knows. I want too much information, not too little." They walked along in silence, gazing at the largely empty streets. "Maybe we should visit the creek and watch the women washing clothes. It might be cooler."

"Perhaps. But what do you expect to find out? If there's going to be trouble, it's not likely to come from housewives." Abdullah stopped and faced Aziz. "Is this about women?"

"No."

"Make sure it's not. Most of the garrison has heard about what happened to the whore two weeks ago. You know the Koran does not approve of drinking wine."

"Don't lecture me. I paid extra for that little slap."

"Look, we've been together doing this for several months now, and I've never interfered with what you do on your own time. But don't bring that with you here. We've got enough trouble on our hands trying to control this whole island and fighting off the Romans from time to time. I know she's only a whore and an infidel. But don't you think that the Greeks are aware of what's going on?"

"I don't care what the Greeks think."

"Well, I do, and so does Abu Hafs. We depend on their cooperation, don't we? They feed us, don't they? Or do you think we need another fight on our hands?" They walked on, with Aziz silently bristling at Abdullah's words. He was aware that Abu Hafs had publicly professed to want his followers to treat the native Cretans with civility.

But, after all, he, Aziz, was a fighter, a warrior, a man. He was wasted being nothing more than a prison guard tending to a bunch of womanish Greeks. His hands curled into fists as he resisted the urge to yell these words at Abdullah.

###

Irene, unusually, had felt good all that morning. She opened her door in order to see how hot the day might be. It was a warm morning that promised a hot afternoon, with the sirocco wind full of sand still blowing across the island at a constant ten miles per hour. Gianni had left early and would return mid-afternoon, hopefully with some cheese.

She had several items of clothing that needed washing. Plus, getting outside early for a few hours and seeing some other women would probably be pleasant, so she returned inside to gather her laundry. She felt like dressing well and put on a white blouse with short sleeves, which she tucked into a blue skirt that ended a few inches below her knees. It was an outfit that she knew Gianni liked to see on her. She wrapped a red scarf around her head and, because it was a beautiful morning, she put on a leather necklace, holding three copper pendants around her neck. She picked up the woven basket holding her laundry and a light shawl of red and blue and left the house.

It was a fifteen-minute walk to the lazy stream that native women had used for washing their clothes for hundreds of years. The water was shallow enough to walk through without having to hike up one's skirts to avoid getting too wet, and there were boulders for sitting and talking as well as pounding and drying wet clothes. Five women were already there, including Miriam, talking to and occasionally laughing at one another. Except for Miriam, she did not know them very well, and they spoke a Greek dialect, which she had to struggle to understand. Nevertheless, soon, she was more or less chatting with them. Many wanted to know what Venice and Italy were like. "I don't know. My brother and I joined the crew of the galley at a small port on the Adriatic. We arrived there from Bulgaria, but we are Slavs.”

“Bulgaria? Where is that?”

“Oh, it’s north of Greece, well away from the sea. And very cold in the winter.”

“But your husband is Venetian, isn’t he?”

“Yes, and young.” Irene shrugged and continued, “It’s a long story,” to which they all started laughing. Soon, a few of them brought some figs, bread and cheese, which they ate as they worked. Irene washed her clothes and laid them on boulders to dry in the sun and wind. She then put out her shawl under a tree and lay down. Miriam came over to her and asked, “Are you feeling all right?”

“Yes. I’m just tired and not used to this heat.”

“Okay. Most of us will be ready in an hour or so. Do you want me to check on you then?”

“No, but thanks. I don’t think I’ll fall asleep, just rest.”

“Okay.”

However, Irene was sound asleep in less than ten minutes. An hour later, Miriam peered at her and gently called her name. When Irene did not respond, Miriam thought, *God knows she needs the sleep. I’ll come back later to check on her*, then walked away with the remaining women.

As they were turning to return to the palace, Aziz told Abdullah that he had to return to the Greek neighborhood. “My wife asked me to bring home some fruit.”

Abdullah, already focusing on what he would report, absent-mindedly nodded acquiescence and said, “I’ll see you tomorrow,” as Aziz turned and walked away towards the small market area. However, after a short distance and now out of Abdullah’s sight, he turned towards the stream and soon stood under a tree, looking across it at the sleeping form of Irene.

Aziz sat down and leaned against a tree and began thinking - Oh what a mistake he had made in choosing to follow Abu Hafs to this Godforsaken island.

He could have stayed in Alexandria; there was always a need for Arab warriors there, perhaps on slaving expeditions to Nubia - mercifully on land. He didn't like sailing, but that was what you had to do on an island. And there were lots of women of all kinds in Africa, women who appreciated a man like he was. He didn't mind the heat of the desert; here, in the middle of the sea, it was the humidity that really bothered him.

Aziz stood and stared into the stream bed.

Then there was Amina. His wife. When he married her he thought he had done all right. She was young, pretty and seemingly obedient. And it's true she rarely questioned him; in fact, only occasionally looked him in the face. Sure, she was inexperienced about the ways of men and women, but that was ok. Anyway, he wasn't going to change his ways of finding pleasure with other women. She should understand that. Perhaps one day they'd have sons, but so far, if she had gotten pregnant, she hadn't told him. All he wanted from her now was her continued silence, obedience and food. He could get the rest elsewhere.

He noticed Irene stirring and slowly sitting up. She yawned and, rubbing her eyes, stood up and started gathering her now-dried clothes from the boulders in the stream bed. Aziz, squatting about fifteen yards away, was staring at her uncovered hair and face, her bare ankles, and her large blue eyes. Irene slowly turned her head around and at last saw him. She stood up quickly and began carrying all her clothes back to her shawl, pushing them into her laundry basket. Aziz rose and slowly moved forward, looking intently at Irene, who turned and, catching sight of him, looked at him fiercely.

She began to walk up the stream bed away from Aziz, towards her house. He followed her about thirty yards behind. She found the path and knew that she had about a ten-minute walk to get home; she walked as fast as she could without running. Aziz, larger and not carrying anything, began to gain on her and was soon only ten yards behind. She came to a turn to her house and suddenly turned towards Aziz and glaringly said, "What do you want?"

He said nothing but walked up to her and asked, "Where is your man?"

"He's on his way. He'll be here anytime."

"It doesn't matter anyway," Aziz snorted. He stepped forward and grabbed Irene by her upper arm. Irene immediately pulled away and stared at him. Aziz looked at her face, her angry blue eyes and suddenly became aware of his rage. He recognized that this was what he had wanted, had even needed all day. He began pulling her to a grassy area beside the path. She tried to yank her arm free, but with a sudden motion, he pulled her past him and onto the grass.

He reached for her blouse and ripped it open, exposing her breasts. She started screaming and beating her fists against his chest and face. He grabbed her head, but she found his hand with her teeth and bit it as hard as she could. He screamed and looked at the bloody gash in his palm. Enraged, he hit her in the face with the full force of his fists. Stunned by the blow to her jaw, Irene fell backward. She opened her eyes when she felt her dress being pulled up and saw Aziz looming over her. He dropped to his knees and pulled her legs apart. Irene felt an intense searing pain course through her as Aziz pushed his way into her vagina.

Aziz now pinned Irene's hands down behind her head as she sobbed. Her eyes were closed, but she could feel the heat and sweat coming from his face and smell the odor of his breath. She felt the spasm in his body and was aware that he had begun to slow his driving into her. Suddenly, she heard two voices yelling. Opening her eyes, she saw Nikolas gripping Aziz by the shoulder, trying to pry him off of her, saying, "Sheik Aziz, don't. Why are you doing this?"

Aziz sat up on his knees and slapped Nikolas so hard that he fell back onto the ground at Gianni's feet. Aziz glared at Nikolas and yelled, "How do you think you can interfere? You don't have any right to touch me!" His rage increasing, he grasped his dagger and, seized Nikolas by his blouse and shoved its blade into his heart.

Gianni stood watching the blood pouring out of Nikolas while Aziz attempted to twist the dagger out of Nikolas' ribcage. To the side, Gianni saw a log about six inches wide and three feet long. Unthinking, he picked it up by one end and, stepping behind Aziz, swung it with all his strength into the side of Aziz's head. Aziz fell to the side, his eyes wide open and blood oozing out of his mouth, eyes and ears.

Gianni went to Irene, who was now bent into a fetal position with blood flowing down her legs. He cradled her head and pulled what was left of her clothes over her.

A group of Cretans soon had formed around them, murmuring, when Miriam arrived. She told one of them to go to the palace and report that Nikolas and an Arab guard were dead. She then asked Gianni if he could help her carry Irene into the house.

Gianni and Miriam disrobed Irene and gently washed her; she only stared at them dully. Miriam asked, "Are you in pain?" Irene weakly shook her head no. Miriam looked at the torn vaginal tissue and said, "There's not much I can do now. Let her sleep and give her mouthfuls of water. Hold her gently and as she needs. I'll be back later to check in on her."

"And the baby?" asked Gianni.

"Yes, and the baby."

###

Abu Hafs had been napping fitfully in the afternoon heat and had to be awakened by Mustafa. "There's been two killings in the Cretan neighborhood."

"Who died?"

"Nikolas, the Greek, our informant, was one. It looks like he was killed by one of our guards named Aziz."

"And?"

"Aziz is also dead. It seems he was killed by the Venetian Gianni as he was trying to withdraw his dagger from the body of Nikolas."

"What caused all of this?"

"Aziz raped Gianni's woman, and they were trying to get him away from her."

Abu groggily sat up and "I see." He thought for a moment and then added, "the Venetian will have to die. I can't have infidels dispensing their notion of justice to my followers."

CHAPTER 14

∽◉∽

The next morning on the dock at Sitia, Rustico said goodbye to Alexios, who asked, "Are you sure you don't want me to accompany you to the harbor at Chandax?"

"No, I'm sure we can find our way. You've been very helpful, and I won't forget it. I'll look for you next year, God willing." Rustico started to turn away but added, "You can look out for the Coptic monk and make sure he finds passage to the Holy Land."

"Certainly."

The galley needed its cargo rearranged after the storm, and Father Theodore and Bono had taken charge of the pork. The sirocco appeared to be tapering off, blowing now at five to ten miles per hour and carrying less sand. Nevertheless, it promised to be an uncomfortably warm early autumn day, with occasional puffs of white clouds scudding across the blue sky. The waters were choppy, more green than blue.

The galley had been rowed eastward within three hundred yards of the Cretan north coast for an hour when Rustico ordered it into a cove. Since there were no apparent inhabitants, the galley was anchored, and Rustico had the shields distributed to the crew. "From positions along the galley's side," he instructed, "prop the shields with their sides abutting all along the perimeter. You'll have to hold on tightly to the shield's handle and be prepared to feel the blow of arrows coming from the outside. Interlacing the shields at the sides should help. It's not perfect, but it will have to do until we get home."

Rustico nodded to Bono, who had brought out the collection of daggers and swords, and said, "These are old also, but they've been sharpened, cleaned of rust, and seem to be in good condition. I know some of you probably have your own knives, probably from Alexandria. Keep them out of view while we are in Chandax. Carlo and Boris will keep these in a box at the front of the boat and will hand them out if needed, probably on land.

"We don't know what to expect," Rustico continued to the crew. "All I can say is that we've done what was asked of us, and I don't see any reason why we should have any difficulties. But it's better to be prepared for trouble, right?" The crew nodded and some murmured amongst themselves. "I want my son back, it's true. But believe me, we would do the same if it were one of you kept there. Now, Let's go and keep your wits about you."

Irene woke with a start. She realized she had been vividly dreaming; however, she also distinctively remembered being nursed by Miriam after being attacked the day before. She looked around and saw her sleeping in a chair. *So that part did happen*, she thought. Irene began to move her legs in an effort to stand up, but a sharp pain in her groin caused her to groan suddenly. Miriam woke up at the sound, rose from her chair and sat beside Irene, gently restraining her. "You need to be careful. You've lost a lot of blood, and you're going to be weak."

Irene slowly sagged back into her bed. "How long have I been asleep?"

"A while, not too long."

"And my face?"

"It's swollen and black and blue. I can't tell if your jaw's broken."

Bleakly comprehending her situation, Irene shook her head slowly side to side and asked, "Where's Gianni?"

"The Arabs have him. He killed the Arab who raped you."

Irene brought her hands up to her face, covered her eyes, and at last, she asked, "Is he all right?"

"So far. Only time will tell what will happen to him." Miriam added, "One other thing."

"What's that?"

"The baby is gone, most likely."

"How do you know?"

"From the bleeding. Last night it was very heavy." Irene put her hand over her eyes and started to cry.

Miriam gently swabbed Irene's forehead with a damp cloth and smoothed her hair. Irene's sobs gradually subsided, and she said, "I started trying to get pregnant just to save myself. I didn't have any real desire to have a child. But Gianni was so attentive. I've never had that kind of attention from a man before. So, over time, I began to change, and suddenly, I really wanted the baby.

"And now, I am alone. I can't imagine them letting Gianni come back to me. And my brother, I don't know if I will ever see him again. What's the point ...?"

Miriam, still smoothing Irene's hair, paused and said, "I can imagine. I'm staying here, so rest now. Tomorrow will be here soon enough."

The Venetians rowed into the harbor surprised that no dhows attempted to intercept them. "It's odd, don't you think, that we haven't seen any Arab boats," Bono said to Rustico.

Rustico, scanning the harbor, said, "Yes. I wonder what it means. Tell Carlo to make sure the men stay alert for any trouble." As they reached the quay, two guards quickly approached the galley and told Bono they were to come immediately to the palace.

"Why should we?" A suspicious and angry Rustico protested. "We've done what was required, and now it's time for them to do as they promised. Tell them to go back to Abu Hafs and let him know we are not leaving the quay. He can come here." Bono nodded, and the guards, muttering about how Abu Hafs would respond, left for the palace.

Rustico, Bono and Carlo disembarked and stood scanning the city. "I'm going to get the shields and daggers ready," Carlo said, leaving.

Twenty minutes later, Mustafa appeared with Abdul and the two original guards. Approaching Bono and Rustico, Mustafa motioned for the guards to stand back. Bono asked Mustafa without his usual bow, "What's going on?"

"There's a problem. Apparently, Rustico's son killed an Arab two days ago."

"Tell me exactly what happened," Rustico insisted.

"The guard had just raped the Slav woman when Nikolas attempted to intervene. The guard killed Nikolas, then Gianni killed the guard."

"Where is my son? Is he alright?"

"He's at the palace. Abu Hafs has been hearing from various people all day. All the available Arab guards are out patrolling, watching for trouble from the Greek Cretans."

"I want my son now."

"I understand, but we need to sort this out."

Unnoticed, Boris and Carlo had emerged from the galley. Suddenly, Boris grabbed Mustafa's hair, yanked him back and put a dagger to his throat. Abdul, seeing this, started to draw his sword, but froze when a Roman sword was pointed up at his throat by Carlo. Bono took Abdul's sword, and both the Arabs were forced to their knees with blades at their throats. The rest of the crew stood on the galley, shields in their hand, ready for any escalation. The two guards, stunned, stood hesitantly looking at Mustafa until Bono said, "Go tell Abu Hafs we have his nephew and we are waiting for him."

After the guards left, Rustico said, "They will send back many more." He then waved–the crew off the galley and ordered them to form a crescent line of shields in front of the galley with only Mustafa and Abdul outside the formation, on their knees, their hands bound behind their backs.

Rustico waved Carlo over and pointed at two dhows moored about fifty feet from the galley and said, "Take two men, unmoor those boats and set them afire. If anyone is in them, bring them here. Quickly."

Bono boarded the galley and found Father Theodore holding the open box containing the relics of St. Mark. "I'm sorry," Bono said," I don't know if we'll leave here alive."

Father Theodore nodded and replied, "I am asking for God's help."

"May I sit with you?"

"Of course. Don't worry. Whatever God wishes will happen."

Bono sat next to Father Theodore, looked at the skull of the saint, and replied, "Maybe."

A short time later, ten Arab warriors appeared. They hadn't drawn their weapons and stood back from the semicircle of shields about thirty yards away, waiting. Soon after, Abu Hafs and Aisha arrived, followed by a coterie of men who brought two chairs for the siblings to sit on. Abu Hafs sat and looked blankly at the Venetians and finally said, "Here I am, as you asked. I believe you've met my sister."

"We had an agreement," Rustico said, ignoring Abu's words. "We did our part, and now it's your turn. Release Gianni and the Slav woman and we'll leave, sparing Mustafa and Abdul."

"Your son killed one of my warriors."

"Mustafa has told us how it happened. Are you saying that if a Christian had raped one of your women, you wouldn't have done the same?"

"Maybe. But you won't dictate how I dispense justice in my land."

"Justice? Is that what I'm to expect? Bring my son and Irene out. I want to hear from them what happened."

Abu looked at his sister and then at his advisors, all of whom returned his gaze in silence. "All right. I'll bring them here. And I'll also bring the dead Arab's wife." He stood, waited for Aisha to rise as well, and then led the group into a room at the port.

Once inside, He turned to Aisha and asked, "What would you have me do?"

"That's my son, your nephew, out there. He can't die over this matter."

Abu turned to his advisors. "Do any of you have a solution to this?"

One bowed to Abu and said, "If we kill them, what will they say in Alexandria? Aren't the Venetians the ones who are expected to bring them slaves? Isn't that what we promised?"

Abu snorted, "What will they say if they knew that I allowed infidels to force their ways upon me? I can't be made to seem to have no control."

"So you are prepared to see Mustafa die?" Aisha harshly asked. "Again, what will they say in Alexandria, where Mustafa is highly regarded? All to protect a rapist?"

"I can't be shown as weak to my followers," Abu said, scowling.

At this time, Gianni was brought out to the dock, wrists bound in front of him. He saw his father standing between two shields and lifted his hands in acknowledgment. Rustico asked, "How are they treating you?"

"All right. The guards don't seem to care one way or another, from what I can tell."

"Did you kill the Arab?"

"Yes. I didn't think about it. I saw Irene, then watched as the Arab killed Nikolas. After that, I just acted," Gianni admitted. He added, "I'm not sorry. Most would have reacted as I did."

With those words, Abu and his group returned to their seats. Abu instructed a guard, "Bring the wife and Abdullah here." A small, thin female figure, dressed in white from head to toe, her head and face covered, emerged from the line of Arab guards and stood looking at Abu Hafs. "What's your name?" he asked.

"Amina, Sheik."

"Was Aziz your husband?"

"Yes."

"Did he have other wives?"

"No, just me." She added, "What will happen to me? I have no one here; how can I live?"

Abu, ignoring her questions, asked, "What's your age?"

"I'm twenty. I have been his wife since I was fourteen."

"No children?"

"No."

"Why not?"

"I don't know. I just did what he asked of me. That's all."

"Was he a good husband?"

"Yes. We had a house and enough food. He hit me a few times when I was younger, But I learned to stay out of his way."

Curious, Abu Hafs glanced at Amina and inquired, "What do you mean?"

"He liked to go out at night, and he would sometimes drink. He didn't like it when I mentioned it to him. He'd get angry." She paused and then started sobbing inconsolably, "But what is to become of me? I can't be left with no one to care for me."

"In good time, Sheika, in good time." Abu Hafs gazed at Amina for a moment and continued with, "We'll stop for the moment, and you can leave. I'll attend to you later." Abu turned to the guard and said, "Bring Abdullah in."

Abdullah entered and bowed to the emir, "Your grace."

"I understand you and Aziz worked together."

"Yes. We often patrolled the Greek section of Chandax together."

"Were you together on the day he died?"

"Yes, we met and then went to Nikolas's house. As you are aware, he kept us updated on what the local Greeks might be up to. We usually saw him a couple of times a week."

"Did Aziz like Nikolas?"

"I couldn't say. I can say he said that Nikolas didn't tell us all he knew, that he should let us know more than he did."

"Did you ever hear Aziz threaten Nikolas?"

"No. He didn't like any of the Greeks, as far as I could tell. But I never heard him single out Nikolas particularly as someone he hated."

"How long were you with Aziz that day."

"Most of the morning. As we were returning to the palace, Aziz said he forgot to get something, some food item, I think - and that he had to return to the Greek section. I said fine and that I would see him later and returned to the palace."

"I understand Aziz somehow ended up at the stream where the Greek women laundered their clothes."

"So, I heard."

"Were you surprised?"

Abdullah answered glumly and said, "No."

"Why not?"

"Aziz had suggested going to watch the women there and I said no. In fact, I told him to stay away from the Greek women, or any women, really. He didn't respond, but I knew he was angry at me."

"He'd had dealings with other women?" Again, Abdullah paused.

"The whole garrison knows about how he beat a Greek whore not too long ago."

"Did you like Aziz?"

Abdullah considered the question and said, "We were colleagues, not friends. I can say he was often unhappy and always short-tempered. But he was reliable, a fearless soldier, and we generally got along."

"You didn't see the killings?"

"No. I heard about it when the whole garrison did."

Abu Hafs nodded. "Thank you, Abdullah, is it? I appreciate your honesty." He then turned to the guards and commanded, "Bring in the woman, Irene."

Miriam escorted Irene slowly to a bench that had been set up for her. Irene sat on it length-wise with her feet on the bench, hunched over her knees. She looked haggard. Her face was black and blue across the entire right side, and her nose was particularly swollen. She looked dazedly around and momentarily glanced at Gianni, not appearing to recognize him, before turning away. Abu Hafs waited for a moment before asking, "Your name is Irene, isn't it?"

"Yes."

"Earlier today, didn't you tell me you had been raped and beaten by our guard named Aziz. Right?

Irene, clutching her knees to her chest, wearily said, "Yes."

"You also said that you saw the Venetian Gianni kill Aziz by hitting him with a piece of wood across his head. Am I right?"

Irene only nodded yes.

Pointing at Gianni, Abu Hafs asked, "Is this your husband?"

Irene looked again at Gianni and answered, "We are together."

"Are you carrying his child?"

"No longer."

"What do you mean?"

"I mean, it's gone." Irene, arms tightly wrapped around her knees, began rocking back and forth. "It's gone now."

Aisha, who had been watching Irene intently, suddenly became aware of a burning sensation in the pit of her stomach and found herself turning away. Abu Hafs looked at the back of her head and asked, "Are you all right?"

Suddenly, Bono pushed aside two shields and walked out in front of the semicircle formed by the shields held by the galley's crew. He stood silently, his eyes moving between Irene and Abu Hafs then he spoke. "Sheikh, haven't you heard and seen enough? What are we doing here? Why are we on this edge of violence? Haven't we done all we could for you and reasonably expected you to honor your promise upon our return?"

He paused briefly, then continued, "I ask that you hear me out. Venice is small and located between two great powers: the Romans of Constantinople and the Franks. Both these powers have tried to control us. In order to survive on our own in this world, we've had to find new ways of acting, which requires taking on new risks. Aren't you also looking for ways to survive? Don't you see that we need each other?"

Taken by surprise, an immobile Abu Hafs sat staring at Bono, who had paused. Bono, in turn, studied Abu Hafs' face for a moment, searching for some sign of a response. Finally, Bono continued, "We have to share this section of the Mediterranean Sea? It is up to us that we maintain some sort of relationship; it's the only way we will survive."

Bono paused momentarily, then stepped further away from the line formed by the Venetians and said, "So I am offering myself in place of Gianni and Irene. Take me instead. Killing Gianni means our killing Mustafa and Abdul as well. And to what end? Many others, Arabs and Venetians alike, will also die or suffer. So take me instead. I'll stay; do with me what you will."

Abu Hafs silently sat for a moment, looking at the ground and then at his sister. He looked at Bono and said, "These two deaths, of a Greek and an Arab, are most unfortunate, but in my eyes, they can be seen as cancelling each other out. The deaths of the Venetian Gianni and my nephew would accomplish nothing more.

"It's true what you say- it is best that we deal with one another as best we can. It appears that we will need your cooperation in the future, and I expect that you will return.... As you have promised." Abu hesitated for a moment and went on with, "It will not be necessary for you to stay. Release the young man Gianni and the Slav woman. Let them leave in peace."

Rustico, stunned, looked at Bono and then at his crew. "Carlo, go get Gianni, and Boris, you go to your sister. When everyone is on board, we will release Mustafa."

"Fair enough," Abu agreed. "However, Signore Bono is to remain where he is under our control until Mustafa is released along with Abdul." Abu signaled to two guards to take hold of Bono.

Irene was accompanied by Miriam and Boris onto the galley, where a rough bed was prepared on the aft deck by Father Theodore. Gianni stood by as Miriam held Irene's face between her two hands and said, "You must rest and let the future happen. One day, this will feel like nothing more than a bad dream." To Gianni, she added as she left, "Don't expect too much from her for a while. Let her mend in her own time." Gianni knelt down and gently touched Irene's hand but felt no response.

With the crew boarding the galley, first Abdul, then Mustafa had their hands released and allowed to stand. Mustafa began walking towards his uncle. As he passed Bono, who was returning to the galley, they both stopped six feet apart and looked at each other. Mustafa bowed slightly and said, "I didn't know how this would end. I don't doubt Signore Rustico was prepared to cut my throat and fight to the end." The two men looked at one another before Mustafa added, "You will be back?"

"I will do as I promised. I can't say what the others will do."

"I hope we will meet again."

"Yes, God willing."

"Yes, Inshallah."

The Venetians quickly rowed out of Chandax harbor, passing the burning dhows and without encountering any Arab interference. Relieved to be back at sea, Rustico approached Bono, who was standing beside Father Theodore. "I owe you for Gianni's life," he said.

Bono looked at Rustico and slowly replied, "You owe me nothing. You see, it was the work of Saint Mark; as I sat there, gazing at his bones back in Chandax, the saint took control of me. I didn't want to die, but I had to act as you saw."

Rustico stared silently at Bono for a moment and could only say, "I see."

###

That evening, Abu Hafs was sitting alone in his quarters when a servant announced that Aisha wished to see him. "Show her in."

Aisha quickly walked across the room and approached her brother. "I know I've said some unfortunate things to you," Aisha began. "But today, you did what you needed to save my son's life, and I'll forever be grateful." She paused and said, "You did the right thing."

"Yes, perhaps," Abu Hafs replied mysteriously. But then adamantly added, "But you see, it was the work of Allah. He permitted it."

"What do you mean?"

"It seemed quite clear to me this afternoon that in Signore Bono's act of offering himself, Allah created a situation where I could choose what to do, whether it was what you call the right thing or not. And so because it was my choice, I didn't appear weak."

"So Allah saved Mustafa?"

"It might seem that way. I think Allah was allowing me the opportunity to choose as I did." Abu rose from his seat and walked around behind it and said, "But now I must do something for the young wife of the dead Aziz."

Aisha stood silently, mulling over her brother's words and then added, "Let me take care of her for you. I'll take her back to Alexandria with me and find her a new husband. It's the least I can do."

"Will Mustafa be returning with you to Alexandria?"

"You'll have to ask him."

CHAPTER 15

The galley headed due north as quickly as possible. Upon reaching the Greek coast, it turned west, staying about five hundred yards from the shore. The sirocco finally diminished into gentle sand-free breezes, and the autumn days remained warm. The nights, however, came early and were cool. Rustico was able to purchase a variety of bows and arrows at a small Greek village where they stopped for one night. Gianni and Boris, now tanned, lean and well-muscled, were back handling the lateen sails while the red and black rowing teams took two-hour shifts.

Irene spent much of her time in bed, often being attended by Father Theodore. She was able to help out when the galley was beached as she and Father Theodore took on the responsibility of serving food, mostly salted pork, to the crew. On the third night, she was sitting on the beach, gazing at the sea, when Gianni approached cautiously and sat next to her. "How are you feeling?" he asked.

"Very sore. It's still hard to move about on a moving boat."

"And your jaw?"

"It hurts but I'm able to eat at least."

"My father plans on stopping at Ragusa so you can be seen by a midwife or doctor."

"That would be nice."

They sat in an awkward silence until Gianni asked, "Are we still together?"

"I don't know. We can't be the way we were on Crete. I don't know how long it'll take for me to be available to a man."

"Yes, I imagined that. I don't know what to say but I'm...I don't care about that now."

"But you will, eventually."

Gianni looked at sand falling from between his fingers to the ground and said, "Most likely." And then, "But I feel I still need to take care of you."

"And I, you. We have to see what happens. Anyway, I would like to see a midwife soon. In the meantime, we're on a boat with twenty-two others, hurrying to a place I've never been. But it's your home."

"It could be yours too."

"Perhaps. We'll see." Irene then gently kissed Gianni's forehead, rose to her feet, and said, "Tomorrow comes early, and I must get some sleep."

###

The next day, Irene was sitting with her arms wrapped around her bent knees, clutching a blanket, when Father Theodore approached her. "May I sit with you?"

Irene looked up and smiled. "Please do."

"I've been told that for your first few days in the galley, you were quite seasick."

"Yes. I guess I've gotten over it. Other pains have taken over."

"No doubt. What did you do before you became a sailor?"

"I'd had never seen the sea before this year. Boris and I are Slavs and grew up in Bulgaria. Boris was always intrigued about what he heard of the sea, so after our parents died we made our to the coast. I could have found work on land, but Boris wanted to go. So we went."

"He seems to be thriving on this boat." Irene smiled and nodded.

"And Gianni? I hope you don't mind me asking."

"Who knows? I don't know... even what I want. Still...."

"What?"

"It's odd, and I can't say I understand it, but...."

"What?"

"In my dreams, or in the first hours of the morning when I'm not really awake, I find myself resenting Gianni. Because he wasn't there. I know he couldn't be there or foresee what happened. But still, I expected him to be there." Irene shook her head and said, "It's all so foolish. He really has been very good to me, even pretending that we were married to keep me from being sold into slavery. I really have nothing to complain about. Still, I have this anger, and I don't know what to do about it."

Father Theodore nodded sympathetically and said, "How awful for you. Not just the violence but the lingering sense of being alone, of not being protected."

"How about you? Were you ever married?"

"Yes, a long time ago. I was married when I was a young man, twenty years old. She was eighteen."

"What happened?"

"She died in childbirth, along with the baby. Twelve years ago now. I am thirty-five now." Father Theodore silently gazed at the horizon before adding, "I was angry too. At everything, everybody. Even at her for dying and leaving me. It took me a long time to realize that one's anger needs a target – someone or thing that you can blame. The realization didn't end my anger, but it allowed me to cope with it until it gradually faded away."

"That would be nice. I still wake up seeing the hate on the Arab's face as he was on me, how he wanted to hurt me."

They sat in silence for a moment before Irene asked, "What are you going to do once we get to Venice?"

"Signore Bono has assured me that I can be involved in maintaining the relics of the saint. I don't really know what that may involve. I can't see that there would be much of a need for a Coptic priest in Venice, nor do I see myself sufficiently changing my beliefs so I can be a Catholic priest. I do know I can't return to Africa.

"Perhaps I could do some translating. I can read and write well enough in Coptic, Greek and Latin, and I know some Hebrew as well. These Venetians appear eager to spread across the Mediterranean world, and they might have some use for me."

Irene shook her head thoughtfully. "I can read too, including some Slavic languages. Maybe I could help."

"That would be nice. We could work together."

###

Amina arrived at the palace mid-afternoon. "I was told to come today and ask for Sheika Aisha," she told the guard, who offered her a seat in an anteroom. He returned shortly and said the sheika was in her quarters waiting for her. Amina followed the guard to a secluded section, far removed from the public areas, where he knocked and she heard Aisha's voice call, "Enter."

Aisha was sitting on a divan, cursorily sorting through a box full of bracelets and necklaces. She merely nodded to Amina's bow. "Thank you for being so punctual. How are you doing?"

"I'm at a loss. I don't know what to do."

"I can imagine. You've been married since you left home as a girl."

"My parents did what they could and arranged my marriage. Aziz told me what he wanted, and that was all there was to it. I've spoken a little with other wives, and my story doesn't seem to be unusual."

"No, probably not. And I gather you have no particular plans for your future."

"No. I suppose I've been waiting to hear something from the Emir."

"Do you want to leave Crete?"

"Yes. But I don't know if I can return to my parents' home in Africa. They were pleased when I was married. We didn't have much money, and I have two younger sisters which they must plan for also."

"Can you prepare food?"

"Yes."

"Shop at the market? Bargain with vendors? Tend to a house and all that is needed?"

"I am very frugal. I am by nature and it was necessary when Aziz was with me. He only gave me a little money to run his household. I didn't mind because I was used to such things."

"He kept most of his money, I gather."

"He didn't tell me much. I knew he spent on things outside our home."

"Other women? Wine, perhaps?"

"I didn't ask. He didn't like that. I knew only that he was often out." Aisha nodded as she stared at Amina.

"I am looking for a woman, a maid I suppose, someone to take care of my clothes, my bedroom, help me dress. She must be diligent and honest; I cannot abide a lazy servant. I can be very direct in my speaking; I don't hand out compliments and I expect to be obeyed *immediately* at any hour of the day. Do you understand?"

"Yes, Sheika."

"I shall be returning to Alexandria very soon. It will be necessary for my maid to make sure that my travels are comfortable and trouble-free. Are you interested in such an opportunity?"

"Yes, Sheika."

"You understand that I am talking about a trial opportunity. If it doesn't work out, then you will be gone."

"I understand. Will I be expected to pay for...?"

"I will make sure that your travel and accommodations are provided."

"When would I start?"

"Tomorrow. Agreed?"

"Yes, Sheika. I will return here tomorrow morning first thing."

Aisha nodded. "I will advise the Emir's company to expect you then. Good night."

Shortly after Amina left, a guard knocked and told Aisha that her son wished to speak with her and asked if this would be a good time. "By all means, show him in," said Aisha. A few minutes later, Mustafa gently pushed his mother's door open.

"Good day, Mother," he said as he bowed.

Aisha bowed in response. "I'm glad you have come. We have many things to discuss."

"No doubt. May I sit?"

"Of course," Aisha said as she pointed to a backless chair and began pacing back and forth-. "I'm concerned about your future. I know this comes as no surprise to you. I also know we have not always agreed."

"I've always *listened* to your advice, Mother."

"I hope so. We have had our troubles in understanding one another. I am aware that you consider me to be overbearing."

"I've never doubted your concern for me and our family."

Aisha looked at Mustafa for a moment and said, "I do hope that is true. I have nurtured great plans for you."

"And I for myself."

"And the family, too?"

Mustafa paused reflectively and said, "Are you referring to my uncle?"

"In large part. I have spent a great deal of time in promoting him."

Mustafa hesitated and then coyly responded, "Perhaps a more accurate phrase is protecting him."

"So it seems."

"It also seems to have become my role," Mustafa ruefully said.

"Let's be candid. We've both tried to protect my brother from the consequences of his own actions."

"That seems a fair assessment. So what would you have me do? You did ask me to follow him to Crete as an advisor. Which I did."

Aisha stopped pacing for a moment. "And the result is that you almost were killed."

"There's no doubt in my mind that the Venetians would have cut my throat. I don't pretend to understand what Signore Bono did, but without a doubt it saved my life."

"My brother would have let you die in order not to look weak in front of his followers. And for what? A thoughtful ruler would have proved his power in other ways. He could have exacted his revenge in other, more subtle ways. He could have pursued them in our faster dhows and fallen upon them as they slept ashore unawares."

"True. But he needs them to do business in Alexandria."

"Abu needs someone to do business for him, but not necessarily them. As long as Abu is not present in Africa, the governor really couldn't care less how the slaves get there."

"Perhaps. But I'm not sure that this new 'someone' is readily available. My uncle hasn't made a practice of trying to make friends in this part of the world. At any rate, I don't disagree with you that the situation with the Venetians could have been resolved without a wholesale slaughter."

"It appears to me that he intends to continue to operate as an outlaw, a pirate, and not as a true emir. How long will it take before the Romans have had enough of him? How long did it take for the governor to tire of his plotting in Africa? He wants to be a leader, someone who is to be taken seriously. But he doesn't realize that a policy based solely on greed and violence can't sustain a true emirate over the long term."

"I've come to believe this too. What do you think I should do?"

"You need to return to Africa with me. There, you can be appreciated."

"Maybe. But I believe I should go to Baghdad and deal directly with the governor."

Aisha paused. "And thereby show your value directly to him?"

"My thoughts are to tell Abu Hafs that I wish to take his case to the governor directly, and I will. The governor might be tempted by a sum of money, but probably an exorbitant amount, more than my uncle would ever agree to. Nevertheless, the governor will see that I'm faithfully attempting to complete my charge, as hopeless as it might seem."

Aisha nodded appraisingly and said, "I now see you to be the son of both your father and me."

###

The galley entered the harbor at Ragusa late morning on a cool, overcast day. Rustico sent Boris and Bono into the town in order to locate a doctor or midwife while the rest of the crew were allowed off the boat in staggered groups of three or four. Carlo, Father Theodore, and Irene remained with the galley. Boris returned with the news that a midwife could examine Irene the next morning.

The midwife was a woman named Anna, about thirty-five, short and plump, with a round red face, black hair cut short and covered with a scarf, and thick, strong arms. Leaving Boris and Bono behind, she led Irene into a separate room and had her disrobe and lay back on a bed.

"When did the attack happen?"

"Ten or twelve days or so ago. I've lost track of the days."

"I understand you were pregnant but lost the child the night of the attack."

"Yes. I had been told by a midwife on Crete that I probably was pregnant; that same woman tended to me afterward and said my blood flow was very thick and that the child was gone." Anna gently probed Irene's vagina and palpated her stomach and abdomen.

After some time, she stood up, wiped her hands cursorily on her apron, and said, "Let's look at your face and jaw." Anna gently moved the jaw, felt inside Irene's mouth, and ran her strong fingers over her head and neck.

"Well, if you were pregnant, you definitely are not now. The tissue is swollen, torn and sore but healing. It may take some time, but the pain will gradually subside, and you'll be able to walk, work, urinate- whatever- without pain.

"Sex, however, is likely to return only slowly and not so much because of the physical wounds. Emotionally, it may be difficult. Your jaw is sore and in place but not broken. It must have been quite a blow, but you may have turned your face with the blow, deflecting some of the force away."

"Will I be able to get pregnant again?"

"Only God knows that. I can only see and feel so much."

###

Abu Hafs stood morosely looking out of a window, awaiting his sister. She was routinely late, and he was startled when her prompt appearance was announced. Brother and sister greeted each other formally, and Aisha sat on a divan to which she had been directed.

"You wished to see me?" Aisha began.

"Yes. Thank you for coming. I understand you have taken the widow of Aziz as your maid."

"I told you I would deal with her. She seems to be fitting in quite nicely. She was terrified at the thought of having to manage her life without Aziz telling her what to do."

"I appreciate your doing me this favor. I really haven't had any time to consider what, if anything, should be done for the young woman." He paused and went on, "I understand you are leaving Crete soon and returning to Africa. Quite soon, I'm led to believe."

"I am. I have seen what I needed and feel there is nothing more I can add."

"Perhaps you know that Mustafa has asked that I allow him to travel to Baghdad to intercede on my behalf with the governor."

"That certainly sounds like a course of action Mustafa would take."

"I also understand he will be traveling with you as far as Beirut, where you will find a boat to return you to Alexandria."

"A mother always enjoys spending time with her son."

"Was this trip to Baghdad your suggestion?"

"Really, brother, do you understand so little about Mustafa that you could ask me that? I assure you that Mustafa came to his own decision without my coaxing him one way or another."

"Does he plan to return to Crete?"

"I have no idea. You should ask him."

Abu Hafs stood silently, looking at Aisha. "Do you think I would have allowed Mustafa to be killed in the standoff?"

"I only know what you said, that you could not be seen as weak. But an opportunity arose which allowed you to avoid such a choice."

"That is what I said, and I meant it. Truly, I don't know what I could have done had not Signore Bono come forth."

"I can see that."

"And Mustafa, what does he believe?"

"I related to him exactly what you said to me. Beyond that, I don't know what he thinks about you. He feels he owes his life to the Venetian."

"Yes, he probably would believe that."

Aisha cautiously responded, "And you believe Allah arranged for the Venetian to act as he did."

Abu Hafs looked up at Aisha and said, "I believe that to be so."

"So Allah saved Mustafa?"

Abu Hafs paused and replied, "I suppose you could say that. Isn't that how Allah operates?"

Aisha stood and said, "There's nothing more to be said. We'll leave within the week and will bid you goodbye then."

###

Later that afternoon, Abu Hafs sent for Abdullah who was then returning from his rounds of the Greek section.

Abdullah bowed and greeted Abu Hafs with "Salaam."

"I appreciate your prompt appearance here. Tell me, do you have someone to replace Nikolas in keeping us informed about the Greeks?"

"Not yet. We are looking for someone, but it's not going to be easy."

"I expect so." Abu paused and then added, "I'll increase what we pay. Let me know what it'll take."

"Yes, Sheik."

"This whole mess was caused by Aziz, I gather." Abdullah only shrugged. "Of course, it's important that we know if any problems that might arise."

"I don't think the local Greeks are likely to cause us any trouble. Still, they are likely to remain suspicious and reluctant to talk."

"Because?"

"They didn't see that Aziz killing Nikolas concerned us at all, that there was going to be any kind of retribution."

"Yes, that, of course. But we can't look like we're too concerned about them, can we? We are their rulers; they must bend to our rules."

"Yes, Sheik. I'm only reporting what I see and hear. They are avoiding any contact with us as much as they can. And that makes it hard to replace Nikolas."

"Do what you can. The whole thing will blow over soon, and we'll be back where we started. I suppose we have to watch out for any more Aziz's. Men who can't control themselves. "

"That's not going to be easy. I knew Aziz was a troublemaker, but I didn't expect him to do what he did. Probably, we'll need to limit the number of Arabs who deal with the Greeks." Abdullah continued, "It's a shame. Before, some of the Greeks were talking about becoming Moslems, and some Arabs were interested in Greek wives. Now, however, I don't see anything more happening in those areas for quite a while."

"Thank you. You're a good man, someone who says things I understand. I need to have more men like you around me. You may go

now. But keep me informed about the doings of the local Greeks as best
you can."

CHAPTER 16

The galley continued north, following the east coast of the Adriatic. One evening, there being no village or port nearby, the crew sat in front of the beached galley, enjoying a large fire. The daylight sailing hours had been short on this late autumn day, and the cool, calm evening came early. Dinner had been fish, purchased from a passing local vessel and roasted over the fire – a welcome change from the normal diet of salted pork. They knew they were no more than a few sailing days from Venice, and the talk was light-hearted and about what might be waiting for them at home.

Bono sat with Rustico and Gianni and asked, "Shall we tell them of our unannounced cargo?"

Rustico sat up and nodded his agreement. Bono stood and addressed the crew: "We will be in Venice soon and, as you know, have brought with us Father Theodore. He has, as you know, been a great help on board in making sure you've had food and water. He's also tended to some of your wounds and helped out on shore.

"He's not the only person who joined us in Alexandria. You're aware that Father Theodore is a Coptic priest and had led a congregation in Alexandria in a church established by St. Mark hundreds of years ago. Now, the Moslems are building their mosques and homes in Africa, using building materials from Christian churches they are tearing down.

"It happens that the remains of St. Mark were interred at Father Theodore's church. In order to prevent their loss, we, Signore Rustico and myself offered to bring those remains with us back to Venice, where they can be tended to with the care they are entitled to. Of course, Father Theodore wished to accompany them.

"As you might expect, we had to smuggle the remains of the saint out of Alexandria. Father Theodore, Signore Rustico and I decided it was too dangerous to try to explain to the Arabs why we wanted to move them. And really, it didn't seem necessary. His remains would mean nothing to a Moslem other than a relic to sell or trade. So we had them hidden in the hold of the galley, covered with the salted pork." Some of the crew chuckled and murmured that they knew something odd was going on.

"It is our plan to present these cherished remains to the Doge," Bono continued, "So that they might be kept safely in the new church being built on the Rivo Alto. We have returned the saint to his current reliquary for the remainder of our trip.

"For me the body of the evangelist, his physical remains, is as close to God as we can hope for in our lives. I, myself, believe that it was the saint who protected us through-out our trip here. Their being in the possession of Venice will provide protection and guidance for all of us Venetians in the future. He will be our patron saint." Bono returned to his seat amidst the animated conversations of the crew.

Father Theodore asked Bono as he sat down, "Shouldn't you have mentioned that the relics will be returned when it's safe?"

"You mean when the Moslems have left Alexandria?"

"I suppose so."

"I wouldn't concern myself about that now," Bono responded. "The Arabs don't seem to be going anywhere anytime soon."

"Very nice speech," Rustico said.

Bono turned and looked at Rustico and said, "I meant every word of it."

"I know that. But you didn't explain the saint's role in the stand-off at Chandax."

"No, not exactly."

"Why not?"

Bono sighed and leaned back against the galley hull. "Since that day, I've been trying to sort out what happened as best I can. I sat in the galley during the standoff, thinking that my life could soon end, staring at his face, what there was of it. I wasn't thinking that I wanted to be a martyr, like Saint Mark. Yet, as I sat there, I suddenly felt like my whole body and soul had been possessed by him. He caused me to walk out beyond the protection of the shields.

"Then the words came, and they were words that I use - my words and thoughts - but infused by a different power or temperament. I did mean that Abu Hafs could have done with me what he wished. I didn't want to die and knew that I could, yet I didn't feel fear. I wasn't thinking about heaven, or the afterlife, or being with God or St. Mark, or anything like that. I was only thinking about what should happen here, in this world. And suddenly, it did. I looked at Abu Hafs, but I had no idea what he was going to do. I wasn't surprised by what he said but I didn't expect it. I suppose the odd thing about it was I had no expectations."

The three men sat in silence until Father Theodore forcefully asserted, "That's why it was a miracle."

"Because it was not expected?" replied Rustico. "Or because there were two souls out there?"

"All I know is that miracles are not expected."

"True enough," Rustico answered. "But who, or what caused it? Was it the force of the relics of a saint or the decision to act by Signore Bono?"

"Does it matter?"

"To me, it does." Rustico turned to the priest and continued. "Was it the result of the will of a man who understands that the choices are his? Or is it truly some force outside of living humans coming through these old bones? I'm of the opinion it is the result of a live human being's choice."

Bono interjected, "I recall making no choice. I only remember the sense of being controlled by the saint."

"I'm sure that's true. But don't you agree that your will could have been formed by an image of the saint acting in the past in ways you admire? Do you believe that your will is formed only by your thoughts and not by your desires as well?"

"But the compulsion to act came from the saint's relics?"

"So you say. But those bones had been lying in that church for over seven hundred years. How do we know whose bones they truly were?" Rustico replied.

"Coptic priests have tended to those bones since St. Mark was martyred."

"But you didn't know that Stauricius had taken a part of his knee. And somebody else's bones are resting what the saint lay, and people are probably no wiser."

"Yes, it's true that I didn't know Stauricius had removed a part of the saint. Nevertheless, there's been a long line of priests tending to the saint, men who have been chosen for their probity and veneration of the saint."

"No doubt. But seven hundred years is a long time, and that means that a lot of different men were involved. Can you be so sure of what a particular priest might have done even one hundred years ago?"

"You're right, of course," Father Theodore paused and admitted, "I only have to look at myself to see how men of good faith can do unexpected things. But what of you? Can you not conceive of an act on earth done by an external power?"

"I believe people are largely the cause of their own actions."

"You're a good Catholic?"

"I try to be. I have raised my son according to the strictures of the church." Carlo and Gianni, having noted the intense discussion, quietly moved and stood behind Father Theodore and Rustico.

Father Theodore nodded to them and continued asking Rustico. "You are aware of the stories in the Bible, the gospels, including that of St. Mark?"

"Yes, I've heard them read."

"So you know that they are replete with miracles. Christ bringing Lazarus back to life, changing water into wine. Not to mention the rising of his body from the tomb."

"Yes, I know the stories," Rustico retorted. "But that happened when our God walked this earth."

"True, but they did happen, didn't they? The supernatural intervened in human life."

"Then, yes."

"All right. You do *now* participate in the holy Eucharist, do you not?" Rustico nodded uncomfortably. "And you understand that the rite is based on the assumption that the bread and wine you consume have been transformed into the body and blood of Christ?"

"Yes. But I've chosen to see this rite as a symbolic story. No one, not even the priest, believes that the wine has become blood in reality. Even at the last supper, no one could have misunderstood what Christ meant when he said, 'This is my body.'" Rustico paused and said, "I suppose the Church might take a dim view of what I am saying. But I don't feel that if you believe in the Biblical miracles, you must also believe that you're eating the flesh of Christ during the Eucharist."

Bono leaned forward and said, "But these relics come from the time of the miracles. They are the remains of one who knew, who saw God in action on earth. They are like a door into that time, left for us to use, to rely on."

Rustico shrugged, "I understand it's possible. I also understand that my belief in the true religion is based to some extent on the possibility of miracles, as you define them, a supernatural intervention. But are they plausible today? Are there no other explanations? I know you, Signore Bono. I can fully understand, now, why you might have done as you did because of the man you are." The men fell silent.

Carlo, shaking his head, said, "I don't know what was going on inside Signore Bono at Chandax. Nor, for that matter, in Abu Hafs. I only know that, but for what they did, we wouldn't be here but dead or on our way into slavery, perhaps in Africa. It came suddenly and unexpectedly, so I'll always see it as a miracle no matter the cause."

Mustafa hired a cart to transport Aisha's luggage to the mole in Beirut, where he met Aisha and Amina. They had purchased transit on a large galley taking goods to Alexandria and had been promised a large shaded space on the aft deck. Aisha embraced her son, who was going to look for passage with a caravan headed for Baghdad and said, "I would have gone with you had you asked."

"It's much better this way. The governor needs to see that I am capable of difficult duties without having his mother there to oversee it."

Aisha smiled, "Of course, you're right. I shall try and be discreet about your whereabouts with those I know in Alexandria."

"I hope you will. It must appear that we are gradually returning to our interests in Africa and that this isn't the result of a falling out with your brother. I don't want to create enemies unnecessarily. I plan on returning to Alexandria after my duties in Baghdad are done. I shall send a message to Abu Hafs that I'll remain there indefinitely but that if he has a specific job in Alexandria in mind, I shall, of course, be happy to help. He can figure out on his own that I'm not going back to Crete."

"Unless things change."

"Yes, of course. But is that likely?"

"No. But he is my brother, and hoping for his best future is ingrained in me."

"Perhaps hoping for a good future for him is all we can do. Anyway, goodbye, mother, and bon voyage."

##

Two days later, on a warm, dusty afternoon in Beirut, Mustafa, unable yet to find passage to Baghdad, was sitting at a small table outside his inn drinking a heavily diluted arak and wondering whether he would be safe if he hired a guide and two camels for his journey. The waiter, bored and irritable, stood nearby and asked "Sheik Mustafa, how are you doing locating transportation to Baghdad?"

"Nothing yet, but hopefully soon, inshallah."

"Yes, God willing. By the way, did you hear about the ruckus yesterday outside the Madrassa? No? Apparently, some crazed Egyptian monk started arguing with some of the students and became quite disrespectful about the true faith."

"Egyptian monk?" Mustafa responded.

"Apparently – recently arrived from Alexandria. I gather he was on his way to Palestine but couldn't go any further because he didn't have enough money. Anyway, he started hanging around the Madrassa, challenging the students about their religious beliefs. They ignored him for the most part, at least initially, but he grew more and more aggressive. I hear that he was enraged that they're tearing down Coptic churches to build mosques and that he had to leave."

"From Alexandria? I left there recently myself and there has been some unrest with the Copts. Do you know his name?"

"I don't. It probably doesn't matter much now. The imam became so outraged when he wouldn't leave that he attacked the old man with a staff. The monk fell and hit his head on a stone and died. The odd thing is, the old infidel was clutching a piece of bone in his fist. No one seems to know why. Anyway, the authorities are looking into it, but I doubt if much will come of it."

Mustafa stared dazedly ahead and thought:

It's too much of a coincidence - it must be the old man the Venetians took with them. He was traveling with a priest, and they said he would leave them at Crete; he wanted to see the holy land. Why did he feel he had to argue with the students over religious faith?

Mustafa sat musing, swirling his glass arak. Exhaling, he thought:

What is the point of arguing with people about such things? Nobody ever changes their mind. That's one thing I have learned from dealing with my mother- there is nothing to be gained by it. It's best to keep such things to oneself. The only thing you can rely on is behavior, not words.

###

By midmorning on a windy November day, the galley entered the Venetian lagoon and docked at the Rivo Alto. The galley had been seen by a fishing boat out on the gulf and then reported to the palace. The Doge was waiting to greet them. "Ah, Signores Rustico and Bono too. How good it is to see you at last. You're much later than you predicted."

Rustico stepped off the galley with Carlo and tied it to the mole. "It's a long story, and we're glad to be home," said Rustico.

Bono appeared beside him and embraced the Doge. "As Signore Rustico said, our trip was very long. But we have something we think you will appreciate. Here is Father Theodore, a Coptic priest from Alexandria. With him, we bring the remains of St. Mark, the Evangelist."

"Here? In Venice?" The Doge, astonished, said. "Where are they?" At that moment, from the deck of the galley, Father Theodore handed the reliquary to a waiting Carlo, who brought it to him. "This is too precious. Let's take it to the palace."

Rustico gazed at Bono and said, "Take it. You and Father Theodore. I'll finish tying up here and letting the crew go; then we'll join you. I assume it's where we first met."

The Doge nodded, and the three men left. Rustico told the crew they could leave the galley and that he or Gianni would pay them off within the next few days. Gianni, along with Boris and Irene, stayed behind with Rustico.

Forty-five minutes later, Rustico, with Gianni and Irene, knocked and then entered the small chapel and found the Doge sitting with Bono and Father Theodore. The Doge stood and embraced first Irene, then Gianni and Rustico. "What a story!" said the Doge, fondly looking at them. "I must say that your journey home had to be under the protection of the Saint."

"Most likely," replied a tired Rustico. "Still, we certainly had to keep our wits about us."

"Signore Bono still wants to return to Crete next spring," the Doge observed.

"With sufficient protections," Bono quickly added.

"Of course," added the Doge. "And Signore Rustico, what are your thoughts?"

"It's a bit soon. But there's no doubt that there are business opportunities in dealing with the Arabs. At least some of them. And as

Signore Bono has said, there needs to be serious precautions in place. But what of the Saint?"

"Yes, indeed, what about St. Mark? Anyone would be excited to have him as their protector. And that includes the Bishop of Grado who claims already to possess the throne of St. Mark."

Brother Theodore asked, "Throne? He was a bishop, not a king; I've never heard of a throne."

"I don't doubt it," said the Doge. "But he might demand the remains of the Saint based on that claim alone. And the Pope might agree, putting us in an awkward position. I suggest I retain the remains here under lock and key until the church is complete. We'll notify the bishop that our church will be named after Saint Mark."

Bono spoke up, "And his remains will be supervised by Brother Theodore, of course. That was our pledge to him."

"Yes." said the Doge. "We may have to deal with some irascible priests, taking orders from a Coptic priest. But we will manage. Brother Theodore will, of course, be housed here. I'll see to it."

"Thank you," said Father Theodore.

"You see, of course, that he cannot return to Africa safely," Bono added.

"I can see that," the Doge said. He paused and added, "Signore Rustico, I'm afraid I have some unfortunate news for you. I feel I must tell you now, before you get back to Torcello, that your father, Leo, died six weeks ago. I'm sorry."

Rustico stared dully at the Doge for a moment. "What happened?"

"As I understand it, he was working in the ditches of the salt works when a gush of water knocked him over. He didn't drown but came close. Nevertheless, he developed a bad cold and died in his bed ten days later.

I believe his widow and her daughter, Claudia, remain in your house and are managing the salt works on your behalf."

Gianni slumped into a chair, and Irene went behind to embrace him. The group fell silent until Bono spoke up. "What a fine gentleman he was." Then to Rustico, he added, "Please let me know if I can be of any help."

Rustico, who had been staring blankly at the floor, looked up and said, "Thank you." Then, to Gianni, Irene and Boris, he added, "We must be going."

CHAPTER 17

The galley was tied up on Torcello at a recently constructed dock and left with the hold covered and secured. Rustico, Gianni, Irene and Boris walked the short distance to the house and salt works, where Rustico rapped on its door and then pushed it open. Angela sat in front of the fire next to her daughter, Claudia, about thirty-two, short, full-figured, with long black hair and large dark eyes. "Signore Rustico," Angela said, rising from her seat. "A passing fisherman said he thought he saw your galley at the Rivo Alto. Welcome home!"

"Good day, Signora. There are two besides Gianni and myself. This is Irene and Boris, a brother and sister who we took on at Kotor and who have returned with us." Angela smiled and bowed as did Boris and Irene in return. Rustico, now solemn, added, "The Doge told us that my father has died."

Angela sighed and said, "It was all so sudden. I tried to persuade him to hire a younger man to work the ditches, but he wouldn't hear of it."

"I'm not surprised."

"Please sit down and rest. Claudia and I are preparing soup for the evening meal. Are you hungry?"

"Famished, in fact. Gianni and Boris are now going to take a cart back to the galley and bring back some of our belongings. We have returned with a fair amount of items for sale – silks largely and some herbs. We'll bring the merchandise here tomorrow for storage."

The six sat around a table close to the fire, eating their meal. "The table is a nice addition. I see you've also curtained off sections of the house. How did my father react?"

"Once they were in place, he liked it," Angela responded. "We did fine, really, after some initial concerns. I was happy, and I believe he was too."

Claudia smiled at Angela and said to Rustico, "They grew to be like an old married couple as if they had been together for years."

Angela smiled wryly, nodded her head and said, "It's not easy, at my age, to learn to accommodate a new person in your life, but you work at it. But enough about that. Tell us about your journey." The remainder of the evening was spent with Gianni and Rustico, sipping glasses of wine, relating the events of the journey to Angela and Claudia with Boris chiming in on occasion. Irene, tired, had excused herself right after eating and was shown a sleeping area, which she was to share with Boris, where she quickly fell asleep.

"How horrible," Angela said afterward. "For everybody and especially for Irene. And Gianni."

Gianni silently sat staring into the fire. "Thank you for the meal, and especially your taking care of my father," Rustico said and then added, "I want you to know that, as far as I'm concerned, you're my father's widow, and as such, you are always welcome here - whether to live or not, at all times."

Then, addressing all, he continued, "There is plenty of work ahead of us and many decisions too. Boris, you and Irene are welcome to stay here as long as you like." Ostensibly to Angela, Rustico said loudly enough so that all could hear, "Boris has developed into a fine seaman, as good as anyone on the galley. If he wants, I'm sure he can make a life here as a Venetian sailor. Still, there's no need for anyone to be in a rush and make any rash decisions. We have time to work out what's best for each of us.

"I'm certain that the family business will expand to include trade throughout the eastern Mediterranean Sea as well as maintaining it up the rivers. And we will have to maintain our salt business without Leo's assistance. But now it's time for some well-deserved rest; Signora, perhaps you will show us where we can sleep."

###

Two days later, Rustico, Gianni and Boris continued to unload the goods from the galley and haul them on a wagon to a storage building behind the house. For the last load of the day, Rustico sent Boris and Gianni by themselves to the galley and sought out Angela. He found her by the fire pit and, looking around, asked, "Is Claudia here?"

"Not now. She has helped me often during the day but feels that it is best for her to return to her home at night."

"I see. Does she live alone?"

"Claudia and I still share a small home not too far from here in the village. She has no children; as you probably recall, she's been widowed for many years."

"What happened to her husband?"

"He was a fisherman and older than her by ten years. He fell from the boat and drowned."

"That happens a lot. Do you have any concerns about staying in a house full of men?"

"I am an old woman, so no. But people might talk about Claudia. She is still young."

"True," Rustico rapidly responded and then added, "Then do you wish to stay here? As I said, I consider you like family."

"I think I'll return to live with Claudia. But we both need to earn money to live."

223

"Of course. I can understand that." Rustico fell silent for a moment. "I need someone to manage the salt works. Gianni has become a man, as you can see. He wants to travel, whether it be up the rivers or out into the sea. I've decided that I want him to take over most of the travel in the next few years."

Angela looked expectantly at Rustico and finally asked, "What are you saying? Are you asking me to manage the salt works?"

"Yes, if you'd like. Either temporarily or permanently. You already know what is necessary, and you're capable, and I trust you. Of course, you can't do the hard manual labor, but we should be able to get that done."

"What about the Slav woman?"

"I don't know. She doesn't know anything about the salt trade, and I don't know whether she has any interest in it either. I'll do what I can to take care of her for the time being. Are you concerned about her?"

"I hope you don't mind my asking but what of her and Gianni?"

"I will deal with any consequences of that. Anything else?"

"I know nothing of her. But I'd like to understand what my responsibilities would be. As well as authority. Sometimes women don't get along."

"I'm sure. Just think about it, and let me know what you might be interested in doing. I'd like to work with you if possible."

"I will."

###

Irene found Rustico inventorying the newly added contents of the storage shed and asked, "What can I do?"

Rustico paused and said, "I should ask you the same question. What can you do?"

"I feel I can work. In fact, I believe I should work. What do you need done?"

"I need someone to harvest salt and move large bags of it. But that's hard physical labor."

"I've done hard work in the past. I'm sure I could manage it. But how about what you're doing now?"

"I'm figuring out what I've got and considering who would be a likely buyer and for what price. It's different from salt because all salt is the same, and I know who needs to buy it. Lumber is the same in this regard."

"So you have various silken items, some completed silk garments and others swathes of fabric, and you need to have a method for remembering what you have and what you paid for them. Is that what you have in mind?"

"True. And the same for the various types of herbs."

"I can read and write, and I can add and subtract. Why don't I do this for you? Boris can help you load and move salt."

"I suppose we could try it. Do you know much about silk?"

"I know something about women and what they like and need. I also know that this storage unit is not going to be adequate for the long-term storage of silk. You're going to have to find buyers soon or else find better storage."

"What will you need?"

"Writing implements and supplies to begin with. And some idea of how you want all this categorized."

"I'll see to it."

###

Two days later, Bono knocked at the door of the Doge's temporary chapel and heard the Doge's raspy voice say, "Come in." He pushed the door opened and found the Doge sitting with Father Theodore around a small table covered with building plans. "Ah, Good morning, Signore Bono. Please sit. Father Theodore and I were just discussing the best way to manage the relics of St. Mark. But first, I suggest we all walk to the site of the church where I hope to have them eventually interred?"

The Doge, leaning on a staff and breathing hard, led the way. Bono asked, "Are you all right?"

"Yes, yes. I do get winded a lot."

"And the staff....?"

The Doge stopped and paused. "It's awful, but I need it. I'm old, it's true, and I know I'm not the man I used to be. But I will see this project completed." He pointed the way towards the church and urged Bono and Father Theodore to continue walking on. The Doge continued, "Many years ago, I had the opportunity to visit Constantinople and all the marvelous buildings there. I was particularly taken with the Church of the Holy Apostles. I want something like that for Venice.

"As you can see, this church will be more square than a Roman church, formed like a cross comprised of two equal arms - like a Greek cross, if you will. There will be a large dome in the center, with smaller domes at the ends of the cross. The saint ultimately will lay at rest directly under the center dome." The Doge paused, looking at the partially constructed church, smiling contentedly.

Father Theodore asked, "Where will the saint be until the church is completed?"

"Under lock and key and guarded in a corner of my residence."

"How long will it take?"

"Years, probably. We are also, as you can see, building a new palace. This square will be the center of a new Venice, off the mainland, safe and secure from any land-based marauders." The three began to walk slowly back to the chapel.

The Doge added to Bono, "You don't have to say so, but I know what you're thinking. What if something happens to me? I've discussed this with my wife, Felicita; I'm also having a new will prepared, which will contain my commands regarding this project."

"And a new doge?" Bono asked.

The Doge sighed. "I've asked my brother, Giovanni, to return from Constantinople. I know we've had many disagreements in the past, but I believe he will have the same vision as I over the future of Venice." Bono and Father Theodore glanced at one another, nodding noncommittally, as they walked on. The Doge, eager to change the subject continued with, "But let's talk about our plans for the both of you.

"Father Theodore, of course, you follow a separate form of Christianity than that found here in Italy. Are you interested in adjusting your beliefs so that you can minister in a Roman Catholic church?"

"I've been praying for guidance in this matter, and I really don't know yet. I probably need to discuss this more with some of your local priests and see if I can fit in. Possibly I will retire from the clergy and look for some other way of making my way in the new world for me."

Bono replied, "Be assured that we, the Doge and myself, will do what we can for you. You're an educated man with knowledge of Africa and the Moslems. That alone makes you valuable if you wish to enter the secular world."

Changing the subject, the Doge said, "Signore Bono, I'm eager to have your services back as my aide and consultant, much as it was before your trip," He added, "By the way, I believe I have some interesting information for you. Your friend from Constantinople, Signore Eugenides, is due to arrive in Venice within the next few weeks and is authorized to continue the discussions you had begun with him while on your voyage. He will be bringing some Roman shipbuilders and at least two dromons for our use."

"That's sounds promising," Bono thoughtfully answered.

Laughing, the Doge turned to Father Theodore and said, "That's Signore Bono's effusive response to good news!"

###

Boris and Gianni were emptying the galley of any unneeded items, preparing to sail it to Ariosto's for a full evaluation. Gianni began, "My father has asked Signora Angela to remain as manager of our salt works."

"Is she interested?"

"I'm not sure. She hasn't responded yet. But we'll need a man to work with her. She couldn't do all the labor involved. What about you?"

"Me? I don't know. I'd like to sail or at least be involved with ships."

"There is also a need for someone to sail up the rivers into the lands of the Lombards and Franks," Gianni countered.

"Selling and trading, I gather."

"Of course."

"I'm not sure I could be a trader, to be honest. Right now, I'd prefer to work on ships, building or sailing them, even as a fisherman if necessary. What about you?"

"I'll definitely work with my father in our businesses as a merchant, buying and selling in different ports. That's been my father's goal in all this, as well as mine."

"I'd like to think we could work together."

"There's no doubt about that. This place is dependent on sailors and on moving things around on water."

###

Angela and Claudia sat wrapped against an overcast, cool autumn day in front of a small fire in their cottage. Claudia asked, "What are you going to do?"

"We need to do something, don't we? I know how to manage the salt works. I watched and assisted Leo in running it for several months. I'll need some help, perhaps from Gianni, at the beginning. I'm waiting to see what Rustico offers. We'll see."

"I don't see how they can add sailing throughout the Mediterranean to what they were already doing without adding help. It means at least one of them will be gone for months at a time."

"That's certain. But it will undoubtedly be profitable. Rustico is just like his father: a savvy businessman who knows how and what to buy and sell. He's in the prime of life, but I'm sure he knows he'll have to remain in Venice and do some of the things Leo did." Angela paused and then added, "There's another possibility, you know."

"What?"

"What do you think of Rustico?"

"What do you mean? I really know little about him."

"Do you find him attractive?"

Claudia, surprised, glanced at her mother and said, "Attractive enough, I suppose. I haven't really given it any thought."

"You've been alone for some time now. I can't help but think you must have thought of a second marriage."

"Occasionally. I can't say that I have a lot of fond memories from those five years."

"No, probably not. But you're still young and attractive. I'm over fifty now and unlikely to find another husband. We've been taking care of each other for several years now. What would happen if I died tomorrow?"

Claudia was silent, then said, "I don't like to think about it."

"Neither do I, but we've both lost husbands, and I'm not going to live forever. Look, all I'm saying is to come around when Rustico is there and talk to him. He asked about you the other day, so I know he's likely to be interested. Just ask him about his son, his galley, the business, that sort of thing. Show some interest. Wear your hair down from time to time. And bring some soup."

"Soup?"

"Yes, soup. I learned this from Leo. There are many things men like, and one of them is soup."

###

The next day, Angela was preparing fish for the evening meal when Irene entered. "Good evening, Signora."

"And to you, Signorina. You've been busy in the storage area, I gather."

"Yes, sorting through the various garments and items of silk. There's also a fair amount of herbs that need to be repackaged for sale."

"Do you like that kind of work?"

"I suppose so. One must work in life, so there's no point in disliking it."

"Very true."

Pausing, Irene then looked at Angela and asked, "Is there something else you wish to know?"

Angela put down her cooking, turned, and said, "I suppose so. I, of course, expected Rustico and Gianni back; you and Boris were a bit of a surprise."

"No doubt. And you would like to know what we plan to do?"

"I don't think that's unreasonable."

"Nor do I. Boris wants to work on or with boats, so he will likely find work on a fishing boat or perhaps with a shipwright. I don't imagine he will end up a merchant.

"As for me, I need to work and don't mind what I'm doing. Boris and I may soon look for lodgings on the Rivo Alto, not here in Torcello. I don't know when that will happen, but we don't plan on being unwanted guests."

"It's not my place to see you as wanted or unwanted. I'm here only as Leo's widow. I didn't mean to seem nosy or proprietary. But I'd like to know what to plan for."

"I understand. And I took no offense."

###

The next morning, Rustico, Gianni and Boris took the galley to Ariosto's boat works, where his entire crew was eagerly waiting for it. "It's still afloat, I see," said Ariosto loudly to Rustico as the galley approached the dock.

Rustico tossed a rope to Ariosto and said after he climbed out, "She performed well but didn't like the storms from the sirocco off Africa."

"This galley was not built for sailing in stormy weather away from the shore. Let's take a look at it." With that, the crew drew the galley out of the water and began poring over the hull, with both Rustico and Boris pointing out areas of concern and asking questions.

Afterward, Ariosto stood next to Rustico, both admiring the galley and said, "The galley looks good. Maybe there is something we can do to lessen the rocking from side to side in high winds. I'll look at it again."

"I wouldn't have tried to cross the open sea south of Crete but was forced to." Rustico said, "In any future trips, we'll follow the shore like we usually do. You heard, too, that Stefano drowned when he was hit by a loose mast?"

"I heard about that. We'll look at that, but in a bad storm, there's not much we can do. By the way, Boris, your Slav worker, seems to understand a lot about boats. Some of the questions and comments he made reflect real knowledge of ships."

"Yes, and this was his first real experience on an open sea. He quickly became quite expert in handling the sails."

"I hear the Constantinople Romans are coming soon with some of their ship architects," Ariosto commented.

"So I understand. They've been sailing on the open seas for centuries. Maybe they have some secrets to tell us."

"Maybe. We'll have to see. In the meantime, I have some boats to build. But how about Boris? Is he working for you?"

"I have him working on shore. But his love is for sailing. Talk to him if you like. Just give me a good deal on all my future work."

"Don't I always," Ariosto snorted.

Three days later Boris found Irene in the storage looking at her notes. "Is this a good time?"

Irene looked up and said, "Yes."

"I was offered a job at the shipwright's today. I'm starting as a basic worker, but I've asked long term to be involved in ship design and testing. It's at the Rivo Alto, though."

"That sounds like something you'd like. Did you say yes?"

"I told him I had to talk to you first."

"Take the job. That's what I say."

"What will you do? I can't leave you alone."

"Don't worry about me. I'm pleased for you."

"We could find lodgings together. I could make that part of the job."

"I'd like that. But I am working here, at least for a while. I owe these people a lot."

"I know. But I'm going to ask for space for you, too, anyway."

Irene looked up and smiled and said "Okay."

###

On a cold winter afternoon, Irene asked Gianni if he would walk with her into the small village on Torcello. They spoke little until reaching the town square, where they found a small inn run by a friend of Rustico. Giovanni, the proprietor, greeted Gianni, "Good day," and they asked for a warm herbal tea popular with the locals. They sat in silence until their drinks were brought, and Giovanni discreetly disappeared into the kitchen area.

"How do you like working with the silks?" Gianni asked.

"It's fine. I've had to put them in some kind of order, and I'm guessing at their relative values." Gianni nodded silently. "Listen, Gianni, I've done a lot of thinking about what happened, not just about the Arab but about you too. You were very good to me, even putting your life at stake. But I don't think we have a future together. I haven't thought of being with a man since…"

Gianni looked at Irene and said, "I suppose not." He leaned back and went on with, "I will be gone more and more, traveling. So I won't be around much anyway."

Irene studied Gianni's face silently and toyed with her cup. "You understand then that things can never again be how they were between us?"

"I do know that. And it's fine."

"I don't regret a thing, I want you to know. But I have to put those memories behind me in order to go forward."

Gianni nodded and said, "I wish you good luck in whatever happens."

Irene, more relaxed now, smiled and said, "Boris is going to get us lodgings on the Rivo Alto soon."

"Does my father know?"

"About our move? I don't know."

"Are you going to continue to work with us?"

"I would like to. I must speak with your father, I suppose, and see what he wants."

That evening, Gianni found Rustico at the galley and told him of Irene's words. Rustico paused and gently said, "Gianni, it'll be all right. There will be other women."

"I know. I knew it was coming and wasn't surprised. I'm not sure what I wanted anyway." Gianni, wishing for a change of subject, asked, "What about the silks and spices?"

"Irene has suggested warehousing them on the main island with other high-value items, and that sounds prudent. If she wishes, I'd like to keep her working with me on those items. I haven't decided on how to approach selling them and I don't have much time to learn. It's probably more efficient to find a middleman to distribute them. We'll see. Anyway, with Boris and Irene leaving the house, we only have ourselves to tend to."

"And Signora Angela of course."

"Yes, and Signora Angela, at least during the day. It looks like we have an understanding that she will continue to manage the salt works for the time being. Talking with her, I've really come to realize how much my father meant to our business. The Signora can do much of what he did and just as well, or even better. I've also come to understand that some men who wouldn't work for my father will work for Angela."

Gianni responded, laughing, "Oh, I know he could be demanding." He paused and then innocently asked, "And Angela's daughter? Claudia?"

"What about her?"

"She's very nice... and pretty, too," Gianni noted.

"Yes. She seems very pleasant."

"And the Signora Angela may come to need her daughter's help more and more. I mean, the Signora is not much younger than my grandfather was."

"True."

"Didn't Claudia bring a tureen of soup for us yesterday?"

"Yes."

"And it was quite good."

Rustico looked skeptically at Gianni for a moment and then turned and said, "I'll think about it."

CHAPTER 18

On a cloudy December morning, the Doge, Bono and Father Theodore stood watching the construction activity at the church building site. The tide was high, and water flowed over the Rivo Alto, across their feet, and up to their ankles. "We need more land obviously and higher," said the doge.

"Where's that going to come from?" asked Father Theodore, shivering. After years in Africa, he was uncomfortable in the cold climate of a Venetian winter.

"I don't know yet, but it has to happen and soon," said the Doge, unsteady on his feet and leaning on a stake.

"What about concrete?" Bono asked. "The old Romans used to build breakwater and aqueducts, not to mention their buildings out of it."

"I know, but apparently, no one in this part of Italy remembers how it was made," the Doge answered. "And even if we could find someone with this knowledge, the water here is around twenty feet deep. That would require an awful lot of concrete to add the space we need."

Father Theodore noted, "There are a lot of trees north of the lagoon and up in the mountains. What about them?"

"That is what you are building this island with," added Bono.

"Ariosto and some others have been driving long wooden poles, notched at the bottom, into the lagoon floor in order to provide additional space. Ariosto guides boats up onto them for shore work. It will be interesting to see if they survive long," replied the Doge.

"Venice needs to become a city the size of Ravenna in order to survive. Come. Let's walk back to the chapel. We need to talk about the relics of St. Mark." They began to walk slowly, with the Doge needing to lean onto the other two men, one on each side.

Father Theodore said to the Doge, "It's a bad idea for you to be out walking in this water. You must take better care of yourself."

The Doge responded, "I'm sure you're right. But you know these high waters occur all the time on these islands. Most often in the winter when the tide is high. I can't let them stop me or the work."

Once inside the chapel, the three men sat around a table adjacent to a small fire over which the Doge warmed his hands. "I am afraid that we may have some trouble over retaining the saint's relics. I told the Bishop of Grado that we had come into possession of them. He grew indignant that we hadn't offered them to him. Like us, he is sure that these relics will provide their holder with much prestige."

"What did you say?" asked Bono.

"That they will remain here under our control and the supervision of Father Theodore, of course. The bishop has suggested that he will take the matter up with Rome. He insists that Grado has a greater claim to them because of the throne."

"What might this greater claim be?" asked Bono.

"Oh, I don't know. Some association Grado had with the saint while he was alive, perhaps. Or maybe a promise of some sort."

Father Theodore said, "Some of us - particularly Signore Bono and myself- believe that he was the cause of miracles on our way here. Brother Stauricius was adamant that the saint saved our galley from sinking on the voyage to Crete."

"A miracle at sea?"

"Yes. I believe it too," replied Father Theodore. "What do you think, Signore Bono?"

"I'm not sure it's a significant enough connection to Venice."

"What did St. Mark do during his lifetime?" The Doge mused.

"He preached on Cyprus as revealed in the Book of Acts. Of course, he had to sail there, as well as to Alexandria. But he was in Alexandria for many years and occasionally returned to Palestine, I believe," said Father Theodore.

"Could he have gone elsewhere? For instance, Rome or other parts of Italy?" asked Bono.

"It's conceivable, I suppose." Father Theodore paused and added, "Now that I think about it, recently, I've heard some of the old priests relating a story of how St. Mark preached at Aquileia once, not too far from here. All that happened hundreds of years ago, so how would we know?"

Excited, the Doge said, "Or better yet, how could it be denied today? What if he came up the Adriatic and stopped here on the islands?"

"He might have been shipwrecked," said Bono. "Shipwrecks happened all the time."

"And he might have preached afterward somewhere around here and claimed that his life being saved was a miracle," Father Theodore added.

The Doge nodded enthusiastically. "Of course! I will relay this to the bishop. I think I can safely add that many of the oldest residents of the Gulf have heard this story when they were children.

"Thank you, gentlemen. You've been very helpful. But I must rest now. I am weakening with age."

###

Two days later, the Doge was still in his bed, ill with a fever. His wife entered his room and said, "Giustiniano, a flotilla of Roman dromons has been sighted, and it appears they are headed here."

Awake but tired, the Doge responded, "Most likely, it's Claudius Eugenides from Constantinople. Have Signore Bono greet them. And help him take them to the lodgings we had arranged for them. I'll be prepared to meet with them, maybe tomorrow. Have Bono report to me after they have been made welcome."

###

Bono stood on the makeshift mole on the Rivo Alto as the Roman war galleys came in to dock. There were five of them manned, with each galley pulling an empty one behind. Eugenides emerged from one of the dromons and saw Bono waving at him.

When safely on shore, a smiling Eugenides said, "Ah, Signore Bono, how nice to find you here. I hope your problems with the Arabs on Crete were resolved favorably."

"That's a long story which I'll save for tonight. Suffice it to say that we made it back with the two hostages. The Doge is suffering from a winter illness or else he'd be here to greet you. His wife will lead you to lodgings which have been set aside for you. It looks as though you're prepared for war."

"I have brought five dromons for your use. Let's call it a down payment for the services of Venice in policing the Adriatic. I also have brought two experts in constructing and piloting warships. I'll introduce them to you tonight."

"Excellent. We will eat in the newly completed dining area in our palace. Fish, of course. I'll tell you the story of our trip then."

"Will Signore Rustico be in attendance?"

"I don't believe so. These were the plans of the Doge, and Signore Rustico has been busy dealing with his business. I'm sure he will be happy to see you again and will be involved in our discussions regarding our future relationship."

###

Bono met Eugenides and two other Roman gentlemen at the door of the dining area. Eugenides started with, "Signore Bono, let me introduce you to two of our finest naval experts." Pointing to the taller of the two, a man about forty with a full head of curly grey hair, a broad nose and thin lips. "This is Signore Alexander, who will provide advice about the construction and maintenance of warships." Eugenides then pointed to the shorter man, perhaps thirty years old, pale, with thinning brown hair closely cropped, brown eyes closely-set and said, "This is Signore Orion, a sailor who is knowledgeable in handling a galley, particularly in battle." Both men bowed as introduced, and Bono bowed in return.

Bono said, "Come this way. I have asked two Venetians to join us in our discussions. This is Ariosto, the shipwright who built the galley in which we sailed to Constantinople and then to Alexandria. And Signore Ariosto is accompanied by Boris, who sailed with us in the galley and now works for Signore Ariosto at his ship works. Please have a seat. I'm sorry the Doge cannot be here but he has stated he believes he'll be ready to meet you tomorrow."

"I assume that you have been delegated by the Doge to enter into any understandings we come to," said Eugenides.

"That is correct. Although I will confer with the Doge before coming to any final agreement."

"Of course."

"We have some Italian wine so let's toast to our joint success in dealing with the pirates and keeping the Mediterranean open for Christian boats. Then, over dinner Boris and I will relate what happened at Chandax on our return from Alexandria."

###

Eugenides sat looking into his glass of wine before saying, "You, of course, now understand what we are dealing with on Crete. An emirate! From what we can see, Abu Hafs is nothing more than a thief and a

240

brigand. We have no intention of giving him any sort of pretense of respectability or peace. We both must live with him until we can manage a full-scale war to remove him. I wish I could tell you when but I can't. In the meantime, we'll have to work around him."

"We Venetians plan on expanding our trade into the entire eastern Mediterranean Sea and in order to do that, we will have to reach some sort of understanding with him. He, however, needs to be under no illusion that we won't fight if necessary," Bono said.

"He apparently witnessed that while you were at Chandax. I gather that you were willing to do what was necessary in order to get back your people."

"That's true. We were. But we intend to engage in trading with the Arabs when it can be done successfully. We feel that can be done in Alexandria."

"Transporting slaves to the Moslem infidels?" Eugenides asked.

"Yes.

"From where?"

Bono paused before responding. "You have a slave market in Constantinople, I believe."

"Yes."

"And some of the slaves are Slavs or Bulgars from your wars with them?"

"Yes," said Eugenides uneasily.

"I see. And so might some of the slaves we'll sell. Of course, we won't transport true Christians knowingly to slave markets in Africa."

"Knowingly?"

"We will do what we can to ensure that. In the meantime, we'll do what we can to keep the Cretan pirates back in their port. That includes fighting them as needed. We will also police the pirates in the Adriatic, many of whom purport to be Christians of a sort. It's in all of our interests to maintain trade relations with a variety of peoples."

"I understand that you somehow prevailed upon some Coptic priests to bring back to Venice the relics of St. Mark."

"You are well informed."

"Word has spread among the many churches in our territory. His relics obviously will be a boon to the credibility of Venice."

"He will likely be our patron saint."

"Quite a coup," Eugenides said and continued. "I believe I understand what you want. I trust you understand that we Romans want much of the same. It's doubtful we'll have much official business dealings with the Arabs. But we won't care what you do with them as long as you do not increase their ability to make war on us."

"I cannot conceive where we would knowingly aid in their military ventures. We are interested in buying and selling things people want, like salt, spices, and clothing items. And lumber, of course."

"Ok. I believe that the most pressing commitment we want from you is that of policing the waters. We have brought you the five dromons and are providing you help in their maintenance as well as how to fight in them. Other items, such as trade concessions or tax reductions, shall have to wait."

"But not for too long."

Eugenides sat silently for a moment. "Do you recall from your time in Constantinople a gentleman named Benedetto, from Genoa? I think you met him at the Hippodrome and then the Hagia Sophia."

"I do remember Signore Benedetto, actually quite well," replied Bono. "He took quite an interest in our business dealings, as I recall."

"He's still quite interested, as it happens. He came by the palace shortly after you left and nosed around for any scraps of information about you. He seems to be of the opinion that you are asking for privileges not otherwise extended to other Italian merchants. And, of course, you are, aren't you."

Surprised, Bono said, "I would say we are asking for payment for various services we are going to provide for the empire."

"Of course, that's what you would say. But what am I to say? That this is payment for Venetian mercenaries? Then why not pay the Genoans for security services, too? And, further, could it appear to the Genoans and others that Constantinople can no longer police the seas like it once did?"

Eugenides paused for a sip of wine and then continued. "The empire views our arrangement as benefitting both of us. We do not want to be seen as favoring one Italian city over another. As a consequence, the empire may have to move on your requests perhaps slower than you would like."

"Why should we care how you treat the Genoans?"

Eugenides stared at Bono and responded, "If the Genoans feel mistreated, what's to stop them from acting as pirates just like the Cretans? There are Italian pirates, as you must know, just like there are Croat pirates up and down the Adriatic. Do you think the Genoans will not be concerned about their business arrangements with us? That they may perceive that they are at a competitive disadvantage with Venice? That we are obliged to favor Venice? Are you prepared to police the Genoans, too? What I'm saying is that we - the empire - have to be able to deal with the consequences of our special arrangement."

Bono silently mulled this over, and Eugenides finally asked, "What do you propose for us now?"

"We have identified an inlet on the north side of this island as an appropriate place to erect a facility to build, house and maintain warships. Tomorrow Aristo and Boris will take you there. We will ask that Signores Alexander and Orion be made available to Ariosto and other shipbuilders and shipowners for consultation. How long will you remain here?"

"Until early spring. That gives us time to show you what we know, and we don't want to sail in the wintertime."

"Perfect. I'll let the Doge know, and we'll meet again tomorrow after you've had a chance to see what we have in mind for a place to maintain a navy."

###

Father Theodore knocked on the door on the ground level of a two-story building about three hundred yards from Ariosto's shipworks. Irene answered the door and smiled. "Father Theodore, how nice to see you."

"May I come in?"

"Yes, please. My brother is at the boat working with the Romans."

Father Theodore entered and sat on a bench in front of a fire. "I heard you left Torcello and are living with Boris."

"Yes. We were only on Torcello until we could find our way in this new world."

"You're working for Signore Rustico?"

"Yes, I am for the time being. He has agreed to warehouse silk items and spices here on the Rivo Alto, where they are better protected from the weather. I'm inventorying these items for him, and we are discussing how to sell them."

"Are you happy?"

"I suppose so. The work is fine and the weather's not any worse than Bulgaria."

"And Gianni?"

"There's nothing. No hard feelings either. I think Rustico is happy because he wants Gianni to be available for a lot of travel. What about you?"

"I don't know what the future holds. I'm not interested in being a Roman Catholic priest. And I am not needed for anything related to the relics. They said they would take him back when the Arabs were gone. But when would that be?

"I don't know that I'll stay here. The Romans are planning on returning to Constantinople in a few months and I am thinking of going with them. It's a world I know very little about, but I really don't think there's much of a future here for me."

"I understand. Neither of us can return to where we came from. And what are we to do here? Boris is quite happy with his lot. He's already made himself indispensable to Signore Ariosto, and he's doing something he loves."

"So you could leave him?"

"I suppose so. And what then?"

"Come with me to Constantinople."

Irene paused looking at Father Theodore with wonderment. "And do what?"

"What you want, I suppose. It's a big city, with all sorts of different people. We both can read and write. We should be able to make our way."

"Our way?"

"Yes, our way." Father Theodore stood and paced before returning to Irene. "I've been thinking about this a lot. I'm not much more than an old priest, but I'd like to try and make you happy."

"You mean....?"

"Yes, we'd marry. I mean, I'd like to; It'd be up to you, of course. But I'd like to be with you - if you can."

"I don't know what to say."

"I'm sure you don't. But if you think you might be interested, think about it. On the other hand, if you're never going to be interested, just say so, and I'll never bring it up again."

"Okay. I have to think about all this."

"I'm presently staying with Bono near the palace. Send me a message if you wish. I know this probably comes as a shock to you - but not to me. I've been thinking of you for weeks, since before we reached Venice, and how we seem to belong together. But enough. Send for me if you're interested in going to Constantinople. Either with or without me." Father Theodore leaned over at Irene and took her hand. He then gently pressed it to his chest, smiled and said, "Goodbye."

In Alexandria, Aisha sat on a chair in her bedroom in front of a window, looking down at her courtyard. She held a plate of figs and was slowly eating them. Amina was busy folding Aisha's clothes and putting them away when Aisha asked, "Are you happy being back in Africa?"

"Oh, yes, Sheika, very happy."

"And your parents, too?"

"Yes. I spoke with them yesterday. They are busy arranging the wedding of my youngest sister. It'll be next month."

"Who is she marrying?"

"A carpenter, Sheika. A man my family has known for years. He is twenty-seven already but does well enough that they can start a family."

"And you, Amina. Do you wish to marry again?"

"I don't think about it, Sheika. I'm happy in my position with you."

"Ah, good. You do your duties well enough and I am satisfied. I do recognize that I can be difficult to satisfy."

"Oh, Sheika, no. I have no wish to leave. Or remarrying."

"Very well. But I will keep an eye open for someone for you. Someone who would not wish to monopolize too much of your time. Someone who will realize that you have a duty to me and my family first."

"Of course, Sheika. I would always heed your advice." Amina then turned her attention to a knocking on the bedroom door which she answered. An older man bowed to Amina and said, "The Sheika has a visitor waiting downstairs."

"Amina, go see who it is," Aisha commanded.

"Yes, Sheika." Amina left and returned a few minutes later, saying, "Sheika, your son, Mustafa, is here. Shall I tell him to wait?"

"No, have him brought here. And have some fresh water brought up."

Entering Aisha's room, Mustafa bowed and asked, "How are you?"

"I'm fine," responded Aisha. "Please sit down and tell me how are you? When did you arrive in Alexandria?"

"Two days ago, mother. It's a long trip from Baghdad, as you know. I needed some rest. But here I am, and I'm fine."

"And the governor?"

"He's in good health and sends his regards."

"Now, Mustafa, you know what I mean."

"I suppose I do. Generally, things went well. There is no chance that Abu Hafs will ever be allowed back into his service. The governor is quite convinced that your brother incited a rebellion against him and that Abu would have 'eliminated' him without a second thought. I could think of nothing that might have changed his mind, and I more or less told him that."

"And what of you?"

"I was candid about my uncle's activities on Crete and what he asked me to do on his behalf. I also said I went to Crete with him because he and other members of my family asked me to go."

"Meaning me?"

"He didn't ask which members I meant. He's no fool and I figure he had an idea. At any rate, the governor said he 'admired' my loyalty to my family. He also said he admired my candor even more and my ability to see Abu Hafs' shortcomings."

"What does that mean for your future?"

"He offered me a position as a secretary in a posting here dealing with trade matters. I admit I was surprised, but I gratefully accepted."

"Does my brother know?"

"I haven't informed him of it yet. I'll start work next week, and I want to be sure it's not a dead end first. I should be able to see where I might go from there in a few months."

Aisha rose from her chair and started pacing back and forth. "So, you're back in the city administration at some level."

"That's correct."

"And your plan is to see what advancements might be available, correct?"

"Yes."

"And you need me to mention that you're back in Egypt, looking for better opportunities?"

"No, Mother, I don't need you to do anything of this kind at this point. Perhaps in the distant future, but not now. Most people here are aware that Abu Hafs is your brother and that your rather shamelessly promoting him even when he was behaving badly. Your 'help' at this time would be counterproductive for me." Aisha stared at Mustafa who then added, "I know this is hard for you, but you must try and understand.

"I'll do what I can for the Arabs on Crete, but primarily, I'm going to try and do as good a job as possible here, in Alexandria, and see where it goes. At this point in my life I'm not interested anymore in tackling impossible projects, even for family."

Aisha nodded and said, "All right, I understand. There's nothing I can do for you now, but perhaps in the future, there may be."

"I have to compose a letter to my uncle explaining that I'm not returning at this time to Crete," said Mustafa and rose to leave.

"How about finding you a wife?" Aisha suddenly asked Mustafa as he stood up.

"Honestly, Mother! Can't you leave well enough alone? Goodbye."

###

Rustico, damp from the light rain falling on a bitterly cold day, entered his home on Torcello and found Angela adding wood to the hearth. "Ah, Signora Angela, you're here. Good day."

Angela nodded and said, "Yes, thank you; come over and sit by the fire and warm yourself. I hope the rest of the winter isn't going to be like this."

"Yes. But at least we have been able to prepare for a bad one."

"Where's Gianni?"

"He's on the Rivo Alto going over some sailing issues with the Romans. He shouldn't be long." Rustico sat and then asked, "Where's Claudia today?"

"She's on the mainland, helping out Signore Farina. His wife died earlier this year, and he's at a loss raising two daughters."

“That’s very nice of her.”

“She’s known him for many years and, in fact, had been a close friend of his wife. He’ll need a lot of help.”

“I can imagine. When my wife died, Gianni was nine years old, I believe. But then I had my father to help. Otherwise, I don’t know what I would have done.”

“Claudia was twenty-five, I believe, when her husband died. They didn’t have children, as you know, but she is very good with them.”

“I can imagine.”

“We’ll see what happens.”

“What do you mean?”

“I mean with Signore Farina. He has grown quite dependent on Claudia. I don’t think she’d like to be a stepmother, but she’s so soft-hearted.”

“I don’t think I know Signore Farina. What do you know about him?”

“Oh, he’s very pleasant and treated his wife quite well, or so I heard. He must be about forty and makes a living doing construction work. He’s very good with his hands.”

“What do you think Claudia will do?”

“Do?”

“I mean, will she be interested?”

“Oh, I don’t know, really. Claudia is a dear and very proper. She might very well be interested; she was widowed so very young. But she doesn’t tell her mother everything that’s on her mind.”

“No, I suppose not,”

“I must be going home. I want to have her evening meal ready for her. If she gets home first, she will start making a meal for me, even after a long day. Good night, Signore." Rustico pulled a shawl around his shoulders and wondered what he and Gianni would eat that night.

###

That night, after Boris returned to his lodgings and they had their evening meal, Irene told Boris about Father Theodore's offer.

"What are you thinking of doing?"

"I was completely taken aback, as you might guess. I've been thinking about the voyage back and how much help he was to me. He was very kind and sympathetic. I don't mean the others weren't good to me. It's just that he took the time to listen to me, and I felt I could tell him all that I felt."

"But he wants to marry you. Isn't that a bit more than being a good listener?"

"Possibly. Maybe, I don't know. What do I know about marriage? All I know is that I have expected someday to be married. But to whom?

"What I believed was that someday *somebody* was going to ask me to marry him, and bear his children, and tend to his needs. And now there is this real person, a real man, really asking me. What do I know of him? What are his needs? I don't know. I don't know what to do.

"Then there is the real matter of making one's way in the world. And for a woman, it's not the same as it is for a man. I can't be a sailor, priest, or whatever. But I still need to be able to get by."

"You know that I would take care of you."

"I know that. But you want to spend your life on boats, all across the world- what would I do? And you're my brother; that's not the same as having a husband."

"I guess some women enter a nunnery."

"I've thought of that. But I suppose, in my heart of hearts, I see myself as a woman married to a man and all that entails."

Boris silently looked at his sister. "Are you ready for that?"

"If I can now think of it with pleasure, I may be. At any rate, I've been asked to accompany Father Theodore to Constantinople - with or without marriage. So would I be better off there where I might find myself ready for marriage to him. Or here, possibly working for Signore Rustico and watching after you? I have some time to think about it before the Romans return to Constantinople.

"All right."

###

The Doge lay on his bed propped up with pillows as Bono entered his bedroom and sat on a chair next to him. "Good day. How are you feeling?"

"Tired and concerned."

"I can imagine. What does the doctor say?"

"Nothing of interest, frankly," the Doge gloomily responded. "How much confidence do you have in doctors?"

"Some, I suppose. I'm lucky, I guess. I've been healthy all my life."

"And you're still young. What are you, thirty-five?"

"Thirty-seven, actually."

"I'm sixty-seven. An old man with not much time left."

"Only God knows that," Bono remonstrated.

"Yes, yes. But I know how I feel. Tired and unhappy about how much still needs to be accomplished. How much I won't get around to. My wife worries about me; thinks that I'm trying to do too much with what's left of my life."

"It's only normal for her to feel that way. Apparently, she loves you."

"Yes, she apparently does," the Doge chuckled. "God only knows why. I've been consumed with the affairs of this city and have not paid enough attention to her." The Doge, off-handedly, added, "You're not married, of course."

"No."

"Why not?"

"I don't know. I've thought about it from time to time, but never very seriously. I suppose because I'm a lot like you. I've spent my life involved in the affairs of this world and never felt a strong urge to try and maintain a private relationship with a woman."

"Perhaps you haven't yet found the right woman. That makes all the difference in the world. Felicita has been my rock. She's provided me with love, steady companionship and understanding. We've not been able to have children. I don't mind, but I recognize that this is a regret of hers."

"You're a lucky man."

"Yes, I am," the Doge chuckled. "But now to business. How are our Roman friends?"

"The Romans have been as good as their word," Bono replied. "Not only have they provided us with five satisfactory dromons, but their experts have been very accommodating in advising our sailors and shipwrights."

"But they're reluctant to speak about our trade arrangements?"

"True. But neither they nor we know exactly how successful we will be in policing the Adriatic. It seems to me that we need to demonstrate that Venice can successfully control the trade lanes of the Mediterranean before demanding much more.

"It's also true that we might want to establish trading outposts throughout the Adriatic and into the Balkans first, without Roman involvement. Then maybe even in Africa, or at least Palestine. Clearly, we will need to trade with the Romans, but maybe we should make it seem like it's a necessity for them that their arrangements be made for us.

"Lastly, it appears that the Genoans are making problems. It seems that a businessman from Genoa we met in Constantinople became suspicious about what we were up to and is now demanding equal treatment by the Romans, much to their consternation."

The Doge sighed and said, "Yes, I see. There are problems. But do what you believe is necessary. Has anyone heard from my brother?"

"Eugenides said that he heard that he was preparing to return to Venice soon. As you know, this is not normally a good time to sail; he may be thinking about a land passage. He'll get here."

"Hopefully, I'll be here too. I have told my wife that if something happens to me before a new doge is appointed, you are to have temporary control."

"We'll see. You are looking stronger today, and I'd never count you out."

As Bono was leaving, the doge added, "We'll need a flag, an emblem."

"Yes, I suppose so."

"One with St. Mark on it."

Bono smiled and responded, "Of course!"

CHAPTER 19

Rustico slowly came to recognize how he was now acutely aware of when Claudia was at the house. She came often during the day to bring her mother her mid-day meal and returned in the evening to walk her back to their house. She was invariably pleasant to him and addressed him as Signore Rustico. On one occasion she asked him if he'd like to share the meal she had brought Angela. "There's enough for all of us," so the three enjoyed a delicious meal of bread and broiled fish garnished with a sauce Claudia had recently learned how to make.

Once, Rustico asked Claudia how she spent her day, and she responded, "I have much to do and I like to keep busy."

"I understand from your mother that you are helping a recent widower with his young daughters."

Claudia smiled and replied, "From time to time," and went about her work. Rustico sat wondering - he hadn't planned on asking Claudia about the widower and his daughters. He thought

It's true. It's obvious. You are taken with this woman. Why else would you ask about Signore Farina? And why not? She's very attractive and pleasant.

You haven't been around a woman in a long while, and you didn't seem to miss them. So why now? Gianni is a man now, and your father is gone. Those two used to occupy your time: that and business. Now your life is changing, for the better mostly. You miss Leo, of course. Gianni is more like a partner now than a son. It's likely that he will do much of what you have had to do for the business.

So why not a woman in your life? This one seems quite acceptable.

###

That evening, Claudia found her mother sewing and said to her, "Today Signore Rustico asked if I was helping a widower out with his children. Where do you suppose he got that idea?"

"I might have mentioned it." Angela looked up over her sewing and added, "He does ask after you on occasion. I was merely making conversation with him."

"No doubt."

"You're not interested? I don't know why not. He's still vigorous, and his son is a man now and will be gone soon. He does well financially, and I think he would be a fine husband. Distracted by his business, of course, but I doubt if other women, or drinking too much and beating you, would become a problem. As I said before, you are young and beautiful now and would make any reasonable man happy."

"I remember."

"And I do remember that you weren't particularly happy being married to Pietro. But you were a young bride then and had some rather romantic notions about marriage. It's time for you to be more practical."

"Perhaps."

###

The Doge, after languishing in his bed for several weeks, died on a late winter afternoon. His widow, Felicita, sent for Bono and said, "He asked me to contact you first, even if his brother had arrived."

"He should arrive this spring if he's taking the overland route. Did the Doge leave any instructions?"

"Simply to not allow the construction of the palace and the church to stop."

"That certainly sounds familiar. I'll advise the Bishop of Grado and arrange a funeral mass. The Romans will want to return to Constantinople soon; however, I'm sure they will remain here long enough to see him buried.

"I plan to sail with a flotilla of Venetian galleys to Crete, and we plan on leaving with them. We won't sail until spring, so there will be no need for an interim doge, at least at this point."

Gianni and Boris sat at Ariosto's boatworks, discussing some naval combat techniques Orion had explained to them. Boris said, "I hear that a group of galleys will sail back to Crete this spring. Some of these might prove to be necessary."

"Signore Bono promised them he'd return and transport the emir's slaves and I want to go also. But we'll go armed and prepared for a fight, if necessary. Rustico is going too: he thinks that if a Venetian makes a business promise, it must be kept; otherwise, people will doubt our words."

"That makes sense to me. I want to go too, you understand."

"Of course. I am planning on suggesting that you and I have command of two of the newly renovated galleys. We probably know as much of what the Romans have told us as anyone."

"It's good your father is also coming."

"Yes, and Carlo too. He goes wherever Rustico goes."

Boris was silent for a moment. "Irene may go with the Romans to Constantinople."

"I see."

"She doesn't see that she has much future in Venice. Like I do."

"Perhaps Constantinople will suit her better."

"She's going to travel with Father Theodore. He also feels that there's not much for him here. The priests have not been interested in his Coptic beliefs."

"I suppose not."

"Father Theodore wants to marry Irene." Boris silently waited for Gianni's response.

"And Irene?"

"She doesn't know. Physically, she's over what happened on Crete. But the memories are still bad. Are you bothered by this?"

"No. Not really. For me, it seems like a dream, something from a long time ago. Everything happened so fast."

"Many of the sailors still think it was a miracle we got out of there."

"It seemed like one to me when it happened. But now I don't know what to think. It seems like a dream. I know Signore Bono saved my life - of that there's no doubt. But a miracle caused by the bones of St. Mark? I don't know. Really, I don't see the need to have an opinion on it.

"Anyway. I'm not bothered by Father Theodore and Irene. If she had had a baby, I would have married her. And, who knows, maybe we would have been happy. But now I'm not interested in marriage. Are you?"

"Not now. But maybe someday."

"Like my father said, there'll be lots of women."

###

Shortly after the funeral for Doge Giustiniano Participazio, the Romans announced that they planned on departing for Constantinople the first week of April. They agreed to form a flotilla comprised of their five galleys plus five Venetian ones. Giovanni Participazio, the late doge's brother, finally arrived in the last week of March and was quickly elected as doge by the Venetian assembly. He was too busy exerting his control over his new office to involve himself in the planned expedition.

The ten galleys were loaded with food and armament, including newly acquired shields, which could now be securely affixed to the ship's gunwale and afforded protection against arrows. The weather had turned cool, rather than cold, with only occasional sprinkles of rain.

Two days before the departure, Father Theodore appeared at Irene's lodging and knocked. When inside, he asked Irene, "Two days. Are you ready to go?"

"Yes, more than ready. Eager. By the way Signore Rustico has been pleased with my work on his silks and has given me a letter of introduction to a Jewish merchant in Constantinople named Jacob. He apparently owns a factory where silk is formed into fabrics and may have work for me. Who knows, maybe for you too."

"We'll see. The Roman Eugenides, in whose galley we will be sailing, has said that a literate African priest should be able to find an occupation. We'll see if he helps. In the meantime, we'll see how we travel together."

"Yes, so will we."

Gianni arrived home just before dinner and found Rustico sitting with Angela and Claudia. They looked up and greeted Gianni, their faces smiling and red from the reflection of the fire, each holding a glass of watered wine.

"Good evening. What's for dinner?"

Claudia answered, "Your father brought home a chicken, which I am stewing. I hope you don't mind- my mother and I are staying for dinner."

"I'd like that. Who knows when we'll enjoy a good meal again after we sail."

Rustico walked over and stood next to Gianni, handing him a glass of wine. As they took in the aroma of the stewing chicken, Rustico said, "I have some news for you. Signora Claudia and I will be married upon our return from Africa.”

“Really? I’m surprised. Happy for you but surprised. You teased my grandfather mercilessly, as I recall.”

“I know I did. But I’m sure now he was happy with his marriage. Signora Angela will remain here and continue to manage the salt works. She is undecided about whether she will continue in the work after the wedding, but we’ll have time to sort that out later. She knows she is always welcome here.”

“Thank you again,” said Angela. “But I think that I most likely will remain in my house after Claudia moves in here.”

“Congratulations to all.”

Rustico continued, “And then there is you. It seems to me that it is getting time for me to stay in Venice and manage our family’s business matters here. So, I plan to sail once or twice more and then let you take over the business travel. That, I believe, is what you wish too. Isn’t that true?”

“So, in two years, I will be in command?”

“Yes, more or less,” Rustico quickly replied. “We will, of course, work together in deciding where we go and what we trade.”

“And the river trade?”

“We’ll still maintain business relations with the Franks. But I would expect the bulk of our trading will be in the Mediterranean. We’ll have to find some help for that part of the business.”

Claudia interjected, “I believe our dinner is ready. Shall we eat?”

###

The galleys sailed out of their protected inlet and met at Rivo Alto before the palace, where they were blessed by a priest. Eugenides, Bono, Rustico, Gianni and Boris met and determined the order of the flotilla.

260

The two newest Roman dromons were to lead, while the Venetians followed, two abreast. The other three Roman boats, including that of Eugenides, were to bring up the rear. They were to stop at Zara if it could be reached before dark. Other stops included Ragusa and Kotor before leaving the Adriatic and heading east.

Eugenides said, "I propose we advise the cities we stop at that they can expect some protection from pirates in the future. Don't you agree?

Rustico looked at Bono and said, "I was thinking about that but on our way back home."

"Why then?"

"We would have more time to negotiate the terms of providing protection then. You wish to return to Constantinople as quickly as you can. Right?"

"Yes, of course. What terms had you in mind?"

"Signore Bono and I believe that a halt to the piracy on the Adriatic involves quite a lot of expenses. We'll need to have galleys patrolling at least half the year, and that has costs. If Ragusa stands to gain from being protected by Venice, we feel they should expect to bear some of these costs."

"Many of these cities are Roman colonies expecting the protection of the empire."

"But they are not our colonies, are they? In fact, many that may be expecting us to help protect them are really our competitors. They should at least expect to house and feed our sailors, right?"

"Yes, I see your point. But please remember you're going to receive an annual payment from Constantinople for doing this, aren't you?"

"It's not going to come close to covering our expenses. It'll be Venetians doing the fighting, won't it?"

"Keep me informed as to what comprises these agreements."

"Of course." The galleys, one at a time, slipped away from their moorage into the Gulf of Venice.

###

The flotilla stopped at the towns of Zara and Ragusa for one day each and reached Kotor on the fifth day, where they stayed for two days due to foul weather on the Adriatic. Rustico took the occasion to see Angelo and inquired about the availability of lumber.

"Ah, Signore Rustico, isn't it? I see your journey to Constantinople last year must have been a success. I can lay my hands on some lumber if you'd like. Are you bound for Constantinople again?"

"Actually, Africa this time. I understand that lumber might sell well there due to a lot of new construction. Can you have any ready for me today or tomorrow?"

"Certainly. I see you're traveling as if you're expecting trouble."

"It's certainly possible. As you can see, we are accompanied by some Roman galleys. We've come to an understanding with the Romans in Constantinople that a Venetian navy will patrol the Adriatic on their behalf, trying to safeguard sea-going vessels from pirates."

"Very good, indeed. So we will see the occasional Venetian warship here."

"Yes, and particularly during the sailing season. We're going to the towns that are being protected, like Kotor, and requesting some financial and logistical aid. Who would I speak to in Kotor?"

"I'll need to think about that. I'll have the lumber delivered this afternoon, and I'll see if I can find a city official for you."

"If you can't today, that's fine. We'll stop here later this year and plan on staying longer. And how much will the lumber cost?"

##

262

The galleys set off the next morning and soon entered the Mediterranean, heading east along the southern Greek coast. The weather was cool, and the seas were often cloaked in a dense, low fog. The first night after leaving the Adriatic was spent with the galleys beached in a cove. Eugenides found the Venetian captains standing around a fire on the beach. "How do you plan to contact the Cretan pirates? Do you plan on entering the harbor at Chandax?"

Bono replied, "We're assuming that they will have some boats manned by pirates on the sea outside of Chandax. That's what happened last year. It's probably best for our purposes that they think that they have found a lone galley on its way east, laden with lumber."

"So you expect to be stopped?"

"Most likely. My galley will be slowly sailing along the southern shore; the remainder of the flotilla will be closer to the shore and shrouded by the fog but still within hearing distance. When the Arabs appear, probably with three or four warships, we'll let out a loud drum beat on the galley's side 'and the flotilla, with all hands rowing, will emerge and surround their dhows."

Rustico added, "We'll seize some of the dhows and send the one back to Chandax with a demand that Mustafa bring out a galley loaded with slaves and our payment, which we will then take to Alexandria. You'll head north back to Constantinople, and we'll follow the shoreline to Alexandria."

"Who will be in the first galley?"

Bono said, "It will be my boat. I speak Arabic and I was the one who made the promise to return. I am not as good a sailor as Rustico, but Carlo will be with me. There will also be a group of armed men with me. Hopefully, they won't be needed until the flotilla arrives."

Eugenides nodded and said, "Our dromons will follow Signore Bono's."

Rustico interjected, "I'll have the lead boat if you will, and you can follow me. Boris and Gianni will linger in the fog and come out late in case additional Arab boats are arriving unexpectedly."

"I see. You've thought this out. See you tomorrow morning."

##

The next morning, Bono's galley, low in the water as it was laden with the lumber from Kotor, was moving slowly about five hundred yards off the Greek coast, which was still shrouded in fog. Carlo pointed out to Bono a dot on the southern horizon and said, "That looks like fast moving boat."

"Do you see any others?"

"They'd likely come from other directions." The men stood surveying the sea when Carlo pointed to the east and said, "That looks like another. Shall I have the shields made ready?"

"At hand but not visible yet. Let's see if they start shooting first."

"All right. A typical merchant ship might not be able to identify such ships at this distance." The dhow coming from the south soon drew near, with the dhow from the east not much further away. Bono and Carlo stood in the front of the galley, open to view and seemingly oblivious to any danger. A handful of sailors continued to oar at a measured pace. An Arab on the first dhow shouted in Arabic towards Bono, "Where are you headed?"

"East to Cyprus."

"These waters are under the control of the Emir of Crete. Come to a halt and prepare to be boarded."

"Who is this Emir of Crete?"

"You'll find out. We're coming by and will lash our dhow to your galley. Understand there is a dhow directly in front of you and one behind."

Bono looked at the dhow ahead while Carlo turned and looked for the one behind them. Bono replied to the Arab demand. "I'm going to give my rowers the signal to stop," and he and Carlo began beating on the gunwale. The dhow glided to the side of the galley, carrying a crew of eight Arab sailors. The lead Arab grabbed hold of the galley and started to climb aboard when twelve armed Venetians appeared and stood pointing their arrows into the dhow. The pirate captain said, "You are making a mistake, you know. The other dhows are filled with many more armed men."

"Take another look around, if you will," Bono said as six dromons emerged from the fog, each filled with armed men, protected by shields; soon, the three dhows were surrounded on all sides by seven galleys.

Bono addressed the pirate captain, who apprehensively stood on his boat and said, "My name is Signore Bono. You may recall that we were here last year. You are to take your dhow and return to Chandax, where you will tell the Emir that I have returned as I said I would. He is to have Mustafa bring out a boat filled with no more than twenty slaves. We will accompany this boat and Sheik Mustafa to Alexandria, where he will be allowed to disembark with his cargo of slaves. We are to be paid <u>now</u> in gold for one-third the value of these slaves.

"If you are not back here by noon tomorrow, we will cut the throats of your men and destroy any pirate boats we find. Do you understand?"

"Yes. But understand Sheik Mustafa is not on Crete at this time but remains in Alexandria."

"All right. Then have the Emir choose another or, better yet, come himself. Understand there are to be no armed men on this boat when you return. We will search for them, and any found will be immediately thrown into the sea. We will also kill and any other pirates we are holding. Finally, what you see here are seven warships. I warn you that there are twenty more hidden in those Greek coves. So here's the choice the Emir has- either business on our terms or a battle at sea you cannot win."

After the dhow left for Chandax, the galleys headed into a nearby cove, pulling the two remaining dhows. They beached eight dromons and tied up the Arab sailors. Two dromons remained on guard on the sea outside the cove. Eugenides sat with Bono and Rustico and asked, "What do you expect?"

Bono said, "Abu Hafs will have no choice, as I see it. He wants to sell his slaves, but he has to come to grips with the fact that we will be treated as equals, one well-armed and not to be taken advantage of."

"And well-paid ones, too," said Rustico. "I'm confident that other pirates in this area, Christians ones too, will hear about it. It's a demonstration that we mean to be taken seriously.

Abu Hafs sat glaring at Abdullah, who had just returned from interviewing the pirates who had been sent back to Chandax by the Venetians. Abdullah bowed and said, "Sheik, apparently, three dhows manned by pirates attempted to stop a merchant ship just south of the Greek mainland. As they tried to board the merchantman, the pirates were surrounded by six or seven more Greek style warships, dromons, fully armed.

"Signore Bono, whom you dealt with last year, was on the targeted merchant galley and told the pirates that he had returned as he promised and was ready to convey slaves to Alexandria on your behalf. No more than twenty are to be placed on one of our ships and brought to them tomorrow morning. Signore Bono said they wanted payment in gold in the amount of one-third the value of the slaves to be delivered to them along with the slaves. Signore Bono also threatened that they had twenty more warships hiding in nearby coves and would emerge in the event of any trouble."

Abu Hafs continued to stare at Abdullah as he thought about how to respond. "Signore Bono keeps his word; I knew that he would. But now prepared for a fight. It was a trap, of course." Abu drummed his fingers and then asked Abdullah, "What would you advise?"

"If even some of what Bono said was true, it's unlikely we could beat them in a battle on the water," Abdullah advised. "As you said, you were waiting for him to appear and do as he said. If you wish to have the slaves transported, here's the opportunity. I've no reason to believe any others would take your slaves to Alexandria."

"No, probably not."

"It appears they were exercising caution by not entering the harbor," Abdullah idly commented as Abu Hafs silently sat thinking over his options.

"No, whatever Signore Bono is, he is not a fool. So I guess we'll have to agree to their terms." Abu scowled and said "I do hate to be dictated to in this way."

The next morning, as the ten galleys sat waiting on the water outside the cove, a dhow followed by a larger galley appeared on the southern horizon. Bono and Carlo watched as it neared and ordered the crew to stand by armed. The galley stopped two hundred yards off while the dhow headed for Bono's galley. The dhow came to a distance of five yards from the galley when Abdullah stood and shouted, "Sheik Bono."

"Yes."

"The galley contains the slaves, and I'm to travel with you and see to their disposition in Alexandria." Rustico's galley meanwhile sailed up the far side of the dhow so that the dhow was now lying between the two Venetian ships. Rustico silently stood among his armed sailors, watching Abdullah intently.

"Abu Hafs is not here?" asked Bono.

"No, nor is Sheik Mustafa, who, as you were told, is in Alexandria. Sheik Abdul, who accompanied you with him last year to Constantinople, is on the galley and will meet with Sheik Mustafa and give him the emir's instructions."

"You look familiar. Aren't you the Arab guard we heard speak last year about the deaths of Nikolas and another guard, Aziz, I believe?" Rustico inquired coldly.

"Yes, I was there," replied Abdullah slowly.

"I thought so," Rustico said and then added thoughtfully, "Nikolas was a good man."

Abdullah stood anxiously for a moment and said, "It was a tragedy for all concerned. I understood we all agreed to let that moment go."

Rustico stared at Abdullah and finally said, "Maybe."

Bono interrupted with, "And our money?"

"Abu Hafs asks that you accept as payment one half of the value of these slaves, to be paid in Alexandria by Sheik Mustafa," Abdullah nervously responded.

Bono, seething, leaned over the gunwale towards Abdullah and shouted, "What do you take us for? I said it's in gold and payable now." Bono then looked up at Rustico for confirmation, who nodded. Rustico stood up and said to Carlo, pointing to Abdullah, "Leave this one for me, but kill all the others and burn their ships." Carlo nodded to a group of sailors who raised their bows and readied flaming arrows.

"Wait! All right, I have the gold here," Abdullah stuttered. He added, "I'm only doing as I was commanded."

"Take the gold to Signore Rustico," said Bono, and Abdullah had the dhow moved closer to Rustico's galley and climbed aboard. A second Arab in the dhow handed a bag to Abdullah, who in turn handed it to

Rustico. "Have it counted, please," said Bono to Rustico. As the gold was being counted, Rustico asked Abdullah, "What's on the galley?"

"Just slaves and Abdul." Bono stared at Abdullah, who finally said, "I swear."

"You'd better be right. Two of our ships are on the way to check them now. Understand?

"Yes," replied Abdullah. "I will see to it that we will honor our word."

Eugenides stood in a nearby dromon and watched as the Venetians counted the gold. He turned to Irene and Father Theodore and said. "It looks like the Signores have everything under control. Three of our dromons will accompany their boats for a few more days. This galley and another will head back to Constantinople now. All right?"

As the dromon prepared to sail, both Eugenides and Father Theodore gazed expectantly at Irene, waiting for her response. She had been intently staring at Abdullah and Rustico silently facing each other as the gold was counted. Suddenly aware that they were waiting for her, she turned to Father Theodore and said, "I'm sorry. I'm ready now."

ABOUT THE AUTHOR

Harry Gandy lives in a small town in Southern Oregon, having retired ten years ago, after having practiced law for thirty-two years. He developed an interest in history and historical fiction some twenty plus years ago, particularly due to reading, among others, Patrick O'Brien, Paul Horgan and Don Berry. Somewhat as a result of enjoying all things Italian, he became interested in the history of what is now called Tate Antiquity, a period beginning roughly at 400 C.E. and extending to 1000 C.E., a span of time in which the major monotheistic religions, based on books, gradually supplanted the polytheisms of antiquity.